I CAME TO

Jaq Hazell is the author of *London Tsunami & Other Stories*. She has been shortlisted for the Jane Austen Short Story Award and The Virginia Prize for Fiction. Her work has been published in various anthologies and she has an MA in Creative Writing from Royal Holloway, University of London. She was born near Portsmouth and now lives in London.

Visit her website at www.jaqhazell.com

ALSO BY JAQ HAZELL

London Tsunami & Other Stories

I Came to Find a Girl

Jaq Hazell

4Media Publishing

London

This is a work of fiction. Names, characters, organisations, places, events, and incidents are either products of the author's imagination or are used fictitiously.

Published by 4Media Publishing Ltd, London.

ISBN-13: 978-1518731563
ISBN-10: 1518731562

For D, Z & B

I Came to Find a Girl

One

I was happy to hear Flood was dead. I wasn't as happy as I thought I'd be, but I was happy all the same. His demise was both painful and premature which was only fair and things were as they should be. Only it didn't last, it couldn't, because Flood stories sell newspapers.

The initial news reports and obituaries quickly dissipated to virtual Flood hysteria as art critics, columnists, and even business correspondents had their say and that's when I thought, *enough*.

You can take two or three hours or whatever it was, but you can't take my life. I never wanted to be an artist's model – never agreed to anything – I was young, stupid even, it hurts to admit that but that's how it was. And now this, Flood's video diaries or whatever it is.

I kick off the shoes Marcus Hedley had admired. That's Marcus Hedley, art dealer, always in *Art Review*'s Power 100 list of movers and shakers in the international art world. "Stunning shoes – girls get to wear such wonderful footwear," he said, and I just shrugged because it wasn't my shoes that mattered.

I spread my toes; rubbed raw from walking too far, too fast in heels I'm not used to – and for what? Days before I'd told my flatmate Tamzin that Drake Gallery wanted to see me. "No way," she said and she was right.

I sigh and reach for my bag. The DVD is on top with a red sticker saying 'Limited edition'. While the black and white cover photograph shows a woman's naked torso – model-thin and translucently pale with Celtic-style lettering like a tattoo round her navel. 'The More I Search the Less I Find' it says, and at the bottom: 'The Jack Flood Video Diaries'.

I pick at the cellophane wrapping, my hands shaky. *Get a knife.* I cross the Kermit-green carpet to the kitchenette where our one sharp knife is half submerged in the greasy bowl. *Bloody Tamzin.* I knock on her door. "Tam, you there?"

The double duvet is plumped and smoothed with the Zippy toy her boyfriend bought resting between the pillows – funny how she makes her bed but never washes up. *We are not students any more.*

I go to the desk in my room and sieve through my sketchbooks, pens and paints. I have a Stanley knife somewhere. A blunt Stanley knife, there beneath a folder marked 'NEW IDEAS'. I force the blade downwards and slice into the cellophane that envelopes the DVD's plastic casing.

Back in the living room, I insert the disc and press 'play'. The blue-blank screen turns black: no copyright warning, no trailers for forthcoming releases. It's not like an ordinary DVD. I should've known that. "Do watch this, if you can," Marcus Hedley had said. "You're an artist yourself, yes?" I nodded, and he said, "Well then, you'll understand."

Words in white typescript move across the screen: 'The More I Search the Less I Find – The Jack Flood Video Diaries'. And in the bottom right hand corner, the date and place: 'Thursday 26 May 2005, the Merchant's House Hotel, Nottingham'.

Immediately, I burn up and have to change out of my interview clothes. I press 'pause' and glance up as legs pass the barred window – an old man in khakis with a skanky dog. No one notices me down here. *I like that.* My first London flat, down a curl of slimy, uneven steps. Too hot in summer, cold and dark all day in winter, but it's private and the area's not bad.

I rush down the corridor to my room where I lay my

trousers and shirt on the bed. They don't look so smart any more. They didn't work. I pull on an old Santa Cruz surf T-shirt and shorts then head back to the TV. The disc resumes. I feel sick and clench my fists as I watch a figure emerge from the gloom of the low-lit room.

It's Jack Flood, of course, and as he walks towards the camera my stomach tightens and I have to grip the edge of the sofa to force myself to stay and watch.

Jack Flood's dark hair frames an intense, inscrutable expression. He's dressed in a black shirt open to his navel – whippet thin, wasted even. And he's in a hotel room, that hotel room, the one with the bronze satin bedspread and crystal chandelier amongst other empty trappings of a boutique hotel. To think I was so impressed by that place, by its look – its obvious statement of nowness.

Movement in the window above catches my eye – another pair of old, slow stranger's legs, but no Tamzin. *When's she due back?* I try to remember what shift she's on but all I can recall is her wishing me luck. We had assumed Drake Gallery were interested in my work. *How stupid was that.*

Jack Flood looks directly at me. He's contained within the box of the chunky old TV but still it makes me shaky to see him like that, looking out, blatantly staring. "I never stop looking," he says. "Got to keep looking and seeing – it's a lost art." He walks around as if he's searching for something, then pauses and slowly turns to face the camera. "My name is Jack Flood and I am an artist."

"Yeah, a fucking shit one," I say, even though he won awards and made heaps of money, and still does.

What do I ever make? Call yourself an artist, Mia; you're having a laugh. I remember that day, the morning-after, when I arrived at college, in my studio space, took one look at the sketches pinned to my white boards and immediately pulled them down in a silent frenzy before seeking out the black bin to dump them in. *But that was then and this is now, and still I'm getting nowhere fast.*

"What is art? How can you tell? Is it all rubbish?" Jack Flood says to camera. "These questions will probably go unanswered but what I can provide is an insight into the life of an artist: where I find my inspiration, what motivates me, how I make art. What do artists do all day? Is it, as many suspect, a piece of piss?"

He retrieves a piece of paper from his pocket. "Rough guide to Nottingham – literally," he says. "I asked the concierge, where's best avoided? Forest Fields, St Ann's, Mapperley, the Meadows – they may sound all right, but Forest Fields is the red light area and the Meadows and St Ann's are notorious for gun crime – they've got territorial issues. It's the drugs – it's gang warfare. Then there's the binge-drinking in the city centre – the fighting, the puking and fucking in alleyways." At a side table piled with photographic equipment he selects a small camcorder, turns, and approaches the camera that's filming.

I move back from the TV, to the furthest corner of the sofa, as if he could come out and get me.

The film cuts to Flood's handheld camera as he films his exit route out of the suite and down a narrow corridor. He opens a fire door and makes his way down the hotel's winding backstairs and through the circular reception – decorated in Schiaparelli-pink, paisley-print wallpaper. He spins round the revolving glass door and out onto the cobbled street.

Daylight: his camera does a 360-degree scan taking in the museum across the road, the pub next door and a nearby church. *It's the Lace Market area – streets I know well, streets I loved until Flood ruined it all. Again, I force myself to unclench my fists in an attempt to feel less tense.*

"Taxi!" Flood shouts in that assertive, arrogant way of his.

A white saloon car draws up alongside, and Flood points his camera lens through the open passenger window towards the driver. He is a youngish man with a large head, sandy hair and pitted skin. My stomach twists. *I recognise him.*

"I want to see Nottingham," Flood says.

"Why you film?" The driver's accent is deep and guttural – Eastern European.

"I film everything – a sort of cultural record, if you like. Are you free or what?"

The driver nods his fat head and Flood enters the cab's spotless black vinyl interior.

"Show me the real Nottingham," Flood says.

"I am not clear what you ask of me?"

"The real Nottingham – not the castle or the Robin Hood Experience – I want to see where people live. I have a shortlist." Flood passes him a piece of paper.

The driver shakes his head. "These places – they are no good."

Through the side window Flood films blue sky and the church's honey-coloured stonework. An empty street – he cuts back to the cab's interior with its black vinyl seats and the back of the cabbie's sandy-coloured head. "I need a driver for a few hours," he says. "I'm sure we can come to some sort of arrangement?"

The driver's frown is visible in the rear-view mirror. "These places you want to go – there are shootings."

"It's hardly Jamaica."

"A girl – she was killed after Goose Fair. She was I think thirteen, and a few months back a boy was shot in Radford. It is crazy place."

Flood films the street. Sunlight on sandblasted stone contrasts with adjacent dark Georgian brickwork. The restored period buildings are immaculate and on the road pristine cobblestones remain intact.

"Drive me around; I'll make it worth your while – an extra twenty quid, say."

The driver looks in the rear-view mirror. "Okay. Where you want to go?"

Jack Flood consults his list. "Meadows, St Ann's, Forest Fields – actually, my friend, let's start in Forest Fields."

5

The driver checks his mirrors and pulls out.

"Where you from?" Flood asks, as he films a blue, bejewelled elephant hanging from the rear-view mirror.

"Poland."

"What's your name?"

"Maciek."

"Magic." Flood laughs.

"To English it sound like magic, but say like *ma-check*."

"You like art, Maciek?"

The driver shrugs. "Old paintings I can appreciate."

The camera moves outwards shooting: shops, bars and restaurants as the cab loops round the one-way system and stops at traffic lights where Flood focuses on a couple of teenage girls with long, straightened hair and matching black and white polka dot skirts. As if he's talking to himself Flood says, "It's all art."

Back at the suite, Flood takes a call. "Hello – yes – okay – okay, if I must. Tell him five minutes." He changes into black jeans, a T-shirt, trainers and jacket, and from the bedside table he lifts a glossy white card that he reads aloud: "Now That You've Gone Were You Ever There?" He half-smiles and goes to a side table, where he selects a small, compact camcorder and exits.

Did he film everything? A sickly feeling rises in my throat and I pause the disc, aware of what's coming next.

The glossy white card was the invite to the private view for Flood's show. 'Now That You've Gone Were You Ever There?' it said, with a close-up of a pubic hair like a question mark, and there was small print on the back that I read aloud to my housemates. "'Future Factory is proud to present work that engages with the more pressing issues in contemporary society. As a result, some work in our programme may cause offence' – that has to be worth a look, don't you think?"

My housemates were sitting on the collapsed green sofa and two rest-home-type chairs in the living room of our three-storey

Victorian terrace in Forest Fields, Nottingham. There were five of us back then, all students, and I was standing in the doorway, having rushed back, excited that I'd managed to secure enough invites for everyone.

But Tamzin rolled her eyes and Kelly groaned. I didn't get it. This was just the sort of happening event I'd been looking for, but then I was more easily impressed than the others having come from 'Bumblefuck', as my friend back home calls it.

Stowe-on-Sea is a bland, sprawling suburb next to a pebbly stretch of grey water on the South Coast: one curry house, one amusement arcade, a couple of caffs left over from the Fifties and endless retirement flats with sea view. 'Stowe' actually means 'place', so it's Place-on-Sea, like it may as well be Nothing-on-Sea. The sort of living hell you have to escape to such an extent that I dared not live while I was there. Boyfriends were out of the question. No one was going to get under my skin; nothing would bind me to that place. So, once I got out I needed to catch up. I'd missed out and that made me desperate for glamour and excitement and to have a good time. So it didn't take much to impress me back then. Even so, we were all into art, apart from Slug who was the only non-art student among us, having filled the small, dark room no one wanted. (We'd had to advertise it on the Student Union notice board and Slug was the only respondent. I had wanted to hold out for someone more interesting, but it would have meant we'd incur more rent and none of us could afford that.)

"Jack Flood's been shortlisted for the Prospect Prize. He's only doing the Nottingham show as a favour to Mike Manners. Then it all moves to London."

Mike Manners, head of fine art, was also known as the Golden Turd thanks to his first lecture when he placed a plastic 'joke' dog-turd on a desk and told us we had three years to find a way to turn it into gold. He had previously been a lecturer at Goldsmith's in London and it was there that he had taught Jack Flood.

"I managed to get enough tickets for all of us," I said.

Kelly, a Londoner who was pretty cynical at the best of times, scraped back her dark hair and said, "Shock art is too Sixties, like shit in a can."

"You what?" Slug curled his lip. He was a Scouser, called Slug on account of his bed linen – a brown polyester sleeping bag (never washed).

"There was this artist, Manzoni, who canned his own shit," Kelly said. "He even called it Artist's Shit."

Slug stopped eating his chicken. "People bought cans of shit?"

Spencer nodded. "It *was* limited edition."

"Didn't some explode?" I added.

"Gross," Tamzin said.

"Yeah, but nothing shocks any more," Kelly said.

"What about the news?" I said.

Slug discarded his plate by the side of his chair, ignoring the chicken bones as they slid onto the carpet. "It shocks me the stuff you lot call art. When is this so-called art show anyhow?"

"Tonight."

"It'll be full of pricks."

"There's free wine," I said, knowing full well that none of them could argue with that. And there it is on film – a moment from my life. It makes me think of the Nepalese, I think it's them who believe being photographed captures your soul. He certainly took something from me. I bite my lip as the film cuts to the college gallery: all white walls and a complicated glass roof, and the chatty, stylish crowd stand in cliques sipping wine, talking, and occasionally viewing the art.

The camera sweeps over Flood's work – more concerned with recording who is there than the art. A sparrow-like woman in a bird of paradise hat beams at the camera. There's a man with a white bouffant, my tutors Mike Manners – ageing hipster – and Mike Cherry in a crisp floral shirt, and briefly, I see myself: talking, laughing. I look young, pale and I hate to say it vulnerable. I'm wearing a simple charcoal dress, my hair is casually pinned up and my eyeliner is thick, and flicked upwards at the corners. Laughing with Kelly as we knock back free Chardonnay, I am carefree and unaware of being filmed. It is my 'before' before the 'after'. My stomach knots at that thought and I have to wipe my eyes.

Meanwhile, the camera moves in: a man in a wheelchair gives a nod, while an older guy in a red shirt studies a painting up close, and there's Marcus Hedley, art dealer. How did he get to be so special? Rich kid of course: Eton, Oxford, the universe. It must be more of a challenge to fail for some people. He's wearing his signature heavy-framed specs. He runs a hand through his shock of white hair and beckons to the camera. "Jack, over here, there's someone you really must meet."

That 'someone' Flood 'really must meet' is in his late forties, dressed in a well-cut dark suit. It's Nicholas Drake, balding hedge funder turned art collector.

"Jack, put that thing away now," Marcus Hedley says. "I've hired someone else to film tonight."

The film cuts to Flood's hotel suite, some time after the private view. I guess the whole event didn't mean much to him, while I still have the invite. "Can I keep it?" I had asked the sharp-faced woman on the door making her look me up and down as if I'd never been out before.

My heart raced as I entered. The gallery was buzzing. There was sparrow-woman, the tiny man in high heels with a white bouffant, middle-aged people in black talking art, a Barbie lookalike (there's always one), other students and the tutors. We accepted wine and canapés, and hung out: looking, viewing, considering, taking it in.

We stopped at the title piece – *Now That You've Gone Were You Ever There?* – a single pearl earring on a small velvet cushion, placed high on a plinth, surrounded by the outline of a body with prominent breasts marked out in yellow tape on the floor.

It looked like a weird crime scene.

Slug laughed and said, "Looks like a murdered porn star."

There was a small pot of dust, toenail clippings and a couple of black pubic hairs lit from beneath by a pink light-box entitled *I Owe You Nothing*.

"This guy is bitter," Kelly said. "Which one is he?"

"That's him, I saw him in *The Sunday Times*." I pointed at a tall, dark-haired, thirty-something deep in conversation with an older man in a wheelchair.

"Not bad," Tamzin said, but then Tamzin said that about everyone.

"I need another drink," I said.

"Get us one," Tamzin said.

"And me," Kelly said.

I crossed the gallery and wove between the cliques; careful I didn't trip in my high ankle boots. I felt good in that charcoal dress. One or two men stared my way. I could sense it. I recognised one particular face – nice looking but not single. I didn't need it. I wasn't interested in unavailable men and I resented the way they kept looking around, checking to see whether or not there was anyone better.

At the bar, I collected three glasses and turned back to find the gallery busier than ever. I could no longer see the art and crowds of people were blocking my way.

"Excuse me, please." I was so going to spill something, but then somehow a path cleared before me.

A man in a black jacket, T-shirt and jeans with artfully mussed up hair was standing aside to allow me through. "Thank you," I said.

The man watched me return to my friends. I couldn't believe it. It was Jack Flood, the artist, and he was still staring, watching my every move. I didn't know how to stand or what to do with my hands. It was like walking endlessly through customs. I drank fast and headed back to the bar and that's when something flashed.

I turned around. Jack Flood was standing right next to me. "You've just been papped." He nodded towards a guy with bleached hair. I'd seen that photographer before; he was always at various clubs, lurking round the fringes pointing his equipment at one girl or another. "Is he press?"

"No, he's on the photography degree."

"He sees something in you. He's not stupid." He smiled. "What's your name?"

I told him.

"Where are you from?"

"Bumblefuck."

"And where is that?"

"The South Coast – a small place you won't have heard of."

"You're a long way from home."

"I'm an only child. I needed to get away – too intense. What about you – where are you from?"

"I've lived all over, but London is home. What do you do?"

"I'm a student – fine art."

He kissed me then, just closed in on my mouth before the possibility had even crossed my mind. And it was a good kiss, I hate to admit it, but I liked it. I liked him; there was something about him, or so I thought.

Jack Flood broke away. The kiss was over almost as quickly as it had begun. He decided. He decided when it started. He decided when it stopped.

"That was nice," he said.

Is everyone staring? What is he doing? It was his show. I looked up at him, took in his light brown eyes. *Is that eyeliner?*

"I came to find a girl," he said, "and that girl is you."

"Sorry?"

"I wouldn't bother otherwise."

"What – you wouldn't go to your own opening night?"

'I came to find a girl' – *what sort of a line is that?* I thought.

I don't like flattery; I know I'm girl-next-door – nothing without the make-up.

11

But I'd never met a true artist before, let alone a highly acclaimed one. *Is this how they are?*

"It's a really interesting show," I said, "but do you like women?"

He laughed. "Some of my best friends are women."

"How come they just become these remnants?"

"How much do your lovers leave you?"

He'd got me there. Sometimes I was lucky to even get a surname, not that I wanted it that way. All I wanted was to meet someone interesting – not easy to find – and I couldn't or wouldn't compromise.

Jack Flood waited for me to say something. I felt a little out of my depth but managed to ask where he thought his work was going, but my tutor Mike Manners interrupted then, saying he had to introduce Jack to someone. And I rejoined my friends. Much later, after several red stickers had appeared to indicate works that had been sold, I felt a hand slowly stroke down my spine and turned to find Jack Flood behind me. "We should talk some more." He handed me his card.

'Protect Me From What I Want' – the following day I sat taking cuttings from a magazine article about the artist Jenny Holzer. It was from her Truisms series: *Protect Me From What I Want* LED light installation 1982. I glued it across the front of my sketchbook.

The microwave pinged in the kitchen below. I collected my lasagne and went downstairs to the dingy living room where we ate our meals balanced on our laps in front of the TV.

"Not the fucking news." Slug came in as I changed TV channel, turning the screen camel-coloured with dust, sand and explosions.

"You've got to know what's going on," I said.

"It's all the same, nothing but bad news."

"That's the world we live in," Kelly said.

"It's not my life," Slug said.

"The Simpsons is on..." moaned Spencer.

"Have what you like," I said. "I've got to get ready for work."

"You're working?" said Tamzin. "I thought we were going out."

"Did you hear that?" Kelly nodded at the TV. "They said Forest Road East – someone's been murdered."

"It'll be a prostitute," Slug said.

"It's so close," Kelly said.

"Don't worry, we'll look after you, girls," Slug said.

"Will you be okay getting to work, Mia?" Spencer asked.

"I'll get the bus or tram back."

Back in my room at the top, I looked out the window to see if there were any girls out on the corner at the crossroads. The wall where they liked to sit was empty but I sketched it anyway – the waiting-for-a-trick wall with its bricks falling from one end.

I reapplied my eyeliner and pinned up my hair, gathered my uniform together, and raced down the two flights of shag-pile carpeted stairs. "Seeya," I shouted out in the greying light of the hallway, and slammed the front door behind me, pressing my fingers against it to check.

Two women with bare legs were now sitting on the wall opposite. It's too cold to dress like that, I thought. What are they doing there? Have they not seen the news? I wondered if Mum and Dad had. Probably not, this was local stuff. They didn't even know I was living in the red light area.

As I turned onto the main road, I saw the police cordon further up the hill by The Vine, our local pub. Nottingham and particularly our scrappy corner of the city suddenly seemed more dangerous, and yet nothing had changed. The threat of a madman roaming the streets had always been there. It's probably safer than normal – police everywhere, I thought. But still, to make the twenty-minute trek across town to Saviour's Bar and Restaurant, I slipped my keys between my fingers. The sharpest, jagged-edged Yale was between my index and middle finger, and gripped discreetly by my side. *Everyone needs keys.*

Two

Jack Flood's DVD cuts to his hotel suite: dark panelled walls, velvet mocha club chairs and a crystal chandelier, beneath which Flood is face down, fully clothed, on the bronze satin bedspread. He stirs, rubs his eyes and rearranges his black T-shirt. He takes a whisky miniature from the mini-bar and switches on the TV.

"Welcome to Sky News at five," the male newsreader says.

"Same old," Flood says. He knocks back the whisky, grabs a leather jacket and camcorder and exits the suite, taking the winding stairs down to reception.

"Good morning, sir," the concierge says. He's a tall, long-faced man, immaculate in black against the hot pink, paisley wallpaper.

The camera moves with the revolving door and out onto the cobblestones. "Why the long face?" Flood laughs to himself.

Outside it's dark, misty and damp. Flood films his way downhill towards the main city centre: there's a man muttering in a shop doorway – Flood homes in on him, spots a mobile headset and loses interest, a couple of women in saris scuttle past and the camera then lingers on a bearded heap asleep in a battered sleeping bag. "Look at that – the original *Nomad*." Flood refers to a painted bronze cast of a figure in a sleeping bag by the artist Gavin Turk that Saatchi used to display in the foyer of his gallery to confuse the public. Flood nudges the bag with his foot. There's little response beyond a muffled grunt.

"Stick it on a skip," Flood says, and moves on towards a pedestrian thoroughfare, where he spots a convenience store – inconveniently shut. "Call this a city?"

"You wanna film me?" There's an old man with matted hair and a gappy grin who gives Flood a thumbs up.

"Any newsagents round here, squire?" Flood asks.

"Don't go there, pal – they're all terrorists."

Flood turns the camera away and films a small blue toy monster that's lying amongst fag butts and beer cans.

"Wait!" The man points ahead. "Tesco is just down there," he says, like he's seen the light.

"Thank you, my friend. Here, have a drink on me." Flood hands him some cash.

"Bless you, sir, most generous."

"Always happy to help the destitute die a little sooner." Flood walks on past Monsoon, Gap and Marks & Spencer and finds the fluorescent-lit temple that is a 24-hour Tesco Metro. There are newspapers tied in bundles by the door. Flood retrieves a small knife from his pocket and slices open the plastic binding.

"You read a lot." The girl on the till has round cheeks, large hoop earrings, a blonde ponytail and black roots. "Are you filming me? What you filming me for?"

Flood zooms in on her pink frosted smile, before the camera shifts to survey the conveyor belt: a pile of the day's papers, a Kit Kat, and bottle of orange juice. "It's all about me." Flood flicks through *The Guardian*. "Here I am." He points at a feature.

The cashier toys with one of her hoop earrings as she reads. "Wow, I've never met a famous artist before."

"It must be hard to meet anyone the hours you work."

"Yeah, but it's all right, you earn more on this shift."

"Have you ever had your portrait painted?"

Wide-eyed, she shakes her head, her hoop earrings hitting against her jaw-line.

16

"What's your name and number? I'll key it into my phone."

The girl checks around before quietly relaying her details.

"Carmen – now there's a name. Do you know the opera?"

"Yeah, well, not really – I've heard of it though."

"She lured men with her beauty – is that you?"

She looks blank. And the camerawork is shaky as Flood gathers up his purchases. "I'll be in touch."

Flood's hotel suite: the bronze silk curtains are drawn and the lights are dim. Flood spreads the newspapers across the king-size. "The show's a sensation – five stars." He pores over the arts pages of the broadsheets, and moves on to the tabloids. His face darkens and his eyes are hard.

There's a knock, and Flood stares at the door. "Who is it?"

"Jack, it's me – Marcus, open up."

Flood moves slowly towards the door.

Marcus Hedley is dressed in crisp jeans and a navy sweatshirt with his usual horn-rimmed glasses. "Jack, thank God," he says.

"It's a little early for a social visit."

"I know you don't sleep." Marcus Hedley glances round at the luxury suite. "Can we sit down? There's something I must tell you."

"Save your breath, I already know." Flood nods towards the pile of newspapers lying open on the bed.

"Oh my God, I'm so sorry. You shouldn't have had to find out like that." Marcus tries to put an arm round him.

Flood moves back and away. "When did you find out?"

"I was trying to protect you."

"When did you find out?"

"Jack, please sit, we need to talk this through."

"Did you deliberately not tell me?"

Marcus removes his glasses and rubs at his eyes. "I only ever have your best interests at heart you know that. I was trying to protect you."

"You couldn't risk the star of the show not showing up..."

"It wasn't like that."

"When did you know?"

"Late yesterday – it was shortly before the private view. I didn't know what to do. I didn't want to spoil your moment; you've worked so hard, and I wasn't sure how you felt about Angie. It's been a while..."

"Why didn't you tell me after the show?"

"You disappeared. Where did you go?"

Flood frowns. "When did it happen?"

"I don't know exactly. The coroner's report will look into it but I'm told she was found yesterday but probably died the day before."

"On the eve of my show..." Flood looks towards the window. "Is it true what the papers are saying?"

"It's too early to tell."

"I saw her that day."

"Oh?"

"She was fine – she seemed fine."

"I'm so sorry, Jack."

Flood moves across the room and retrieves a Bible from the back of the hairdryer drawer.

"Oh, Jack – don't do that, not now."

"How else do you suggest I get through this?"

"Come back to London. You can stay at mine."

Flood sits back down carefully placing the Bible on his lap, dark curls half-cover his face.

"How about I take you for breakfast?" Marcus says. "There's a great little place around the corner and it'll do you the world of good to have a large hearty meal."

"I can't eat anything – not now." Flood opens the Bible to reveal a hollowed-out cavity.

Marcus stands up. "I'm going to leave now."

Flood carefully removes a small plastic wrap from the hollowed-out book.

Marcus shakes his head. "You'll be okay?"

Flood doesn't reply. And Marcus sighs and lets himself out.

Again, there's a knock at the door.

"Is that you, Marcus?" Flood closes the Bible and puts it aside, then redirects the camera ensuring it will encompass the door.

Outside, stands a petite woman in a pink, tailored skirt-suit with blonde waist-length hair and stilettos.

"Can I help you?" he asks.

"I am Tatiana."

"You've got the wrong room." He goes to close the door but the woman reaches out to stop him.

"This is suite 12?" she says.

"There must be some mistake."

"You book me online, no mistake."

"I can't see a tall Russian blonde with flawless skin."

"You booked me. I know – photographic memory." She taps the side of her head with a perfect pink nail.

"You're about five four at a push, yellow hair – I'll give you that, but you're orange. Fake tan does nothing for me, sweetheart."

"You saw my picture online, you know what to expect."

"Look, putting the Trade Descriptions Act aside, now is not a good time."

"You want – I come back in little while?"

"It's inappropriate right now."

"I come all this way. You pay my taxi?"

"I thought I already had."

"No – you must pay – you take up my time."

"You're all the same, here, take that and lose the tan – we may have a future then." The woman snatches the cash and deposits it in her slim Chanel clutch bag.

Flood shuts the door and then immediately reopens it. "Hold on a moment."

The woman pauses and turns around, and Flood says, "I want a closer look."

Maciek's cab, after dark: the car is stationary in a built-up area. Flood must be filming from the backseat, as he's not visible and yet his voice is audible.

"The work is by Douglas Meek. He made two identical pieces – *Catch Me If You Can I* and *II*. The first was displayed in an exhibition and allowed to melt as Meek had intended. Nicholas Drake bought the second one and he insisted the gallery deliver it frozen to his home so he could enjoy the melting experience in private. Only he didn't do that, he's had a special freezer installed to house the piece."

Maciek frowns. "In Poland we have many power cuts. He could go away for a day, come back and find only water."

Flood laughs, and says, "That's like the urban myth about Saatchi's blood head."

"What is blood head?"

"It's a piece by Marc Quinn. It's actually called *Self.* Basically, it's a cast of the artist's head filled with his own blood. There was a rumour that Saatchi had it stored in a freezer at home that got switched off by builders who were refurbishing a kitchen for his wife. But it wasn't true. He sold it to America for a decent profit. I hate to admit it, but Drake's on to something."

"And he will buy your work?"

"He's making the right noises, let's put it that way."

"What is this man who can spend so much on ice?"

Flood snorts. "He's a vulgarian."

"You do not have respect for him?"

"These collectors are all the same. They buy to feel alive – to terrorise themselves. They long to feel like their lives are volatile when they are not."

The camera focuses in on a man across the street as he doubles up and vomits by the wheel of a parked car. Maciek tuts. "What is the matter with your people?"

"There's no poetry in their lives," Flood says. "It's all so disappointing."

"You have too much."

"Don't think your country won't go the same way now you've joined the EU. Everyone wants to be someone whether they have talent or not."

The camera shifts to a figure standing outside the curved window of Saviour's Bar and Restaurant: jeans, a T-shirt, long brown hair and a slouchy bag. *It's me.*

A sick feeling rises within me again, and I wipe my hot hands on the sofa, as I force myself to watch my younger self. What was I – twenty or twenty-one? It's only a matter of a year or so. I look better than I realised at the time, but apprehensive, as I search up and down the street.

Run, leave – get away. I wish I could shout at that girl who is me, but isn't me. *Go home – save yourself.*

Three

I had arrived early at Saviour's that night and gone straight through the bar area to the backstairs and storeroom where we could leave our stuff. My mate Donna was already there, sneaking a quick fag as she teased the cockatoo hairstyle that added an essential two inches to her five-foot frame.

"What you doing here, Mia? It's not your night."

"Covering for Mags – her son's ill."

"What, serious?"

"No, I think it's man flu."

"Isn't he about twenty-five?"

"Yeah, I know, weird isn't it? How busy are we?"

"You don't wanna know. Jason's in a right bad mood. There's something wrong with the cooker."

In the kitchen everything appeared as normal, well, better in fact as it was head chef's night off. Jason, my favourite, was at the main station, his whites pressed, his hair gelled, sauces prepped, cuts of meat portioned and wrapped, ready to be ordered. Even so, something had obviously kicked off.

"How can I work without a stove? I'm not a fucking magician," Jason said.

Our boss, Vivienne Saviour looked agitated, as she flicked her blonde highlights. "I've got someone coming in on Friday to fix it," she said.

"We're fully booked and I've only got two poxy gas rings."

"You'll just have to manage, Jason. You're a professional – surely they train you to cope with unforeseen circumstances." Vivienne turned on her patent court heel and walked out of the kitchen.

"It's a fucking joke. She could have got someone out today. She's just too tight to pay the emergency call-out fee."

"Is there anything we can do to help?" Jenny asked. She was the commis chef. She'd only been there two months but was considered the best commis chef ever. She was lovely looking too, in an understated way, with long mousy hair that she wore in a plait down her back.

"Jen, you just keep doing what you do. It would help if Mia and Donna get the first tables' orders in quick so we can get them out the way."

There were people waiting: a balding man of about fifty and two women. "Party for four – Drake," the man said. He was about my height, and well dressed in a dark suit, his forehead deeply lined. It was Nicholas Drake, the art collector, but I didn't know that then.

I showed them to the best table by the limestone fireplace, and gave them menus and a wine list. "Can you do the crab and scallop cakes without the crab?" the blonde woman asked. She was dressed in a flesh-coloured top that from a distance made her appear naked.

"I'll have to ask chef."

"I'll have the duck," the other woman said.

I returned to the kitchen: "Jase, we've got an awkward anorexic on table two." I passed him the order.

"I can't do the crab and scallop cakes without the crab. They're prepped." He was calm considering.

"Can you see to that other customer?" Donna said.

I looked out the porthole window of the kitchen's swing door at the solitary figure in a pinstriped jacket over jeans and T-shirt. *Jack Flood*. A rush of nervous excitement went through me and I returned to the restaurant.

"Hello, I didn't know you'd booked?"

"We meet again," he said and smiled. "There should be a table under Drake."

He's not single, was my first thought. *And what is he doing dining with them?*

"Jack, at last," Nicholas Drake said as soon as he saw him. "Let me introduce you. This is Mandy." He gestured towards naked-top woman. "And this is Christine. We've ordered, so hurry up."

"Can I get you anything to drink?" I said.

"My lady friend would like to change her choice of main," Drake said. "She'd also like the cod without the roasted garlic potatoes and paprika oil."

"It may be too late, I'll have to check," I said. And yes, Jason was already cooking the duck she'd previously ordered, but I mentioned it anyway and unfortunately Vivienne had made her way back into the kitchen.

"Change it," she said.

"What?"

"Do as they ask."

"Whatever you say, boss. It's your profits going straight in the bin." Jason flicked the part pan-roasted duck into the rubbish. Vivienne glared and walked out, and Jason said nothing for once, which meant he was really pissed off. And, to make matters even worse, Drake also changed his mind.

"Jase, the guy on table two's now changed from pork to spiced rump of beef."

"Where's the chit?"

For some reason, I hadn't thought to write it down.

"I need a chit." Jason's eyes were hard – the way he looked at Vivienne. "Look, I've got ten fucking chits here, if you just say it to me, I don't know what you're on about. It has to be written down."

I tried to reply but it was all getting too much and I slipped back outside to calm down.

"You all right, Mia?" Donna asked. But there was no time to stop. Another table had arrived, and my table of six needed their wine and table three's starters were due out. I seated the new arrivals, sorted the wine and went over to take Jack Flood's order before collecting table three's starters.

"Ah, my water, thank you, Mia" Jack said.

"You got her name already?" Naked-top said. "Fast work."

"We've met before, although I had no idea she worked here."

"Well, I haven't got much choice if I want to study and eat regular meals," I said.

"Fetch another glass for the champagne, will you?" Drake said.

They liked the food in the end, sending compliments to the chef, but they declined dessert. Jack said they'd drink in the bar, and they relocated leaving a hefty tip. Drake and the anorexics didn't stay long after that but Jack was still there in the bar as the restaurant emptied.

He called me over. "I must apologise for being such an awkward table," he said.

"They were happy in the end."

"Some people are never happy."

"I suppose not."

"Are you finishing soon?"

"I'll be another half an hour."

"I'd like to take you for a drink. I'll wait outside."

It was so decisive, assumptive even and I liked that, but it had been a long night, I was tired and felt I should go home.

But it's Jack Flood, I thought, I might not get another chance.

In the ladies I screwed up my uniform and changed back into my Diesel jeans and Blondie T-shirt. I wished I'd worn something else, something sexier. I didn't even have any jewellery. At least my make-up looked okay. The eyeliner had stayed in place, still thick and flicked up at the corners. I pulled on my Bambi-coloured suede boots and zipped up the zip that started inside the foot and travelled round the back of the leg and up the other side. I loved those boots. Mum had bought them as a special back-to-college present. "That's it for now, don't ask me for anything else," she had said, but I could tell she'd enjoyed buying them for me.

In the bar, Jason was sat with Clint the kitchen porter.

"Are you gonna join us, Mia?" Jason asked.

"Not tonight, sorry."

"You always have a drink."

"I can't, I'm meeting someone."

Jason nodded as if letting me go.

And so I left, expecting Jack Flood to be there, waiting, but I couldn't see him.

The dark street was noisy. It was a thoroughfare that led to various clubs: Indigo, Oceana, the Forum, a neon-lit kebab shop and other fast food joints. There was a group of lads in shirts and jeans on their way elsewhere. Don't notice me, I thought, wanting to melt into the chocolate woodwork that framed the curved glass at the entrance to Saviour's. *I should go.* Jack Flood was a no-show, but then I heard my name. *It must be Jack. Where is he?*

Groups of lads and girls passed one another, shouting and laughing. I noticed a cab across the road, its engine running as its back door opened. "Mia, over here."

I hadn't expected a car. I crossed the street. "Why do we need a cab?" I asked.

"We can avoid the drunken idiots. Come on, jump in."

"I thought we were going for a drink?"

"I know a great place, come on."

"Hi Mia." Jenny said, as she crossed nearby.

"Jenny." I waved, and she came over. "This is Jack Flood. He's an artist – quite famous," I said. "Jenny's one of the chefs."

Jack said, "Great meal, I enjoyed it."

"We're just off for a drink," I told Jenny. "See you next

week." I climbed in the back of the cab next to Jack and it took off immediately as if the driver had already been instructed where to go.

A glittery blue elephant hung from the rear-view mirror. *Lucky?* I thought, as I watched it gently sway.

Initially, Jack didn't say a thing. I felt awkward and racked my brain for something to say. "I liked your show," I said, though I hadn't been that keen. "Where did it all come from?"

"Didn't we have this conversation?" He stared ahead.

"I don't think so."

"You grilled me at the private view."

"Hardly a grilling."

"Your tutor had to step in and save me."

"You're kidding right?"

He smiled.

"I like the untitled piece. Why is it untitled?"

"Words can sometimes pin a work down too precisely."

"You weren't just being lazy then?"

"A lot of thought went into settling on 'Untitled'. Who do you like art-wise?"

"That's hard. There are so many: Peter Doig, Sarah Lucas, Rachel Whiteread, Gary Hume. Do you like Gary Hume?"

He nodded. "Some of them are neighbours of mine."

"Where do you live?"

"Spitalfields."

"You have a studio there?"

"I have the whole floor of an old wire factory."

"Oh yes, it's on your card – The Wireworks, Quaker Street..."

"That's right. You should visit – bring some of your work. I'd like to have a look."

"Really?" I said, unsure whether he meant it or not, and if he did – would it help?

"What sort of work do you do?" he asked.

"I'm not sure I've found my thing yet. I draw a lot."

"Is drawing not passé?"

"I don't think so."

He smiled, and said, "What do you draw?" And I was about to say, anything really: what's outside my window, people, me – when the cab stopped.

"Thank you, my friend," Jack said.

"What's this?" We were outside the Merchant's House Hotel.

"I need to change. One of those silly tarts spilt beer over me."

"What – deliberately?"

"No, though you never know."

"Who are they?"

"Tarts."

"Don't say that."

"It's true. They were with Drake, the art collector. He recently divorced. It was acrimonious to say the least."

"And now he has to pay?"

"He prefers it that way after his wife took him to the cleaners."

"They're really prostitutes?"

"Yep."

"My God."

"It's not unusual."

"I guess not, it's just…"

I didn't want to sound naïve but I'd never seen the high-class sort before. I was used to watching them outside my window, but they were all drug addicts and alcoholics, or so I assumed, and that meant they had little choice.

"It's whatever turns you on in this world – you'll learn. Anyway, come on, I need to change."

The elephant hanging from the rear-view mirror stilled. "I'll just wait here in the cab," I said.

"Maciek has to go." He passed the driver some cash. "I'll call you tomorrow."

The driver nodded and turned his pitted face in a way that let me know I had to get out.

I slammed the car door behind me. "Sorry," I said, and the driver looked away.

"Have you been here before?" Flood asked.

I shook my head. "No."

"You'll like it." The Merchant's House Hotel was *the* place to stay, and I was curious. Jack Flood stood back. "After you." He gestured for me to take the revolving door into the reception. It had hot pink, paisley wallpaper that eventually gave way to pared-down elegance. It was a picture of minimalist chic within its Georgian shell: pale limestone floors, framed architectural prints, leather Barcelona chairs, Perspex coffee tables and huge exotic floral displays, while the bar was a black-panelled room with club chairs and glass coffee tables with mixed salted nuts in little white bowls.

"I'm sorry, sir, we're about to close." The barman was about my age. "I can bring drinks to your room?" he said.

"You have Cristal?"

"Certainly sir, can I take your room number?"

I had no intention of going to his room. "Hold on, we're going straight out aren't we?" I said, and stopped.

"This way." Jack ignored my hesitancy and walked ahead, turning the corner into the stairway. I waited a moment before curiosity got the better of me. I hurried and caught up as Jack opened the door to room 12. It was the sort of hotel suite I'd only ever seen in magazines. There was a huge crystal chandelier, a large bed with a dark padded-leather headboard, a bronze satin bedspread, a couple of velvet club chairs and a pile of camera equipment on a side table.

"What's all this equipment? You must have a different camera for every day of the week."

"Something like that."

"This room is amazing. We're still going out though, aren't we?"

29

"I just thought you'd be more comfortable having a drink while I change." He gestured to one of the two armchairs. "Please, take a seat and enjoy a small drink before we go."

The barman rapped on the door and Jack directed the drinks tray to a side table. "Shall I open the champagne, sir?"

"No, it's fine. Thank you." Jack tipped him and showed him out. "More fun to pop the cork yourself," he said, smiling as he passed me a flute. "Cheers," he said, pulling up a chair and sitting down opposite. For a moment our knees lightly touched. "Have you had Cristal before?"

"No. Isn't it what footballers and rappers like Puff Daddy or P Diddy or whatever he's called drinks?"

"I've no idea."

"It's what Kylie likes; she mentioned it in an interview once." Flood laughed – and I felt myself redden. "I sound celebrity-obsessed – I'm really not."

"I'm not going to judge you," he smiled. "You have pale skin."

"It takes me ages to tan. I don't really bother."

"We couldn't be friends if you did."

"What?" I thought he was joking but he didn't smile.

"Help yourself to more champagne. I'm going to get changed."

"Then we're going out?"

"Mia, relax or you'll never have any fun in this world. I won't be long, and then we'll move on, I promise."

Flood selected a fresh shirt from his wardrobe, entered the bathroom and shut the door.

Why am I making such a fuss? I took another sip of champagne. *I'm going to tell Kelly and Tamzin that Cristal's overrated.* I flicked through a glossy magazine on "Best British Hotels", impressed at the Merchant's House Hotel's inclusion. *Who'd have thought I'd get to go here tonight?* I drank a little more then got up to have a nose round the room. I looked through the CDs and put on Norah Jones, then checked out the free stationery, twirling a silver pencil stamped with the Merchant's House Hotel between my palms. For a moment I wanted to keep it, but then I thought better of it. What would I say if Jack noticed? *Oh sod it.* I slipped it into my bag then moved over to one of the tall multi-pane windows.

Outside, a hen party was shrieking up the road. They were dressed in pink wigs and plastic tiaras while the bride had an 'L'-plate pinned to her back. "Last chance to knob our Laura," one of her mates shouted. How naff, I thought, and turned away but I must have moved too quickly as I felt odd, a little light-headed, like I'd drunk too much. *I've only had one glass.* I looked down at suede brown boots. *Are they my feet?* My vision blurred and I tried to focus. *My head? What's happening?*

Jack Flood was standing in the bathroom doorway with a brown towel round his waist. *Why is he smiling? I feel funny – how embarrassing.* A phone rang – a mobile. *Is that mine? Where did I leave it?* I'd only had my bag a moment ago. The ring-tone stopped. There was muffled talking. I tried to concentrate, and looked back at Jack, but he was all blurry.

What's the matter with me?

Four

I lifted my head. *Oh God, I'm dribbling. How come I'm lying face down?* I never lie on my front. I lifted my head a little more. It hurt.

What is going on?

My cheek was wet where I'd been lying. And as I moved away from the dark damp patch my spit had made on the satin bedspread I looked back at myself – naked. *Oh my God, shit. What is going on?*

The earnest words of a Sky News correspondent resonated in the background. *Where is that coming from?* There was a plasma TV in the corner, and seated in a dark armchair, dressed in a hotel-issue white towelling robe was Jack Flood.

I grabbed at the corner of the bedspread to cover myself. I checked my watch. *Jesus!* It had gone four. *How did that happen?*

"How come I fell asleep?" I touched my forehead, confused by the throbbing pain. *I don't get headaches.*

Jack Flood gazed trance-like at the TV. "Just a spoilsport – one of those girls that talks a good game but can't take the pace."

What? A thundering wave of panic washed over me, and my heart raced, as I shifted off the bed still wrapped in the bedspread. I stumbled trying to find my feet. I felt dizzy and disorientated. I shuffled round the room searching for my clothes. I couldn't remember undressing. *Who undressed me?* My jeans were scrunched on the floor. I almost fell as I tried to retrieve them.

"Steady," he said.

"Where's my underwear?"

"I'm thinking of that Sarah Lucas piece right now – *Two Fried Eggs and a Kebab*." An image of that artwork – literally two fried eggs and a kebab on a table representing a reclining naked female body with emphasis on her genitalia – flashed through my mind.

Bastard – what a bastard. I gave up on the missing underwear and struggled into my jeans, mixing up the legs like a three-year-old. *Shit, shit.* I tried to fasten them, but the metal button had gone. I looked at the floor. I couldn't see it anywhere. "I need a cab. Call me a cab."

"I'll call Maciek, if you like? Where do you live?"

Don't say. It dawned on me I mustn't say. *He mustn't know any more about me.*

"Forget it, I'm getting dressed." I gritted my teeth, fists clenched, in an attempt to stem the panic that kept rising within me.

"I can see that." He looked me up and down, his face all sneery and hateful. "Here, make yourself decent." He threw over my Blondie T-shirt.

"My boots – where are my boots?"

He looked round slowly and pointed to the side of his chair.

I'd have to walk over near him. *Do I need my boots?*

Flood raised his chin and eyed me like it was a challenge – are you brave enough to reclaim your boots? It was a long way home. *I have to get them. I love those boots. Mum bought them.*

"This is a hotel. I can scream the place down."

"Go ahead. They'll assume you're yet another of my whores."

Fuck it. Fuck him. I lunged for my boots and quickly edged round the side of the room as far from him as possible. And the door handle was finally in my hand. I turned it. It wouldn't open.

"Open it, why won't it open?"

He rose from his chair, and his eyes met mine. Slowly his lean, tall frame approached, as he let the robe hang lose.

I looked away – it was obvious. *Look anywhere but at that.*

But Flood's smirk told me he knew I'd seen it.

He was right beside me. What will he do? Every muscle in my body tensed, as I moved back. But that was no good. He was blocking the door.

"Let me out."

"Allow me." He turned a latch – one I should've been able to work out myself.

Whatever, I glanced back briefly and felt my heart bash against my ribs. There was a small camera mounted on a tripod in the corner of the room. *How hadn't I noticed that? Was it there before? Fuck, don't say that cunt filmed me?* But there was no way I could go back in and investigate. I was out of there, running down the corridor.

"Till next time, Mia."

As I got to the other side of the heavy fire door a primeval sound escaped me. It was something between a muffled scream and an involuntary grunt – ugly, subhuman – the sound of an embattled, desperate animal.

I stuffed my feet into my boots and found the stairs, taking them two, three at a time. I lost my footing and stumbled.

Get up. Get out. I felt sick. Gripping the banister tightly, I pulled myself up and stood swaying for a moment before I continued down the narrow stairs concentrating hard not to fall. Another fire door and I made it to reception where it took everything I had to find my way through only once lurching towards the bright pink wallpaper.

"Good morning, madam." The concierge said, as he looked down his long nose.

I pushed hard against the etched glass door, made it three steps round the corner and vomited. It helped. I wiped my mouth with the back of my hand. There was laughter in the distance but I couldn't see anyone. I had to get away, get home and fast. *Stupid girl* – a claustrophobic feeling of self-loathing swept over me as my stomach churned. I lurched to another doorway and retched. I could hear people coming – they'd think I was some useless drunk – if I could just keep it together. Again, my stomach heaved.

I swayed down High Pavement, my boots stomping heavily against the cobblestones as I fled further from the hotel. *Stupid Girl, You Stupid Girl*, an angry, combative song filled my head. It was by a band I really liked but I couldn't remember their name, not at that moment while everything was so hazy and confused. But I could remember the tune and the way the sexy, edgy lead singer, with her kohl-rimmed eyes, spat out the words with such venom.

I had escaped the Lace Market area but still I kept looking over my shoulder, expecting Jack Flood to be flitting between the shadows, tracking me down intent on finishing whatever weird, perverse assault he'd already begun. But no, he'd had his fun. Why would he leave the comfort of his luxury hotel suite to follow me? Oh God, what if it's like he's given me a head start, like he enjoys being in pursuit. That sick feeling rose again and I made another involuntary pathetic desperate sound, something like a yelp.

I rushed on and reached Market Square. It was so late the drunks had mostly gone. There was a police van though, at the far end, its blue light flashing. I considered walking over, wondered if I should talk to someone. But what would I say? I didn't know what had happened. And besides, what if it were a male officer? How could I begin to explain?

I looked towards the taxi stand. I had money; the tips had been good. *Oh God, it's his money – I don't want it.* I searched the square for someone homeless I could give the cash to – *typical, no beggars when you need one.*

I couldn't risk a cab – what if it was that Magic bloke with his fat potato head and small curranty eyes?

I found my keys and manoeuvred them between my fingers; as usual the sharpest Yale gripped between my index and middle finger. *I could slash Flood's face and stab his eyes.*

"You're in a bit of a hurry, love." A bloke in a Burberry T-shirt came at me from a crowded bench. "Come back with me if you like." I looked away and kept walking. "Fit but you know it," he shouted.

Fuck you. I rushed on and soon left the busier streets behind as I headed for Forest Fields, gripping the keys even tighter as I walked uphill past the cemetery and the arboretum towards The Vine – murder territory. The slightest whistle of the wind in the trees or crackle of rats in the undergrowth made me jumpy. I could hear myself breathe. I had to laugh really; there I was, as always, afraid of the dark, my imagination working overtime; hooded rapists lurking round every corner, in driveways and behind bushes. Now the bogeyman had finally come for me and it had been nothing like that. Still, I kept looking behind, checking no light-footed attacker was creeping up close until at last I made it home to the blue paint-chipped door. I looked over my shoulder once more. *Don't rapists lie in wait, ready to jump victims on their own doorsteps as they search for their keys?* At least I had my keys ready. I opened up and quickly closed it again, leaning my back against the door. I slid down to my backside and stared at a patch of orange glow seeping through the fanlight.

Upstairs, the lights in the kitchen were on. It was so late my housemates had to be asleep. I pushed the kitchen door open, taking in the stale smell of spilt lager and the remains of a wilting grey kebab. I filled a glass with tap water and made my way upstairs, my boots silenced by the shag pile.

I unlocked my door, closed it, turned the key from the inside, and went straight to the mirror. I looked pale, paler than usual, with hollowed out eyes, my dark hair straggly over my hunched shoulders. I hugged myself tight. I wanted to be small, wrap myself in cotton wool and post myself back home to Mum and Dad. It wasn't supposed to be like this. Everything was so simple for them – in their day you could pretty much fall into any job you fancied and with a little effort do well, have innocent dates, fall in love, marry and be safe. *Where did all this pressure to experience come from?* They'd cry their eyes out if they knew, their little girl alone in the world, probably violated. And worst of all, it was my fault. I should never have gone. What an idiot. All those years of Dad collecting me from anywhere and everywhere at any time, had I not learnt to be streetwise?

I turned off the light and went to the window, peeking out from behind the curtains, expecting to see somebody else's little girl getting it wrong – keen to know I wasn't the only one. There had been no one out there when I'd walked home but one girl was there now, talking into her mobile, skirt round her arse. Just the look of her scared me – she'd know too much – she'd be unbearably aware of the dark side of the world that I had only just had the misfortune to visit. She was pretty though, slim and anywhere between fifteen and thirty with shapely legs. Her braids made me think she might be mixed-race though it was hard to tell by streetlight. I wondered if she'd ever been attacked. At the very least she'd surely know someone who had. She'd know what to do. I could ask her. Only, it was ridiculous. I knew very well what I should do, but then I'd have to tell people how stupid I'd been. And really I couldn't remember a thing so what was the point?

A large family estate pulled up alongside Girl-with-braids. She leant down to talk at the window, then slipped round to the passenger door and got in where his probable wife probably normally sat. And she was gone, the street empty. The Victorian terraces opposite were dark, the crossroads quiet. I was the only one still up, though of course that couldn't be true. There had to be something going off somewhere in the city at that time whether it was just the last late-night pizza delivery, a little casual domestic violence after a night's drinking, some territorial gun-crime, or a kerb-crawling man in a family estate looking for his next victim.

Five

Did someone knock on my door? "Mia, you awake?" Kelly tried the handle. "You've locked it – you all right in there?"

I felt my head. It hurt – a dull, heavy ache.

"Mia, you in there?"

I stared in the direction of the door: "I'm awake." My eyes felt gritty and I needed a drink of water.

"I'm going now," Kelly said.

"Going where?"

"Where do you think? I'll see you at college."

It's Friday? I felt grubby and wanted to shower. *I can't rush.* "I'll see you down there." I pushed back the duvet to re-examine my pale legs beneath my Santa-Cruz T-shirt. There was nothing there, not a single bruise.

My limbs were heavy, as I forced myself up and went to the bathroom where I took a compact from my wash bag and looked between my legs, momentarily fascinated by the mysterious fleshy shellfish folds.

Surely, if he'd done something it would show. Physically there was nothing – I couldn't see anything and I couldn't feel anything untoward. *I must be okay.* I was tired but then it had gone five by the time I finally got to bed. Sleep had been fitful with images of Flood over me doing something. At one point, I even sat bolt upright, convinced he was there in the room. *Stupid Girl* – that song kept going round my head. Garbage – that was it – that

38

was the name of the band, it had come back to me; maybe other memories would filter through and I'd know what had or hadn't happened and I'd know what to do.

"Who's in there? Hurry up." Slug shouted, as he hammered on the bathroom door.

"All right, calm down." I pushed past him.

"You walking down?" Tamzin was in the kitchen looking like a young Elizabeth Hurley in white jeans and a tight pink T-shirt.

"I don't believe it – where's the milk I bought yesterday?" The fridge was empty apart from some sausages and a couple of eggs. And after all I'd said. While Slug's box of Frosties and a used cereal bowl were on the table. "Bloody Slug, does he ever buy milk?"

"Come on, get dressed," Tamzin said. "I'll wait if you're quick."

We walked down to college in silence. Tamzin was never much good in the morning and I certainly didn't want to talk. As we turned left into Shakespeare Street Tamzin dragged the last few puffs from her cigarette. "You must have got back late," she said. "I didn't hear you come in." Tamzin's room, originally the front reception room, was next to the hallway. "Did you stay for a drink after work?"

Why does she have to get talkative now?

"Have you got your eye on one of the chefs, is that it?" Tamzin stabbed out her fag before entering college. "You love Jason," she said with a smirk. She only knew Jason's name because I'd once mentioned how I thought he was quite funny. "Jason!" She grinned, and turned to go upstairs to Fashion.

I didn't want her to go. I realised it then as streams of students crossed our path on their way to different departments. I wanted her to stay and drink endless cups of coffee with me somewhere. "Tamzin," I said, making her turn around.

"Yeah?" She paused, and for a second I almost said something, but a dark wave of guilt silenced me.

"It doesn't matter," I said.

She made a face like I was acting weird, and I turned away quickly, fearing I might cry. As I walked down the bright, white corridor leading to Fine Art I struggled to compose myself.

My desk was isolated by ten-foot high board partitions that designated my space within the whitewashed studio. My boards were covered in drawings, mainly sketches of friends, strangers and found objects, and there were magazine cuttings and other rough ideas. I'd been working relatively hard but now it all felt wrong. None of it was any longer applicable. I went at it in a frenzy reducing the pinned-up layers of sketches to nothing. *Fuck, shit, damn, piss, bastard.* I scrawled in my sketchbook filling several pages with obscenities before slamming it shut.

"Ah, Mia, what's it all about?" My tutor Mike Manners pulled up a chair in my space, but didn't sit down. "What have you got for me today?"

It was time for my tutorial. Ten minutes earlier he'd have found a space full of rough workings and gathered sources of inspiration but now I'd dumped the lot.

"I'm moving on." I glanced at the bin.

Mike Manners surveyed the stark white wooden boards of my enclosure. "Go on," he said.

I swallowed hard, determined to hold it together. "I want to try a more conceptual approach, looking at communication – how it defines us. You know, how we're perceived." Hot, I wiped my forehead and coughed. "Sorry," I said.

"Where's this taking us?" Mike looked at the one pen and ink drawing I had accidentally left pinned to the wall. It was of a cat, hardly cutting-edge stuff – and he then peered at the postcard from my mate Ant. It was called '*The Perfect Woman*' and consisted of a pair of tits and an arse on legs – no arms, no head.

"The Perfect Woman," he read aloud. "So she does exist. Where can I find her?" He thought he was being funny. "What about sketchbooks?" he asked.

My sketchbook was there on the desk in front of me. It was shut, but still it provided the only colour within my whitewashed space. I had tugged at the book's black covering with a Stanley knife and rubbed coloured pastel into the greying underbelly and then daubed it with thick layers of red acrylic paint. And there, glued on top, was the Jenny Holzer cutting – 'Protect Me From What I Want'. I passed it over. And then he did sit down, made himself really comfy, one leg up on the other, and his right foot on the left knee of his faded jeans that made him think he was still with it. Oh, and God no, he even had cowboy boots on – fucking cowboy boots – at his age.

Slowly, he leafed through the pages to show he was taking it all in because this was a tutorial; our one-on-one moment. Even if I hardly ever saw him from one end of term to the next, we did have this.

"Interesting," he said, as he stroked his salt and pepper stubble. "You could use these words. I don't mind that. I wouldn't want everyone to do it, but yeah..." He thought he understood. But what had he seen? Surely, it was just ranting – the spewed anger of my confused, semi-amnesiac mind. Again I coughed and discreetly rubbed my watery eyes as he studied my work.

"There's a recurring theme." He nodded. "You need to look for a pattern. As I've said before, I don't mind you using words. I wouldn't want everyone to do it..." He stroked his chin, crossed and uncrossed his cowboy ankles. "I think it's about representing one fundamental aspect of yourself, say angry young woman for instance. I'm not sure anyone can represent his or her whole self in one piece, not straight off, first attempt. Artists spend a lifetime working on such projects. Okay, Mia. Let's go for a big push." He pumped his right fist. The tutorial was over. For all his concern, he stuck steadfastly to the allocated ten minutes before strutting off for coffee.

Again I wiped my eyes as I packed away my sketchbook and slung my bag over my shoulder. *I'm out of here.* It was a relief to exit the studio until I realised I'd have to pass the gallery showing Flood's work. A bubble of panic burst within me and I let out an involuntary gasp.

I'd forgotten about it on the way in as I'd been talking to Tamzin and the foyer had been full of people who must have obscured it. *Now, it's just me and over to the left, the brilliant white cube that designates the gallery space.*

What if Flood is here? I could see the show's title piece, *Now That You've Gone Were You Ever There?* The pearl stud earring on a black velvet cushion raised high on a plinth surrounded by the outline of a body with prominent breasts had become more sinister. *Where did that earring come from?* When I first saw it I had assumed it belonged to an ex-girlfriend, but now I had my doubts. *Did he do something to her? And the yellow taped outline on the floor – is that woman dead?*

Burning up, my heart raced as I checked in every direction and forced myself forward, glancing briefly at the few people studying Flood's so-called art. *It's shit*, I wanted to shout but instead I held my breath and made for the glass door.

Outside, there was bright sunshine, a brilliant day, early enough in summer to make the heat a novelty. Students were sitting out on the library steps, removing any surplus clothes. But I wouldn't even roll up my sleeves as I marched up the hill home, my hair soaked with sweat.

There was a ropey yellow-haired prostitute sitting on the wall opposite. I went inside and slammed the front door.

In the kitchen I stopped to check the fridge. It was empty, while Slug's box of Frosties remained on the table. *Sod it.* I took the box and went upstairs. Sitting cross-legged on my bed I would make rough plans for the project in my sketchbook as I ate handfuls of the sickly-sweet flakes straight from the box.

I could hear a car outside. "Look at that – what a dog!" someone shouted.

My room felt stifling with its velvet curtains and old dark furniture but I couldn't open the window. I wouldn't let in any fresh air and besides the dilapidated sash wouldn't stay up.

I had to shut everything out by shutting myself in. I sat back on the bed; mindlessly eating Frosties and took out my phone. I flicked through the names and paused at 'Home'. *Should I call Mum?* I thought of years ago in the garden back home: lush green grass and Mum lying on a sunbed. Something had happened at school that day, I can't remember what, but even aged six or seven I felt I couldn't burden her, not when she was so tired after a hard day. I scrolled down the names on my contacts: Lucy, Tom, Kate – mates from home – they'd all listen, but they were all at other universities or working, getting on with their lives.

Desperate, I thought, wiping at my sweat-dampened hair. I sighed and flopped sideways. And I must have instantly fallen asleep, as I was still like that when Kelly rapped my door. "Mia, are you ill?"

I looked up at the ceiling, assuming it was early evening. "What time is it?"

"It's gone eleven."

"How come? It's so light."

"It's eleven in the morning – what's got into you?"

I'd slept right through – twenty hours or so. I rubbed my eyes and shifted onto my side. My legs were leaden, as though my very bones were sore.

What is up with me? Again I felt shaky, as if I could cry at anything. *Sort it out, Mia. You can't go on like this.*

Six

There was a new club night, Incendiary. I'd been looking forward to it for ages; only it was at Lost and Found, a converted lace factory close to the Merchant's House Hotel. *Can I go near there?* I asked myself. *Can I bear it? Flood's gone. He must have. He has no reason to stay in Nottingham.*

I convinced myself he'd gone back to London, but even so my stomach knotted as I walked the Lace Market's wormery-like streets, checking each passing face, wary of whom I might see. And I hadn't told Kelly or Tamzin or anyone else – that would make it real. *It's best I forget it*, I reasoned – *seeing as I barely remember anything anyhow.*

At the door to the club, a skinny girl in hot pants and a halter-neck top checked us over. And then we were in and on our way up the stairway where I touched the walls – painted Prussian blue and dripping with a glittering film of condensation.

There was a buzzing queue of the city's beautiful people moving into the first-floor bar. Two girls in gold bikinis with matching asymmetric haircuts danced on a podium. A gorgeous gazelle floated by in a dress slashed in a V to her belly; another wore a lime sorbet dress and there was a Boho type in a diaphanous kaftan. Boys with shaved heads and sharp suits stood in a Reservoir Dogs group while a Jesus lookalike in a torn T-shirt popped something in his mouth.

Everyone was looking at everyone else while pretending not to. People were moving in all directions looking for the best place to stand, where best to be seen, or space at the bar. There was my friend Ant in a skintight psychedelic Pucci top nodding from afar, the entire fashion course though Tamzin barely acknowledged them, along with basically anyone who was supposedly anyone.

I stood, bottle of Budvar in hand, looking around like everyone else but I didn't feel good. *Is my dress all right?* It was vintage, sleeveless with gold sequins sewn in a thick collar and I'd felt pleased with it earlier but in the club up against all the other girls it seemed lacking.

That photographer was there, the one with the blonde Mohican who'd been at the private view. Again his camera swept the room, picking people off. I looked away, not wanting the black hole of his lens to rest on me – not again, not while I was feeling so unsure.

Kelly passed me another Budvar. It helped to have something to hold. "Let's look upstairs," she said, so we went up to the quieter, chill-out bar above, which was low-lit with people seated at the sides or standing in groups. I recognised a few faces and quickly scanned the room for anyone interesting.

Luke was there. He stood out as he was tall, good-looking and effortlessly cool, but then again perhaps his nonchalant image of classic T-shirts, jeans and retro old-school trainers took hours of dedicated sourcing. He was also on fine art, a third year sculptor, and I'd always liked him. Luke was the sort that always flirts back just enough to keep you interested. I went over and said hello.

"Mia!" he said, as if he was surprised to see me.

"What have you been up to?" I asked.

"Just working – I've got a lot on."

"Oh yeah, your final year. What are you doing?"

He shrugged. "I don't want to go into it right now."

I should have taken the hint and made myself scarce, but I

wanted him, someone familiar, though apart from looks it wasn't obvious why. I looked back at him, desperately thinking what to say but he got in first. "I've got to find Nick." And that was it, he walked away and I stared after him. *Who the hell is Nick?* I turned back, sensing someone watching me, and found Mohican-man pointing his lens straight at me. He captured my disappointment. And I glared back until he let his camera drop.

Give them nothing and lots of it, I had heard men joke – *is that Luke's approach?* "Arse-hole," I muttered to myself later, staring at my reflection in the chipped mirror that hung over the dodgy gas fire in my room. *I shouldn't have gone. I wasn't up to it.* Clubs like that are for confident days when you feel good about yourself.

My housemate Spencer walked me home. "Are you all right, Mia?" he said in a way that made me think he was asking about more than my inebriated state. But I couldn't tell him anything. I couldn't tell anyone. I stumbled and Spencer caught me. "Steady – how much have you had? It's not like you to get this drunk."

Back home in my room when I looked at my disappointed face it seemed such a shame to wash away the make-up. I liked the heavy eyeliner slightly smeared by sweat and my hair falling forward as it should but rarely did.

"Fucking tosser," I said to the mirror as if it were Luke, and then said it again more aggressively, thinking of Flood.

I reached for the wardrobe door. It was a dark, shiny, upright, mahogany tomb.

From the next room I could hear groaning (Kelly had brought someone back). I pulled at the filigree metal knob and let the wardrobe door swing loose on its creaking hinge as I stared into the black hole of its interior. I knew it was in there, wrapped tightly in carrier bags and shoved to the back. Out of sight out of mind I had hoped, but it kept coming back, haunting my thoughts, coming between me and my life, reminding me I'd lost control, had allowed four hours to slip from my consciousness.

I reached in and grabbed the bag as an image of a hooded man in black pulling me in flashed through my mind.

Got it. I dangled it at arm's length as if toxic, and then let it drop to the floor, its contents spilling out: my favourite Diesel jeans and Blondie T-shirt rolled in a ball, now criss-crossed with a thousand creases.

I held the T-shirt to my nose, determined not to gag, as I smelt for signs of Flood. *Could it be evidence – but evidence of what? I have no idea what, if anything, went on.*

I could detect only the faint hint of my own sweat mixed with the chemical perfume of deodorant, while my jeans had lost their metal button.

I went over to my desk where I kept my art equipment and searched my toolbox. *Damn, no scissors.* I must have left them at college. *Scalpel?*

I placed my drawing board on the floor. It was a board my dad had made from an old off-cut of wood, carefully rubbing down the rough edges. I picked up the T-shirt. It was one of my favourites and I always felt good wearing it. It was fitted and a perfect length. I loved that T-shirt, and I couldn't help but cry as I held the material taut, looking at Debbie Harry's beautiful face from her New York heyday. She was a punk Marilyn, I thought, as I slashed her to pieces.

Seven

Saviour's, like college and the Lace Market area, had been tainted by the fact Flood knew where to find me. I was due back at work and, despite how I felt, I knew I had to go.

Flood's in London, I kept telling myself. It was the only way I could carry on as normal.

Warren, the head chef, was in. Crass and stocky with floppy white hair, he did my head in. "Whatever you do, don't take your eyes off it," he was saying to Jason, as I entered the kitchen. "They can whip right round your arm and paralyse you."

"That's a wind up," Donna said.

Jason plunged his right arm into the shallow tank, grabbed an eel firmly behind its head and pulled it out of the water. Whack! He slammed its head against the edge of the steel worktop and slit its metallic skin, moving the knife in a full neat circle behind its head. The eel twitched as he pulled the skin down and away as if he were removing a wetsuit and chopped the length into portions while the jaws of the severed head gnashed away at the steel surface.

"That is minging," Donna said.

"What's it for?" I asked.

"Lightly smoked eel with eel brandade," Jenny said.

"Sounds gross."

Jenny shook her head and smiled. "Eel is under-rated."

"You look nice, Jen," Donna said.

48

"You don't normally wear make-up," I said.

"Why Jennifer, you're beautiful." Warren said, putting on an American accent.

"Leave her alone," Jason said.

"Interesting – it's not like you to be so sensitive to the feelings of others," I said.

Vivienne looked in. "Girls, there's customers waiting."

"Off you go, back to work," Jason said.

In the restaurant I seated a middle-aged couple, took their drinks order and immediately returned with a bottle of Chenin Blanc and a jug of water.

"Mia, tuck your blouse in, you've got a nice figure, don't hide it." Vivienne was on my case again. I gritted my teeth and slouched back into the kitchen.

"Hear them scream." Warren held two lobsters, their pincers bound, above a huge pot, as he sang Rock Lobster by The B-52s. He grinned at Jason as he lowered them into the boiling water but Jason was with Jenny at the far side.

"You're a very sick man, Warren," Donna said. "It's so cruel, isn't it, Mia?"

"Sorry, what?" I'd been distracted, watching Jason and Jenny.

Jason returned to his post. "It's not a scream – it's just the air coming out of their shells. It's very quick. Shellfish have to be totally fresh."

"Aren't you supposed to kill them first?" I said.

"You can split their head with a knife if you want."

"You do the next lot, Jase?" Warren said, and Jason glanced at Jenny who shrugged as if boiling lobsters (which I knew she didn't like) couldn't be helped.

Back in the restaurant a man raised his hand and snapped his fingers. He'd been difficult all night. "Do that again," he'd said earlier when he'd caught me blowing up at my fringe. No way was I going to repeat something just for his amusement. "Four Tia Marias, please."

I headed back to the bar wishing I were invisible so I could travel like vapour, in and around, seeing who was there but without being seen.

The bar was pleasant enough with dove grey painted tongue and groove panelling on the lower half of the walls and a selection of framed colourful prints – works by Dufy and Matisse, that kind of thing. They brightened the place up and yet were obviously chosen for their inoffensiveness. There should be a law against that, I thought. Companies should be made to buy or at least display original works – imagine the kick-start that would give young artists. I thought of one of Spencer's vast seascapes – good enough to go anywhere – all that passion and turmoil in layer upon layer of thick oil paint that he couldn't really afford.

A balding bloke in a pink shirt by the bar looked my way. "If you were a bit older and had better posture..." he said, and his friends laughed.

Yeah, as if. I scowled back at him. *Hurry up, Duncan,* I willed the barman to get on with my order. There was nothing to do but look around, take it all in – social life without the socialising.

"Mia, what can I do for you?" Duncan finally got round to my order though it wasn't long before Finger-snapper wanted more. In fact, over the next hour all my five other tables emptied while he kept ordering, forcing me to repeatedly return to the bar, worried that Flood could be there. Although I did try to rationalise: he has to have gone. He lives in London. Why would he hang round here? But even so, my heart raced whenever I walked in that direction.

"Are they ever going to leave?" Donna said. Well, not before Finger-snapper had tried to humiliate me once more.

"You have to smile to get a tip," he said, sweeping back an oily piece of hair. I looked back expressionless. "Must be her time of the month." They all laughed, even the two women. Bitches. And then finally, drunkenly, they left leaving a little loose change for my trouble.

I cleared away while Donna cashed up and split the tips between us. "What a load of shit for all that grief," she said.

"How are we doing, girls?" Vivienne turned up, G and T in hand. "Oh Mia, do something about your hair – tie it back properly please."

Don't employ art students if you don't like how we look, I thought.

"Any room at the inn?" Warren sat on the bench next to me and Jason pulled up a chair. "We had some right fuckers in tonight."

"The customer is always right," Vivienne said.

"Yeah, and I'm Wayne Rooney," Warren said.

"Ugly enough," Donna said. "What about Tia-Maria-man – he was giving you some grief."

"They do it to feel better about themselves," I said.

"Here's Jenny." Warren tapped the other side of the bench beside him but Jenny sat down next to Donna.

"Are you going to get yourself a drink, Jenny?" Vivienne asked.

"I've got to get going in a minute." She gripped the strap of her Nike kitbag as if she wanted to leave immediately.

"Come on, Jen, have a drink," Jason said.

"I'm training tomorrow."

"How far are you running this time?" I asked.

"Ten miles."

"Is that supposed to be fun?"

"I'm doing the Midlands marathon next month."

"Rather you than me," Donna said. "You must be a masochist."

"She's good," Jason said.

How would he know? Something is going on. I didn't want to hang around anymore. "I better get going," I said.

"Me too," Donna said, and Jenny stood up.

"Are you okay getting back, girls?" Vivienne asked, which was a joke because we all knew she'd never pay for staff taxis.

"I heard about that murder," Warren said. "That's near where you live, isn't it, Mia?"

"Why mention that? Cheers, Warren, I'll worry even more now." I didn't need reminding. Days earlier, I'd even passed the bundle of wilting bouquets marking the spot where she was found.

Donna frowned. "That poor woman."

We left then, and walked up Victoria Street towards the bright lights of Market Square.

"How did it go with that artist the other night?" Donna asked. She was being a friend. Friends ask questions. But I didn't want this conversation. *What to say?* I felt sick and turned away, as if checking the traffic before we crossed a road. "Where did he take you?" She wasn't going to drop it.

"The bar at the Merchant's House Hotel – I only stayed for one drink," I said, which was true enough. I saw it then – the hotel room with its dishevelled bed and me naked as I desperately searched for my clothes and boots. "He's too old and smarmy." I made a face and changed the subject. "What about you, Jenny? Are you seeing anyone? You never tell us anything."

Again, she gripped the strap of her kitbag. "I'm always working."

"What about your nights off?" I had to know. Jenny was so pretty with poker-straight hair to her waist. If she weren't so shy she'd be deadly.

"I'm usually at running club."

"Is there no one there?"

"They're all too old."

"She wouldn't tell us anyway," Donna said.

"I reckon you'll end up falling for another chef," I said.

Jenny looked at me quizzically. I'd guessed right, something was going on between her and Jason. She smiled and looked away and before I could ask anything more Donna interrupted. We'd reached their bus stop and the moment passed.

I left them then to walk on alone, too impatient to wait for a bus or tram. And, as always, I worked my keys between my fingers.

It had gone midnight by the time I got back. I looked over my shoulder before I opened the door. The house was dark. There wasn't a sound. I listened at Slug's door – nothing. Tamzin's was slightly ajar – again nothing. Upstairs it was obvious no one was about. Spencer had left his light on and there were pots of wet paint on the windowsill. *Lazy shit – never cleans up.*

Kelly's door was shut. She would have locked it. I unlocked my own, went in and locked it from the inside. I was too buzzy to sleep. Service does that to you – all that running around after people. *Sod it; make coffee.*

But there was no milk. *From a restaurant stuffed with fresh produce to this. Black coffee it is then.* I returned to my room, relocked the door and sat on my bed. *What's on?* I flicked through a chat show, two American comedies, the end of a film and the weather and went back to the film, thinking I might recognise it.

Turn off the light, look out the window – it might be more interesting.

Across the street, leaning against the wall of the Asian family's house was Girl-with-braids dressed in a micro-skirt and leather jacket. She checked her nails and paced up and down past three or four houses.

A white car pulled up. It had lettering on the side.

"Go fuck yourself, arsehole!" She stepped back and away, while the car stayed put. *Should I do something?*

The cab pulled away and Girl-with-braids gave it the finger. *Good for you, girl. Don't worry, I'll watch out for you.* Girl-with-braids walked off down the street and disappeared out of sight.

I withdrew from the window, found my sketchbook and wrote "Girl-with-braids, white car," and the date and time. Then I looked around, straining to see. The room was dark apart from the telly's flickering brightness. I moved towards the mirror that hung on the chimney breast, took off my T-shirt and jeans and kicked them aside. Mismatched underwear – *there's a surprise* – pale pink knickers and a black bra.

I switched on my Anglepoise lamp and gathered paints, water and some heavy textured paper, and placed a drawing board on the floor. I unhooked the mirror from the wall, leant it against the unlit gas fire, and knelt in front of it.

The blank paper's whiteness glowed, appearing vast and daunting. *Can I do this? Can I make it work?* I took a medium sable-hair brush and ran its soft bristles over the bare skin of my thigh and dipped it in water, and Naples yellow, more water, titanium white and a spot of carmine red.

The translucent colour punctured the paper's whiteness as I sketched a fluid outline. I thought of the eels in the kitchen, and it was as if the delicate pools of welling, spreading watercolour were skinning me alive as the hard shell I felt forced to wear each day dissolved before me. There I am, that's me: twitching and unsure, I thought, as I let more drops of watery colour drip and spread like the unshed tears I was constantly battling to withhold.

Eight

The woman found dead on Forest Road East had been named as Loretta Peters. She was pretty with a tanned, smiling holiday face shown in an old snap from years before, and she was a mother of two, as well as someone's 'lovely, bubbly' daughter until a boyfriend introduced her to drugs.

Since Loretta's murder, there had been no further squabbles about watching the news. Kelly shushed us so she could hear. "They've found another body," she said.

"It must be a serial killer." Spencer sat forward.

As did Slug. "Loretta – she's not bad. You wouldn't think she's a prostitute."

"I don't recognise her," I said.

"Is there something you need to tell us, Mia?" Slug said.

"Have you not noticed them outside our front door, Slug? We do pass them every day. You must recognise some of them?"

"I don't care what they look like as long as they're kneeling."

"Slug!" Kelly threw a magazine at him.

"Are you working tonight?" Kelly asked.

"I'm not going," I said.

"That's not like you."

"I'm phoning in sick."

"Yeah, I would," Tamzin said. "Say you've got a migraine."

It was a Friday, which meant Neon. Every day of the week had its associated club nights. Friday was Neon, the Forum or

Lost & Found and my housemates favoured Neon. I didn't like it but as I usually worked that night the choice wasn't mine.

There was the usual shouting, drunken queue for admittance.

"Go on, Mia, get in there," Spencer said, as the doorman lowered the rope for the next batch of club-goers. We were in, and immediately I joined another queue for the ladies, as we'd already been drinking heavily at Ruby's. The toilets were packed: girls in skimpy tops, with competing perfumes, vied for cubicles and mirror-space, reapplying lipstick that didn't need to be reapplied. It wasn't easy to gain the space to wash my hands and I was glad to get out, back to the bar area, where Kelly had bought me a vodka.

"Come on, let's go upstairs to the balcony," she said. It was a good place to go to look around and check out who was there. But it was just as busy as downstairs. We walked around and stopped briefly, holding on to the chrome railings, as we looked down below. There was no one I liked, though I could see Spencer at the bar below ordering drinks, while Tamzin was up against a pillar kissing some rugby-type, the size of a small wardrobe.

The music changed tempo. "Bee Gees!" Kelly pulled at my arm, but I hated the Seventies slot – so predictable. Tamzin turned up (minus wardrobe-man), and they rushed to the dance-floor, doing exaggerated disco moves to Staying Alive.

Bored, I looked around even though I didn't expect to see anyone I'd like. *Hold on...* There was a guy with black hair and heavy-hooded eyes, like a Raphael self-portrait, updated and come back to life. He was too beautiful but even so... "Are you French?" I asked.

The heavy-hooded eyes looked my way. "'ow did you know?"

"I've seen you before." It was true. He'd been in Saviour's but he didn't ask where I'd seen him. He must have been accustomed to being admired from afar.

"What's your name?" I asked, as I admired his fine features.

"Bert."

"That doesn't sound very French."

"It's Bertrand." He then asked my name.

"Do you like it here?" I asked, glancing around at the tired chrome fittings and royal blue carpet.

"The whisky is very cheap."

"But it's a bit crap, isn't it?"

"The music's not so good."

Our small talk continued until someone distracted him.

"He was nice." Kelly had returned from the dance-floor. "Where's he gone?"

"His friend dragged him off somewhere."

"He'll be back," Kelly said, but I wasn't so sure.

"I need another drink; do you want one?" I went to the bar, knocking back more vodka, then a few minutes later Kelly nudged me. Bert was there, sitting on some steps at the far side of the bar. And when he saw me look over he stood up and waved. *God he's beautiful – can he really like me?*

"You're in there," Kelly nudged.

And so it was that within a few hours he was walking me home, drinking my coffee, easing me back on my bed, gently pushing my hair away from my face as if he couldn't see enough. *Can I do this?*

He kissed my neck, my shoulder, and right breast, as his hand slid behind the waistband of my jeans.

I could barely breathe let alone speak. I had wanted this. I had wanted him. I liked him. Only, it was as if I were outside myself, like watching a soap opera sex scene that went on and on to underline the fact two characters are an item.

I moved my hips and feigned desire, kissed, licked, nibbled and faintly scratched – all the while willing him to come so it would stop.

He did stop and he lay still, still inside me. I wanted him off. I curled myself away from him, only for him to follow me across the bed, kissing the back of my neck. *What made me think I could cope with a stranger in my bed?*

How did I manage that? I asked myself the next morning. I'd been inebriated of course. My head hurt. *I need to stop drinking so much. It's not helping.* He lay there filling my single bed, his renaissance profile highlighted by a shaft of light eking through a crack in the curtains. I was staring and he must have sensed it.

"I've got to go," I said, though I didn't really.

He shook a little as he got up, his lean, defined torso rock god material. "Can you sing?" I asked.

"No. Why?" He bent down to sort the clothes he'd dumped by my bedside. I gave him only moments to dress – didn't offer coffee, didn't offer breakfast.

"I've got to go this way," I said, after leading him downstairs and out the front door onto the pavement. "What about you?" He pointed in the opposite direction and smiled, his face a little confused. I don't think any girl had ever turfed him out before.

Nine

It was just like any other Sunday, the day I heard. I'd had a hangover all day and was desperate for food. I checked my kitchen cupboard. "Dried pasta and tuna – I can't believe that's all I've got," I said to Kelly, who was sitting on a stool reading *Vogue*.

"Nightmare," she said, without looking up from her magazine.

"Do you think *Vogue*'s advertisers realise it's bought by penniless students?"

Kelly shrugged. "I'm going downstairs."

I flicked through the Student Cookbook. There had to be something I could make. Tuna bake was the best option, but I'd need some Campbell's Condensed Mushroom Soup.

I found the few coins I had left and walked down the road, glancing up at the three-storey terraces. *Are any of the windows watching?* It felt like they were.

On the wall at the crossroads sat a young girl – one I hadn't seen before – in a crop top, short skirt, bare legs and trainers. Her hair was in gelled ringlets and her hands tight in her pockets. She looked fed up. No one was about. Punters would surely be home with their families eating Sunday roasts. And besides, hadn't she heard about Loretta and the other woman? She shouldn't be out. *What is she doing?*

Around the next corner, I entered the tiny over-filled shop.

There were only two aisles, so I soon located a dusty tin of soup. It was too dark to see a Use-By date but I guessed it would be okay. The shopkeeper checked my carefully counted out coins and nodded as his wife stood silently by in her sari and thick cardigan.

"Hey, pretty girl," a guy shouted from a third-floor window in the house next to the shop. He always said something or else he just went 'psst'. I kept walking. I mean, did he really think he could pull from up there like a male Rapunzel?

Back round the corner, girl-on-the-wall had gone. *I hope she's safe. Please let her be safe.*

Mix the condensed mushroom soup with the pasta, tuna and sweetcorn, place in an ovenproof dish and top with buttered bread and grated cheese. *Oh yes, though I'd never eat this at home, I can't wait.* It needed to bake for twenty minutes so I sat in my room with my sketchbook open and thought again of the Frenchman tenderly pushing the hair back and away from my face.

The warm fishy smells drifting up to my room grew stronger so I knew it was time. Downstairs, the kitchen window was fogged as the bubbly, boiling tuna and soup belched like volcanic mud. I spooned a large dollop of the steaming gunk onto one of our mismatched plates and made my way downstairs to join the others.

"Shove up, will ya?"

Reluctantly, Slug and Spencer made some space on the collapsed green sofa.

"Antiques Roadshow – will that programme ever end?" I said.

"This bird's painting's gonna be worth a packet." Slug nodded towards the old woman who was telling the valuer how she was downsizing due to bereavement.

"Yeah, all right love, we're all very sorry, but stop going on."

"It is a most ravishing painting," the TV expert said.

"What you eating?" Spencer asked.

"Tuna Special."

"Looks like elephant dung," Tamzin said.

"Don't diss my cooking."

"You could stick it on one of your paintings like Chris Ofili," Kelly said.

"You what?" Slug said.

"He sticks elephant dung on his paintings."

"Did you hear that – one hundred fucking grand for that picture," Slug said. "I'm on the wrong course."

Kelly curled her lip. "Colours looked muddy to me."

"I don't like it," I said.

"That's the door." Tamzin went to answer, and quickly returned looking concerned. "It's for you, Mia. It's the police."

Oh my God. "What?" I got up, taking my plate with me.

Two dark uniformed figures filled the doorway.

"Mia Jackson?" The younger one asked. He was cute with chocolate button eyes. Is this who they send when it's bad news? I nodded and thought of Flood. *Do they know something?*

The police officers introduced themselves. The cute one was called DC Stanmore or Standard or something? I couldn't take it in.

"Is there somewhere we can talk, Miss Jackson?" The older one had a thick Scottish accent and a miserable, craggy face. "Can we come in? You have somewhere we can talk?" He had to repeat himself. I wasn't reacting but where could I take them? Everyone was in the living room. It would have to be upstairs. I led them up to the first-floor kitchen.

Just say it. Tell me. Get it over with. Don't let it be Mum and Dad.

My plate wobbled as I placed it on the side. And I gathered up two further dirty plates and there were mugs with browning dregs and fag ash. I started tipping slops into the sink.

"Don't fuss," the older officer said. "Please sit down."

Our chairs were rickety and the police officers looked too big for them. I gripped the sides of my old wooden seat.

"You're a friend of Jenny Fordham?" the young officer asked.

Jenny? I only know one Jenny. What's her surname?

"She's a chef. You work with her at Saviour's Bar and Restaurant."

"Oh Jenny, yes, of course. She's okay, yeah?"

Their hesitation was my answer.

"She's missing," the older, craggy-faced officer said.

And I laughed. It seemed absurd. "No, she can't be." They looked at me as if I might know something. All I knew was that people I know don't go missing.

The older officer leant forward. "This is strictly routine, but we have to ask: where were you on Friday night, 11.40pm?"

I gripped the edge of the old wooden chair and glanced at the dirty plates and empty cereal packets. *What to say? I should have been there.* "I phoned in sick. I've never done that before, it's just I couldn't face it. I told Vivienne, that's my boss, that I had a migraine but I went out with my housemates to Neon." I gripped the chair tighter. "Are you going to tell her that?"

They didn't reply. They just carried on looking, waiting for me to say something significant. "If you can think of anything and I mean anything – please give us a call." The older officer passed me contact details. "We'll show ourselves out."

The younger one nodded towards the dirty plates piled on the worktop and in the sink. "Reminds me of my student days."

I poked at my tuna bake. I no longer wanted to eat, and it had congealed anyway, so I scraped it into the swing bin where it landed with a thud.

Ten

Jenny – I saw her everywhere. I looked for her in every face I passed, on every pavement, in every crowd but always it turned out to be just her chin walking around on someone else, or the way she'd shyly look away, or the back of her long, straight hair worn by a less attractive woman. Sometimes, I thought I'd caught sight of her back disappearing down a side street or in a crowd and I'd have to change direction and follow, walking for ages out of my way. It was exhausting, the constant looking, and the willing, wanting her to be alive and back again.

People go missing every day, often because they want to get away.

I took my camera and snapped away at the overflowing bins and relatively empty Sunday streets. Perhaps I'd capture something, a clue, and not even realise till later when I looked over the images on my computer.

Six hundred people disappear every day. It's not unusual.

My housemates wanted to help. They asked what Jenny was like and I zipped through the images on my mobile, determined to find a photo. Eventually there she was in the kitchen at work, smiling and slight in her chef whites, her long mousy hair tied back, and her arm round a grinning Donna.

"She often wears her hair tied up but she should wear it down. If I had hair like that I'd wear it down," I said.

"She looks nice," Slug said.

"She is – way too good for you."

Saviour's felt like a morgue long before we knew anything. It amazed me that anyone would want to eat there while there was a question mark over Jenny's whereabouts, but people did.

The police did a reconstruction with a young female officer in a long, straight wig and the same sweatshirt, combats and trainers Jenny had worn the night she disappeared. And they released a police statement, saying: "Trainee chef Jenny Fordham is a popular young woman who was born and brought up in the Nottingham area. She is a keen runner, as well as an active member of a young Christian group. It is out of character for her to go missing or fail to keep in touch."

Jenny, being considered 'nice' and 'middle-class', had become newsworthy.

It is rare for anyone who goes missing over the age of sixteen to gain news coverage. Girls go missing all the time, girls with piercings, bleached or dyed hair, girls who wear tight, revealing clothes; the media rarely bothers with them unless they're particularly young or vanish in unusual circumstances. Only the wholesome are considered worth looking for – the rest had it coming. But Jenny was good, she was different – her parents live in the Park area of Nottingham, a desirable enclave of period homes near the castle.

The national press picked up on the story and Crimewatch ran a reconstruction. And there was the front of Saviour's on TV, the curved Art Deco windows looked decorative and smart as the Jenny impersonator walked out, Nike kitbag over her shoulder. And that was it, reconstruction over, because that's all they had – one night, Jenny left work and vanished.

"Right now, I could almost believe in alien abduction," Donna said.

We had both sat down in the bar for coffee in the brief lull between preparation and the arrival of customers.

"It doesn't add up," she said, "and you know what really gets me is that normally we leave the same time as Jenny but she didn't stop for a drink that night. She was running the next day and wanted to get back."

"I should have been there," I said. "Maybe she'd be okay if I'd left work the same time as we usually do."

"It's not your fault." We both fell silent as we finished our coffee.

Over 210,000 people go missing every year. I had checked the statistics online. "The police call them mispers," I said.

"You what?"

"Missing persons – they call them mispers, sounds like whispers, doesn't it? Like they're ghosts the rest of us can no longer hear."

"Don't say that, you're creeping me out."

They only search for the vulnerable or where there's been a crime.

The police had already come out and said they thought Jenny had been abducted and yet no CCTV footage of her had been traced from any of the cameras in the city centre. She must have got in a car whether willingly or otherwise. And no significant sightings had been made though the police remained convinced someone must have seen something. But if there was a witness, he or she was not keen to come forward whether due to fear of reprisals or the simple fact he or she was not meant to be on that street at that time.

From my bedroom window I looked out at the lamp-lit crossroads. *Can anyone tell me where to find my friend?*

The street was empty. The girls must have been taking heed or were they in danger in a stranger's car at that very moment?

Windows glowed in the period conversions opposite: other students, the unemployed, the old, low-paid, and immigrants. A car crawled past. Bang! One of its wheels burst a crisp packet. The driver sped away – *Loser.*

I withdrew from the window, closing the heavy curtains; I had work to do. *How can I concentrate? What if it's Flood?* I had introduced Jenny to Flood the night I went for a drink at his hotel. *Did he go back for her?* I couldn't get the idea out of my head. *I should go to the police.* I felt sick. Reporting what may or may not have happened would make it real.

Hold on, no, it can't be Flood. He's back in London. I'd seen him pictured in a newspaper at the opening of the latest Royal Academy show in London.

I'd know if he was here. I would sense it.

I looked back at my self-portrait from a few nights before. The painted figure looked bemused and wary and that was before I'd even heard about Jenny. I had to have something to show. I had a crit the next day. What else could I do but take the watercolour sketch and develop it – thicker paint, texture – put it on canvas? So what if it showed vulnerability, bemusement and even fear – that's life isn't it?

A police siren whirred.

Have they found Jenny or is it someone else?

Please, let Jenny be safe.

Eleven

Flood's DVD. Interior, loft apartment: large multi-paned windows, exposed brickwork and in the middle of the room a calico-covered chair. The date in the bottom right-hand corner states: Thursday 2 June 2005, the Wire Works, Spitalfields, London.

"Who lives in a house like this?" It's Flood's voice. "Let's take a look at the clues." The camera points upwards. "Lovely high beams, perfect to hang yourself from as and when your genius goes unrecognised." He moves into the kitchen area. It's small with the usual fitted appliances and units.

"Cooking may not be a priority for this person," he says. "Although, there is a large fridge freezer..." The camera shifts to a stainless steel American-style side-by-side fridge freezer, and sweeps back towards the living area. "Note a distinct absence of any statement pieces – no mid-century design-classic furniture, no oversized flat-screen TV. We can only surmise this is no flash city slicker's crash pad. But what to make of the generous expanse of empty space?" He points to the corner. "And the large canvases lined up against one wall and the pile of sketches?"

The camera switches to a fixed position and Flood comes into view. He walks over and begins to leaf through the drawings, holding a couple to camera. "Here's a woman's face in ecstasy, this one has a wanton lolling tongue, while she's asleep with legs akimbo – racy stuff. And paint on the floor, turps by the sink – who lives in a house like this?

"In fact, it's not a house; it's a loft, a lateral conversion of an old wire factory – my studio, a live/work space. Eleven years I've been here, watching Spitalfields change from button-makers, hat shops and general decay to a hipster theme park, but at least there's decent coffee to be had.

"I've been working away – just got back, and Dora Maar isn't talking to me, are you, my sweet?" He lifts a dark brown cat from the calico-covered chair. "She's named after one of Picasso's mistresses – the one he only ever portrayed in tears. She adopted me." He holds the cat out in front of him, face-to-face. "She couldn't resist my indifference – it's a girl thing. Look at her, what a beauty, the colour of bitter chocolate." Dora Maar wriggles out of his arms. "Very well, have it your way."

He selects a sketchbook and sits down to flip through the pages. "There she is, that's Angela." His finger traces her jawline and he holds the page up to camera. The drawing is fine, the expression sad, lonely and vulnerable. He snaps the sketchbook shut and tosses it to the floor. Moving up close, he rubs his eyes and looks into the lens. "I have to sleep. It's been a week." *He does look rough.*

He shuts his eyes and holds his head as if in pain. And he goes to a laptop open on a desk and keys something in. "Lab rats deprived of sleep die after a matter of only weeks instead of their usual two years or so. That's what it says. Ten days is the record without sleep, or 260 hours – but that's without drugs or torture."

He walks towards what must be his bedroom.

Interior, Flood's studio: the light pours in from skylights in the roof and the large warehouse windows. Two police officers are seated on paint-splattered wooden chairs. One is young and slim, the other old, fat and nearly bald, like a handsome son next to the disappointing older man he'll become.

"Would you like tea or coffee, gentlemen?" Flood is dressed in a fraying T-shirt and jogging bottoms.

"Coffee, two sugars, please," the bald policeman says.

Flood turns towards a dark-haired young woman busy tidying piles of paper. "Rita, do the honours, there's a love."

"We've been trying to get hold of you for days," the younger policeman says.

"I've been away."

"Where have you been?" the bald one asks.

"I have a show in Nottingham at the moment."

"You know why we're here?"

Flood shrugs. "It's to do with Angela?"

"What can you tell us about Angela?" the bald officer asks.

Flood looks away. "She was special."

"Go on," the bald one says.

"It wasn't supposed to end like that."

"What do you mean?"

"She had talent. But it was getting harder for her out there."

"She was a model?" the younger one says.

"A model, actress, whatever, you know how it goes. She was good, though she didn't get the breaks, not the big ones anyway – came close a couple of times, missed out in LA. It wasn't to be and she was all washed up. Back here in London at the age of thirty-five, she thought it was all over for her. Her beauty was fading." Flood goes to a chest of drawers and retrieves a slim portfolio. He passes them a series of line drawings. "This is Angela."

The policemen rotate the sketches, trying to work out what it is they are looking at. "They're very modern," the older one says.

"Do you have any recent photographs?"

Flood shakes his head. "I never filmed Angela."

"You normally film your models?" the older officer asks.

"I record what's around me, whether I'm filming, sketching or taking photographs."

"Did you think Angela was depressed in any way?"

"Yes, but only mildly, it was a shock."

"She'd just got back from holiday; surely she would have been feeling relaxed?" the bald officer says.

"I don't know about that."

"When was the last time you saw Angela Fields?"

"It's been a few months since we split."

"Where were you the night of Wednesday 25 May?"

"It was the eve of my show, the night before the private view. I was in Nottingham, staying at the Merchant's House Hotel. Here, I've got their card."

Interior, Flood's studio: Flood is at the breakfast bar while behind him a young woman in her early twenties with black hair in a tight ponytail wipes down the sealed concrete work surfaces. It is the same woman who made coffee for the policemen.

"Have you seen this, Rita?" Flood asks, as she sprays cleaning fluid into the sink. He holds up a newspaper cutting.

Rita holds up her wet Marigolds and peers at the paper. "Why are they dressed like that?" she asks.

"It's a forensic team; they have to wear overalls."

"Where are they?"

"It could be anywhere, but it's Glasgow, Scotland."

She wipes at her brow with the back of her gloved hand. "Why you cut that out? You are interested in strange things."

"It could be anywhere – just your average 1930s semi, looks like so many streets in Britain. That's what attracted Damian Hirst."

"Damian Hirst?"

"You know – shark – you must have heard of him."

"Oh, you mean the shark in a big tank?"

"Yeah that's right, pickled."

"I have seen a picture of that."

"Imagine raking over the putrid remains of the dead for a living?" Flood shakes his head. "Do you think anyone goes to

70

their school careers adviser and mentions that?"

Rita wipes down the cupboard doors. "What does it have to do with Damian Hirst?" she asks.

"At first glance it's just another suburban murder, probably domestic, and yet it could have been something else, something special, because Damien Hirst took an interest. He was having a photorealism phase, ripping pictures out of papers and magazines and getting his team of assistants to phone around for permission to reproduce them as photorealist paintings. Only the grieving family of this particular victim objected."

"That is their right," Rita says. "I would not be happy."

"This is BBC News 24 with the headlines at five."

They both look at the TV mounted on a shelf in the corner.

"As police release details of the woman murdered in Nottingham last week, another body is found. Loretta Peters was a forty-year-old mother of two..."

Flood approaches the TV. "Loretta? What sort of a name is that? I bet she got that from her job at the lap-dancing bar."

"You know her?"

"Where is she in that photo?"

"It is old photo I think."

"She is the colour of a frankfurter."

"That is not nice."

"These girls, they look like they've been working the fields, like peasants out of a painting by Millet – turnip pickers."

"You are critical man." Rita sprays Mr Sheen over a table.

"Skin should be pale."

Rita pauses at Flood's work area. She has a yellow duster in one hand, furniture polish in the other. "What you want me to do? It is difficult to dust your home right now. There are many things. Should I move, clean, and put back?"

"No, don't move a thing – you'll have to work round it." He lounges back in his calico-covered armchair.

"You artists..." She shakes her head.

"You clean for other artists?"

"I do for one other but there are many round here, I think."

"Who else do you clean for?"

"I should not say."

"You have to tell me now you've mentioned it."

"You have that camera on. I don't like..."

"Don't worry about that, it's only for me..."

"I let you guess. She is untidy also – messier than you."

"I dunno, Tracey Emin, Sarah Lucas – Paula Rego?"

"It best I not say. That reminds me; I wanted to ask you something. On television there was artist who left a tap running in an art gallery. He said it was to show how we all waste so much."

Flood looks at Rita intently. "What did you think?"

"It is not art. It cannot be. It takes no talent to turn on a tap. Anyone can do that. Does it not make you mad when you spend so many hours drawing and painting and someone just turns on a tap? Look, I can do it now. I am artist also."

"Why not, Rita – you're a lousy cleaner."

"You not happy with my cleaning?" She pauses, hands on hips.

"I'm kidding. Here, turn around, look at the camera."

"Don't film me – I not want that."

"I want to introduce you: this is Rita, my overqualified cleaner from Hungary. Wave, Rita."

"Why you always have that thing on?"

"I won't miss anything." He looks into the lens.

"What you mean?"

"I'm expecting a visitor – Mr Moneybags."

"Who is that?"

"Nicholas Drake, my patron." Flood rearranges his cameras, training one on the entrance and one on the main studio area.

"Why you want to film everybody all the time?"

"Do you not wish to know what lies beneath? I'm going to record his arrival. I have to know whether he gets it or not. Should be fun, don't you think?"

She shrugs. "If you say so."

"That's what I love about staff – they have to agree with you. Right, I'm just going to play that back – make sure it's set up properly. There, beautiful – did you notice how I've positioned it by my Seventies deluxe leather couch?"

"That is new? I like."

The sofa is black and worn and yet stylish in a retro fashion.

"I've had a sudden improvement in circumstances." Flood grins. "Drake has bought five works from my Nottingham show, though he's yet to take delivery – there are still a few weeks left to run, and then it's on to London."

"Then you won't have to travel there the whole time leaving poor Dora?"

"Lovely Rita, artist's maid...." From behind, Flood puts his hands on Rita's waist as he sings. "Uh oh, she didn't like that – better shut up." He wags his finger at the camera.

"This is impossible. How am I supposed to clean when I cannot move a thing?" Rita pushes at the Hoover attachments.

"Don't complain, Rita – that's not part of the agreement. Just do the best you can, love."

"I am not 'love'." She glares at him.

"Spirited, you Hungarians – I like that. You're very pale."

Her face is pale and yet her cheeks appear flushed.

"Is that usual in Hungary – pale skin, I mean?"

"Maybe, I never give it a thought."

"You don't like the sun, sweetheart?'

"I am nobody's sweetheart."

"Stop dyeing your hair black – you'll probably have more luck."

"You are rude man. I promise I only clean your place to take care of Dora."

"That's good enough for me. Anyway, you nearly done 'cause I've got the main man coming round any minute and I don't want to be disturbed?"

"I cannot finish quick enough."

"Call me rude – here, what do I owe you?"

"The usual."

"But you've only been here half the time."

"I come here when you say. It is your choice to let me go."

"You'll go far. What was it you said you were studying in Hungary?"

"Business studies."

"You gonna do that over here?"

"Of one thing I am sure: the word 'cleaner' will not be carved on my gravestone."

"Gothic ball-breaker, perhaps."

"I ignore that. You want me Tuesday?"

"I want you Tuesday."

"Well, I come – for Dora."

"All the best, Rita."

"Whatever."

Flood paces the room.

"That's the door." He turns abruptly. "It's either Gothic psycho-cleaner forgotten her handbag or the man himself. Let's have a look. I've had one of those video entry-phones installed. I can choose not to be in if needs be. It's him all right, Mr Nicholas-don't-keep-me-waiting-Drake. Jesus, look at that – a study in impatience, I'd like to capture that."

Drake's pate appears shiny on the video-entry screen.

"Nicholas, hello, I'm second floor. Come on up."

A few moments later Drake enters, wearing a crisp blue shirt open at the collar, dark cords and pointed shoes.

"Welcome, Nicholas, can I get you a drink?"

"I don't have much time." Immediately he looks around.

"Bear in mind it's all work-in-progress. None of it is

74

finished, as yet." Flood walks to the far end where he's piled sketches on a trestle table. Drake follows. "I like to start with sketches, very fast and free." Flood goes through them one by one, letting Drake look for a moment before placing them to one side. "And that energy – I like to carry it through," Flood says. "These are the canvases. I work on several at once over a number of months, adding layers then leaving them aside for a while – contemplation is part of the process."

"Has Marcus seen any of this?" Drake asks.

"I have a theory about dealers – they're all frustrated artists, think they know what needs to be done, as it were. Best not to leave your dealer any space for meddling, you don't want them trying to make you fit a market. I mean, don't get me wrong – Marcus is supportive on the whole but then they all are while works are selling; it'll be a different story if the money dries up."

"I can't see that happening." Drake is serious.

"You like it?"

"I want to know more. Tell me about the work?"

Flood shrugs. "What can I tell you?"

Drake gestures towards the sketches. "These girls, where do they come from?"

Flood looks away as he talks. "When I find a girl, a good girl, one that inspires me, they're usually willing to get involved and if not, if they are a little reticent shall we say, well... there's ways to work round that – they're all grateful in the end."

Drake snorts. "They can all be bought."

"We're singing from the same hymn sheet," Flood says.

"Where next with these? I'm fascinated to see where you take them – how far you'll go."

"You like your art challenging? I hear you like to take a risk when you buy?"

Drake smiles. "A calculated risk."

"How do you feel about really getting involved?"

The camera cuts.

Exterior, dusk: a city street, lined with tall Victorian buildings. A black cab trundles past followed by a 4x4 and a white van. Coloured lights sparkle in the windows of a grand pub with black paintwork. The camera draws in, focusing on a street sign that reads Club Row, and then back to the pub, Les Trois Garçons.

"That's it," Flood says, as he approaches. He pushes the heavy black door revealing a riotous, opulent interior with taxidermy galore: a stuffed dog adorned with wings, a pouncing tiger, a crowned swan and a threadbare monkey. There are mirrors lining the walls, coloured glass vases, beaded curtains, Murano glass candlesticks and chandeliers. Flood's camera wallows in the contrived chaos.

"Jack, at last." Marcus stands to greet Flood, as does Nicholas Drake, albeit slowly. "You can put that thing away now," Marcus says.

"I always film – you know that. Anyway, excuse me – I must visit the little boys' room." Flood films the heads of glossy-haired women as he squeezes his way through the tables to the magnificent black marble restroom. He places the camcorder on the cistern as he searches his pockets. There are shiny bottle-green tiles on the cubicle walls. Flood is out of view. The toilet flushes and there is the sound of a credit card chopping powder on the ceramic cistern, sniffing and a cough.

Flood returns and places the camcorder on the table. It records a glimmer of cutlery, a shimmer from a wine glass stem, the white cloth and little else apart from the three men's voices.

Marcus: "I have to say, Jack's work will sit perfectly within your collection."

Flood: "Who do you collect, Nicholas?"

Drake: "Big names: Nauman, Freud, Koons, Hockney, Schnabel, Flavin, Gilbert & George, Hirst of course, Gormley, the Chapman Brothers – and I've just secured a Peter Doig."

Flood whistles. "That's quite a list."

Drake's voice: "I'm thinking German right now, buying up

Kiefer, Richter and Rauch, and there's a buzz about the Chinese. I'm always on the lookout for the new."

"To the 'new'." Flood proposes a toast. There is the clink of glasses and Flood says, "Tell me, Nicholas, do you have trouble remembering what you own?" Flood lifts the camcorder from the table in order to study Drake's face as he speaks. It is an intelligent face: thin, with a long nose.

"That's enough, now," Drake says, after a moment.

Flood's attention drifts to the next table where a sleek-haired redhead talks loudly above her ample cleavage.

"I do have trouble recalling my collection in its entirety," Drake says. "That's the measure of a true collector. Naturally, everything is catalogued."

"You didn't mention any female artists?" Flood says.

"What's the point?"

The three men laugh.

"You exhibit everything you own?"

"The collection's grown too big. I rotate pieces around my three homes and often lend out to galleries for particular exhibitions. I also employ a freelance curator to direct how they are hung."

"You need your own gallery."

"It will happen."

Beluga caviar is served. The waitress is young and attractive. Flood zooms in for a close-up of the shiny coils of her dark hair.

"Anyway, enough about me, I want to know about you, Jack," Drake says.

The camera shifts back to Drake, studying his eyes.

Flood says, "I'd like to know what it is that attracts you to a particular piece."

Drake smiles faintly. "I've been called a gambler, but I take calculated risks."

"You have an eye. I can vouch for that," Marcus says.

Drake says, "I like to think I can spot something special."

Flood's camera focuses on the redhead's lips and pale cleavage.

"Do you mind!" A man's hand blocks the lens and Flood swings the camera back to Drake.

Drake says, "I want to be challenged – shaken up a bit. It doesn't matter if I don't understand a particular piece as long as it evokes a strong response in me. You see, when you want for nothing, life can become tedious."

"Trouble in paradise?" Flood knocks back another glass of red wine. "Paradise syndrome – you can't enjoy having it all."

"We'll have another bottle of this," Marcus calls out to the waitress.

Later, after yet another bottle of wine, Flood drains the dregs from his glass and abruptly stands. "Nicholas, Marcus, it's been a pleasure, but you must excuse me, the muse has spoken as it were."

"Surely, you don't have to leave quite yet," Marcus says.

"Let the man go," Drake says. "Just make sure I get to see the new works before anyone else."

Flood nods. "Enjoy the rest of your evening, gentlemen."

Outside, a few drunken suits make their way home.

"Hey!" Flood shouts across the street to a black cab, its yellow light on. The cab does a U-turn and stops by the kerb.

"St Pancras, quick as you can – I must catch the last train to Nottingham."

A hotel room, a different one: smaller and obviously downmarket. The tartan-covered double bed almost fills the room leaving a small walkway and space for a dressing table with a white plastic tray containing coffee and tea-making facilities.

Flood is preoccupied sifting through the complimentary drink sachets. A portable TV is on in the background – the local news.

"Powdered milk, and look at this kettle – did you ever see such a short, pathetic cord?" Flood holds the kettle up to the camera, stretching out its tiny cable. "It can barely reach the plug." He stretches the cord taut and forces the plug into the socket. "Cheap or else it's down to health and safety – prevent the odd auto-asphyxiation or hotel suicide.

"I've swapped hotels. Marcus kept saying, 'What is so special about Nottingham?' Blah blah... 'There's nothing there you can't get tenfold in London.' I told him he was missing the point. I've started something – I can't just abandon it. I've too much invested. If he can't see the importance of what I'm doing and where I'm doing it, I may as well seek representation elsewhere."

"Fears are growing for a young Nottingham woman missing since Friday night. Local chef Jenny Fordham was last seen leaving Saviour's Bar and Restaurant on Goose Gate in the Hockley area of the city at 11.40pm. Police are unwilling to link her disappearance to the recent discovery of two women's bodies in the city."

Flood stares at the small TV.

"Mother of two Loretta Peters was found dead last month in the Forest Fields area of Nottingham while last week an as yet unnamed woman was found on Lenton Boulevard.

"Police say they are extremely concerned about the whereabouts of Jenny Fordham and ask anyone who thinks they may have seen Jenny to call the number below. All calls will be treated in the strictest confidence."

The newsreader's face brightens: "Shoppers at the Broad Marsh Shopping Centre are in for a treat this week as local manufacturers Pork Farms will be offering samples of their new range of Tikka Masala sausage rolls. Sally-Ann Webb reports..."

Flood smirks. "From dead women to sausage rolls..." He picks up his phone and dials.

79

"Carmen, it's Jack Flood – that's right, the artist. Can we talk through the Tesco 24-hour rota? When are you free?" He nods. "See you then." He turns towards the laptop on the dressing table and reads from the screen: "Nothing exists until or unless it is observed. An artist is making something exist by observing it. And his hope for other people is that they will also make it exist by observing it." William Burroughs.

"These girls, for example – what are they before they meet me?"

Exterior, Pukka Palace: an upmarket curry house with purple lettering edged in gold. Inside, there are plush purple seats, white walls and framed black and white prints of the Taj Mahal, Jodhpur and Jaisalmer. Flood, dressed in a black suit and white shirt, is shown to a table.

"I'll take over from here." Flood reaches out to take the camcorder from his driver. "Two Bellinis, please," he tells the waiter as he films a young woman in skinny jeans and a pink shiny top as she approaches. It's Carmen, the Tesco cashier, and she is wearing her signature heavy hoop earrings.

She sits opposite. "Why do you film all the time?"

"It's a search for answers."

"Like the meaning of life and all that?"

"You could say that."

"I can't eat this food. Is there anything that's not spicy?"

"I'll order for both of us," he says.

"Do you know where the loo is?"

"On the left down there." He films her backside as she walks. She looks good in tight jeans, high heels and the pink backless top – her skin flawless.

Camera cuts to the end of the meal. Carmen has barely touched her food. "Have another Bellini," Flood says.

"You were in the paper again. How famous are you?"

"To be honest no one ever recognises me, but then I do usually have a camera stuck in front of my face."

Exterior, a city street. Carmen's heels clack against the pavement as they walk past boarded-up shops.

"Where are we going?" Her face, although heavily made up, appears ethereal in the moonlight.

"I want to film you."

"Film me where?"

"Just down there, on the corner." Flood points the camera towards the end of a dark alleyway.

Carmen stops, her arms folded. "What do you take me for?"

Twelve

Is Jenny already a lost cause? I kept asking myself.

I liked to think I'd find her walking in a daze, a little confused, lost, and suffering from amnesia. She'd be spaced out after some nasty incident that had culminated in her being dumped back on a side street in the city centre. I would find her. There would be a hurried press conference and I'd look a little nervous in the spotlight, uncomfortable with all the media attention and there'd be Jenny beside me battered and bruised but alive, very much alive.

My eyes welled up and I shook the image from my head. It was a wonder I'd made it to university – if people really spend a third of their lives asleep, I had to spend another third daydreaming. I'd try to snap out of it, especially when it went on too long. But really, I could spend half a day and an evening immersed in fantasy land, stopping only to eat or watch TV. Then there'd be fresh opportunity to whisk myself away to a better world where Jenny was safe.

I tried to sleep. Only I couldn't because I was too excited by the prospect of this parallel universe where everything was right and I was the hero.

But the daydreaming didn't help Jenny and it didn't help my coursework.

"It's fucking weird," Slug said. I'd roped him into helping me carry the completed canvas down to college in time for the crit that day. He stood back in order to get a better look. "It's supposed to be you? You're weirder than I thought. How heavy is it?"

"Not heavy – just awkward."

We shuffled out the door and past the crossroads where the prostitutes normally sat and began the walk downhill to college.

"Everyone's looking," Slug said. "It's nothing to do with me, mate," he told a passer-by.

"Slug!" I could have done without it. I was nervous enough about the crit and how my work would be received without him drawing negative attention to it.

"Where do you want it, Picasso? Fucking hell, look at that." Slug was staring at a large, colourful sculpture of what looked like a cross-section of skin. He'd never been in the fine art studio before. "You lot are weird." We manoeuvred the piece into my studio space. "Good luck, I think you'll need it." He shook his head. "Weirdos," he said. "Don't forget those beers." (I'd had to bribe him to help).

I tacked a couple of nails onto one of my boards and hung the canvas, fussing over the angle. *Is it OK?* I couldn't tell and had to walk around to compare other work with my own. The whitewashed studio was full of colour and energy.

The project had sparked something in everyone, although my initial enthusiasm had waned after the hotel incident and now Jenny had gone I wasn't sure anything else mattered.

Ten minutes later, Mike Manners' cowboy boots descended the office steps into the studio followed by Mike Cherry's loafers.

Mike Cherry rubbed his hands together. "Take it away, Graham." We all turned towards Graham's space – the two tutors and twenty-six students all gathered round the 3D model of a sample of skin, which had huge glittering hairs sticking out of the epidermis and subcutaneous layers cut away like a monster slice of birthday cake.

"You doing Damian Hirst now?" Kelly said.

Mike Manners rubbed his chin and said, "It's always a hazard. Everything may very well have been done before but there's always room for a fresh take. How did you get to this point, Graham?"

"I reduced myself down to what separates me from the rest of the world. It is skin that contains me as it were."

"Oh I say, yes, and so well executed, it really is a lovely piece." Mike Cherry's hands were on it then, feeling it, stroking it, and testing its weight. "The colours, they're almost jewel-like – is there a reason for that?"

Graham nodded. "I wanted to move away from the biological model and show that even though my skin is like everyone else's, to me it's special – it represents the ego if you like."

"What does everyone think?" Mike Manners asked.

"It's lovely to look at," Kelly said, "but if I didn't know Graham, it wouldn't necessarily tell me anything about him."

"That's an interesting point," Mike Manners said.

"It's well executed, superb, well done, Graham – moving on." Mike Cherry took the couple of steps to Kelly's space, now filled with a series of huge, spidery drawings in coloured pencils and felt tips. "My word, what texture," Mike Cherry said, and everyone laughed as Kelly's self-portraits included hirsute limbs and luxurious pubic hair.

"Talk us through it, Kelly," Mike Manners said.

"They're hypnotic drawings," Kelly said.

"They've got me hypnotised," Spencer said. And a few people laughed, while others groaned and Kelly ignored him.

"I went for hypnosis – I wanted to be able to draw the way I did when I was a kid to get an insight into my early sense of self before any conditioning or other outside influences took hold."

"The old nature versus nurture," Mike Cherry said.

"I think they're brilliant," I said, but I guessed everyone thought I was just sucking up to be a good mate but that wasn't the case.

"Certainly interesting," Mike Manners said. "I'd like to see you take them further." And Mike Cherry agreed, before moving on to the next person.

We all traipsed round after them: two tutors leading twenty-six students in varying degrees of nervous apprehension. We looked at light boxes, knitting, neon signs and oil paintings. There were found objects in specially made boxes and one student called Gavin even had photographs of his chaotic alcoholic parents. Eventually they came round to me, stopping three feet in front of my canvas. Mike Cherry exhaled a quick puff of air, then silence.

"Well..." Mike Cherry said.

"I like it," Spencer said. And I had never felt such warmth and gratitude towards my housemate.

"Don't you think it's a bit sixth form?" asked Mike Cherry.

My throat tightened. I'd put so much into that piece.

"I wouldn't say that," Mike Manners said.

"So, what have we here? Do enlighten us," Mike Cherry said.

The canvas hung there between us looking inadequate. Somehow it seemed less than it had the night before when I had finally declared it finished with a moment's satisfaction. I was starting to well up. It was ridiculous. I bit the inside of my cheek. *I can't let this silly little man get to me. Jenny is missing – that's all that matters.* I had a lump in my throat as I struggled to speak. "It's sort of what it feels like to be a girl." My nails pressed into my clenched fists.

"The project is *Who Am I* – not how does it feel to be a woman." Mike Cherry pursed his lips. "We went over all that years ago."

"I kind of think my gender is integral to who I am," I said.

"It's perfectly valid, Mike," Suki interrupted. She was one of Mike Cherry's favourites as, even though she was a left-wing feminist, she also possessed a petite Asian figure and doe eyes.

"What do we have here – a victim, an animal?" Mike Cherry

85

pushed his nose up close to the painting's surface.

"There's a decadence to it I find interesting," Mike Manners said. "The crimson mouth for instance..."

"How does this answer the brief? I'd really love to know," Mike Cherry said.

"I was concentrating on how appearance can so easily be misconstrued."

"The face is unexpected," Mike Manners said, "it's not a look I recognise."

I had painted a self-portrait in dull greys – a sad face with vacant, staring eyes and taken on a mock religious pose like a Virgin Mary statuette. This was the quiet me, the dull, sensible one from Stowe-on-Sea. While in the background in small typeset I'd printed: "I came to find a girl and that girl is you".

"It is interesting," Mike Manners said.

Mike Cherry made a dismissive noise and said, "Next!"

Spencer again said that he liked my piece, once the crit was over. "What does Cherry know," he said. "You coming for coffee?"

But I couldn't sit around after everyone else's work had been well received. *What's the point? All that effort and all I got was, 'Next!'*

Back home in my room, I took out my sketchbook, found a clean page and wrote 'NEXT!' in the middle in neat capital letters and drew a box round it – all in black ink. I had a bad feeling. I didn't like everything moving on, stuff continuing as if nothing had happened when all the while Jenny was missing. *Nothing matters any more – nothing but Jenny...*

I went to the window, peeking from the edge of the curtain, conscious I couldn't let anyone see. Girl-with-braids was there, just as I'd hoped. I held my sketchbook below the window and using a black pen began to make marks on the page, sketching her lean body with gazelle-like thighs, a hooded top and nonchalant expression, mobile gripped at her ear. She looked hot, edgy, good enough to get into any club – *how can this be her lot?*

I added the brick wall behind and a couple of lines here and there representing the crossroads, then Girl-with-braids paced up and down and I started again on a fresh page. Girl-with-braids stopped on the corner, I started drawing again, then a car drew up and I added it in, lines over lines, images on top of other images. Girl-with-braids got in. I scribbled down half the number-plate before the car (I didn't catch what make) drove away, and then I turned to a fresh page to draw the scene again – this time empty. The urban landscape: a wall, the tall Victorian terraces, the shadows they cast, and the crossroads.

Thirteen

Exterior, Victorian factory conversion: camera approaches a doorway with an adjacent brass plaque: The Wire Works.

There is the sound of someone fumbling for keys and the camera moves through the doorway into a stark, white entrance hall towards a small silver lift. The doors close, the lift travels upwards. There's a corridor, another door, his door. A key is inserted in the lock but it doesn't turn.

"What's going on?" It's Flood's voice, the camerawork shaky, as he leans in to push against the door. "Rita! Are you there? Open up."

The faint sound of footsteps and the camera jolts as if Flood has fallen through the doorway. "Rita, what you put the other lock on for?"

Rita, the cleaner, looks different, dishevelled somehow, her long, dyed black hair pulled up high in a messy ponytail. She's wearing a brown velour tracksuit. She narrows her eyes. "You piece of shit."

Flood goes to the tripod in the corner of the studio, switches to the other camera and comes into view. He removes his black raincoat. The studio looks immaculate. "What have I done?"

"You no-good piece of shit."

He sits down and kicks off an old pair of Pumas.

"You are sick bastard. You care about no one but yourself."

"Stop talking in riddles, I'm not in the mood. If I've done something to offend you, please tell me."

"It is Dora." She refers to Flood's cat.

"Dora?"

She nods – her mouth downturned.

Flood holds his hands up in surrender. "I give up, what is it?"

"Dora is dead."

"Dead? She can't be."

"It is because of you – your fault. You are useless pig."

"You have been feeding her?" Flood walks towards the kitchen area. He opens a tall cupboard, checks the cans of cat food. There are several tins of Whiskas left.

"I come three times a week."

"And you have been turning up, I take it? I mean, don't tell me I've been paying you for nothing."

"Three times is not enough. You cannot feed cat only three times a week. Dora should have been fed two times a day – you know that."

"Oh come on, that fat Indian woman across the road – she looks out for her – treats her like a temple cat: tandoori chicken, Goan fish curry, you name it."

"I have not seen Indian lady. You cannot rely on neighbour. Keeping pet is responsibility; you cannot go away all the days."

"There is that timed feeding contraption, but yeah, okay, I take your point, but she wasn't really mine. She adopted me, cats are like that – they find someone who suits them. Trust me, I never went out to a pet shop and said: 'Show me your fluffiest kitty for me to love and cherish for evermore'." Flood pretends to stroke an invisible cat. "Anyway, where is she?" He looks around the vast space with its white walls and scant retro furniture.

"Oh –," Rita looks away, hand over her mouth.

"What does 'oh' mean?"

"You don't want to see her?"

"Yeah, I do. Where is she? Let me see her."

Rita's face crumples. "I didn't know what to do with her."

"Don't start crying on me. Where is she? I want to see her."

"I thought perhaps I leave her outside but then she might get eaten but in here she would smell and there would be the maggots and the flies..."

"So, what did you do? Don't tell me you threw her away?" He looks out of the large window towards the bins.

"I show you." Rita walks around the breakfast bar and stops at the stainless steel fridge freezer.

"She's in the freezer?"

She starts crying again. "I am sorry."

Flood takes a deep breath. "Let's have a butcher's." He opens the heavy freezer door and pulls at what looks like a leg. "My God, that is not appetising." The dark cat looks twisted, mangled even. "She's been hit by a car by the look of it," he says. "She came home to see Daddy..." Flood momentarily presses the frozen fur of Dora's belly to his cheek.

Rita's arms are folded. "And you were not here for her."

"My goddess cat."

"She is super skinny." Rita points at the cat's twisted haunches.

"Rock hard." Flood taps Dora against the concrete worktop.

Rita squeals. "Don't do that."

"She won't snap if that's what you think. Oh come on, don't cry, there's no need for that. Here, sit down, let me make you a nice cup of tea – or maybe you'd prefer something stronger?"

Rita raises her chin. "What you got?"

"Wine, vodka, whisky..."

"What sort of whisky?"

"Jacky D."

"Jack Daniels?"

"Yep."

"I have that – neat."

"That's more like it – you want ice?"

"What – from freezer – are you kidding?"

"Good point, maybe not." Flood takes a couple of glasses from the cupboard. "Here, get that down you." He passes her a tumbler – three quarters full.

Rita takes a gulp. She looks directly at Flood. "Can you put Dora back – until we bury her?"

"You want her back in the deep freeze?"

"Please."

"Bit cramped in there."

"You have too much frozen produce – not healthy for a man."

"Saves me shopping, I haven't got time for it. In fact, perhaps you could shop for me. Jesus, you drank that quick – you Hungarians. You want another?"

"Sure."

"So, what to do with the body? It's always difficult – shall we bury her?"

"Yes, of course, but I not know where?"

"I don't have a garden. Do you have a garden?"

"I do not." Rita feels her brow with the back of her hand.

"We'll have to take her down the park in the dead of night."

"You know, I don't feel so good. I haven't eaten."

"That's what they all say."

Fourteen

How extraordinary we look. I had caught sight of my friends reflected repeatedly in the Venetian glass mirrors that lined the walls of Ruby's. It could have been a glossy photo-shoot for a *Vogue* spread: unlined skin and shiny hair with the seemingly effortless style that consists of T-shirts, cut-off jeans, flimsy sundresses and miniskirts. We looked so good I could hardly believe I was part of it. Jenny would have fitted in; I thought, with her strong, slim runner's body and waist-length hair. How had I not seen it before, how wonderful we looked? I could have spent the year feeling better about myself. But then perhaps it was just a moment, something that would slip away unless you thought to pickle it in a jar like a Damien Hirst.

It was early evening, the summer term was drawing to a close and about ten of us had met up in Ruby's before more friends joined us on the slouchy leather sofas.

"What are you doing over the summer?" Beth asked, flicking her hair as she always did. She was on my course.

I told her I was planning to work extra shifts at Saviour's. "That's as exciting as it gets. What about you?"

"New York, New York – I'll be working at a Soho gallery."

"How did you manage that?"

"Billy emailed samples of my work to a friend out there. They loved them."

"Lucky," I said.

"We're going out for the whole summer." It was down to her older boyfriend. I knew it. He'd last as long as he was useful.

I turned away, keen to join Kelly's conversation but she was looking to her right, in hysterics over something. I couldn't get the gist of it, so instead I gazed ahead at the vast Venetian mirror opposite. *Who's here? Anyone I like?* There were other students I recognised, but no one I particularly wanted to talk to. I looked towards the reflection of the door, wondering who would turn up next. Immediately I tensed, my skin bristled and my heart raced. There, right in front of me, or rather behind me, or more like all around me were ten, maybe twenty or even more Jack Floods reflected in the surrounding glass.

Where is he? I froze, my neck locked, too afraid to turn round. *What if he sees me?* A wall of noise rose up around me with nothing I could home in on. I was unable to move. "Kell? Kelly," I said, from the corner of my mouth but she wasn't listening. "Kelly!" She turned around. "Don't look now," I said, "but you know that artist Jack Flood; you know the one from the private view?" She nodded. "Can you discreetly look round and tell me where he is?"

She gave me a funny look then slowly moved her head as if she weren't looking at anyone in particular, while I sank deeper into the sofa. "He's by the window, to the right, near the door," she said.

"Who's he with?"

"I dunno. She looks like a gecko – all pale with white hair – nowhere near as nice as you. Mia, what are you doing? Are you hiding?"

"What's he doing here? He lives in London."

"I didn't think you were into him?"

In the mirror, I could see Flood's dark eyes. It was hard to tell in which direction he was facing. He was reflected over and over, different aspects, different angles. I had to get out. I clutched Kelly's arm. "I've got to go."

Kelly frowned. "But it's Thursday." We always went to

Ruby's followed by Rock City on a Thursday.

I touched my head. "I feel weird."

"What is it? Are you all right?"

I stood up. "I have to go."

"But it's Rock City – you never miss Rock City."

"I really have to – will you come with me?"

"I don't get it – you love Ruby's. Is it him?"

"I'll explain later – just come."

"What about the others?"

"Tell Tamzin, but just say we'll meet everyone else at the club."

Tamzin said she'd catch up, so at last we were leaving, weaving between people, tables and chairs. *But, oh God, it's Bert.* I hadn't seen the French guy since the morning after, when I'd shoved him out the door. *Bloody typical, he's with another girl.* I had to squeeze behind him. I tried to smile, let him know I didn't care, but my heart was pounding and I stopped, frozen, right there behind beautiful Bertrand and his equally attractive female companion.

"Come on, Mia," Kelly said.

"Get me to the door."

She grabbed my arm and pulled me through the bar. I couldn't help but glance at Flood. He gave no impression of noticing and I was through the double doors and out into the warm, wet night air. "What's going on?" Kelly asked.

"Can we just walk?" I crossed over, head down staring at the dark grey sheen of the wet pavement.

"Mia, are you going to tell me what this is all about?"

"Mia! Kelly!"

My stomach flipped. *Who the hell shouted my name?*

"Girls, wait." It was only Tamzin, but Flood must have heard as he was looking out the window directly at me. *Fuck,* I walked faster, almost running.

"Mia, wait," Kelly said.

"What's got into her?" Tamzin asked.

It was nearly three weeks since the hotel. I hadn't said a thing to anyone. I had hoped I wouldn't have to, convincing myself I'd never see him again. But now it all had to come out, right there in the middle of Market Square with the grand columns of Market Hall behind me and the fountains, shouting drunks and leggy girls bantering with boys in baseball caps and hoodies.

"I'm just going to go home," I said. "I'm not feeling too good."

"Was it the French guy?" Tamzin said. "Who was he with?"

I shrugged. "No idea."

"Are you bothered?" Kelly asked.

"No."

"What is it then?"

"It's – well, a few weeks back, that artist, he..."

"He what?"

"I don't know, it's just..." I said what I could, tried to make sense of it. "I think he drugged me, but really I don't know what else – I can't remember."

"I can't believe you didn't tell us." Kelly hugged me, they both did, and went on to say loads of great supportive stuff about what a wanker Flood is and things we could do. "You've got to report it," Kelly said.

"But I don't know what happened."

"Yeah, but even so, what if he keeps doing it, drugging other women, I mean. What if they don't get away next time?" Kelly and Tam looked at me like I was their kid for that moment. They knew best and I had to agree.

"Will you come with me if I report it?"

"Yeah, course," Kelly said. "We'll go tomorrow."

"Oh, I've got a crit first thing," Tamzin said.

"That's okay, as long as someone can go." I looked at Kelly.

I felt like getting drunk then, really drunk. Nottingham was my place, why should I go home? I'd head to Rock City as planned, as a matter of principle.

Rock City, a Nottingham institution, is a vast cave of a place. Its interior walls are painted black and there's a beer-sticky carpet. We usually stood at the far end by the bar, overlooking the dance-floor. It was too much effort to talk – too loud.

I knocked back my first can of Stella and went to the bar for another and, as I'd already had a few in Ruby's, I was tipsy.

Doug, one of those club-friends that you only see out, came over. He wasn't bad-looking with dark hair and thick eyebrows but he didn't do it for me.

"I heard about Bert," he shouted above the music.

"What's that?" I wasn't aware they knew each other.

"Mandy told me – about Bert's girlfriend."

"It doesn't matter," I said, which was sort of true. "Was that the girl he was with in Ruby's?"

"Yeah – Céline – she's over from Paris. They're engaged."

Too much information – did Doug enjoy telling me that?

"Bert's been a prat," Doug added. I shrugged. It was such an effort to talk, the music going right through me, and more to the point I'd noticed Luke, the third year sculptor. I hadn't bothered talking to him since the night at the club when I'd returned home and cut up my Blondie T-shirt. But now he was standing close by, staring over like he wanted to talk.

"Hello," he said, and I went over as Luke knew I would. We talked for a while though it was more like the odd shout in one another's ear in an attempt to be heard. He was going on about what it is to be an artist and whether acknowledgement is important, which was all very well but he was being pretty flirtatious – and didn't he have a girlfriend? Wasn't that her standing alone behind him?

"Isn't that your girlfriend?" I asked. He looked sheepish. *Fuck it.* I wasn't in the mood for this. I turned on my heel, left him to it, and went back to Kelly. "I don't believe it – that's his girlfriend."

"Bert's been watching you," she said.

"What – he's here too?"

I needed to get away, be alone for a moment. I headed to the toilets at the far end of the club. There were about fifteen cubicles in a long line and yet there was always a queue. I waited on the right-hand side, close to the washbasins. All the girls checked themselves in the mirrors at some point. I was next to a particularly smeared patch of glass. I squinted at my reflection, thinking I looked haunted, and then aimed towards a vacated toilet cubicle as its door swung ajar.

The lock was broken. I sat down, leaning forward, one hand on the door to hold it shut as I relieved myself. The walls were metal and covered in graffiti: 'Anita Smith takes it up the arse', 'The Libertines', and then another simply said 'I need love'. Me too, I thought. *I want someone, someone of my own, but not Doug, he bores me. Why am I always on the outside of an already established relationship?*

I ran my tongue around my lips. Then, shakily, stood up, leaned my back against the door to hold it shut while I rearranged my dress. I felt dizzy. The floor was wet. My feet gave way. I slid down the door to the floor catching my bare back on the door's useless metal lock. *Shit, that hurt.*

Back outside, I returned to the bar area at the other end.

"Here, I got you another beer." Kelly put her arm round me. "I love this song – let's dance." So, we all hit the dance-floor for a few tracks, beer cans in hand.

I went back to the bar, bought another round, danced some more, and then went back to the bar, and bought yet another beer... Bert was still there, watching me. *Where's his fiancée?* And there was Luke's 'girlfriend' standing alone, looking at the dance-floor. She talked to some of Luke's friends before dancing alone for a few miserable minutes, then eventually made her way back to Luke who hardly turned in her direction. He stood back and spoke from a distance barely looking at her. She must have told him she was leaving. She must have asked him to leave with her but he let her go, remaining where he was, looking back at me.

What is going on? I can't take this, not tonight. I've had enough. I checked my watch; it was getting on for one thirty – late enough. "I've got to go," I said to Tamzin.

"Yeah, I've had enough," she agreed. "Where's Kelly?"

We spotted her in the corner talking to a guy she really liked. Tamzin had a word. "Kelly's staying, but Spence is coming."

I was unsteady but I managed to follow Tamzin and Spencer out.

"I'm Hank Marvin." Spencer nodded towards the pink neon fish flashing in the window of the takeaway across the street. We crossed over and joined other club leftovers in the queue of the brightly lit chip shop.

"Foxy ladies." A bloke in a checked shirt handed out flyers for another club night, but we were more interested in smothering our cones of chips with salt, vinegar and ketchup.

"Shit, look at that rain, it's pissing it down," Tamzin said, as she stabbed at a fat, ketchup-coated chip.

The rain was heavy and none of us had coats or umbrellas. "Let's shelter down there." Spencer pointed towards the underpass and Tamzin and Spencer made a run for it, rushing ahead down the fifteen or so concrete steps out of the rain.

I followed, and as I paused at the top of the steps to stab at another chip, I glanced up and panicked. On the subway's left-hand side, was Gecko Girl and someone holding a large black umbrella above her bright splash of hair – *Flood*.

Fuck. I lost my footing, stumbled and fell down the subway steps, scattering scarlet chips across the concrete.

Fifteen

Flood's DVD continues with an exterior shot of a city street with wet concrete steps that lead down to a fluorescent lit underpass.

It's the subway where I fell. The realisation sickens me. I don't want to know.

A figure in white with a platinum blonde crop (Gecko Girl) stands over someone lying on the ground.

It's unclear but it must be me.

"Are you okay?" Gecko Girl asks, as she stoops to check on me. I look up but my face is unrecognisable. It has been pixelated.

Can you film anyone you like as long as you pixelate them?

Is that what he's done?

Gecko Girl takes my arm, while Spencer takes hold of my other side. They try to hoist me up but I struggle – obviously out of it. I look pathetic and that makes me now feel even worse.

"Give us a hand, Jack," Gecko Girl says.

"It's okay, she's up," Spencer says.

Film cuts to a close up of the chips splayed across the path – some fat and anaemic, while others are bright red.

Gecko Girl folds her arms. "Hurry up, I'm so cold."

"*Don't go with him.*" It's my voice, and I sound desperate, crazy even, while my face remains pixelated.

"Silly drunk tart," Flood says.

"There's no need for that, mate." Spencer puts his arm round me. "You telling me you never had one too many?"

Cut to interior, the basic hotel room: tartan bedspread, bed almost filling the room and Flood's washed-out face in close-up.

"We've met before – the girl in the subway and me, and I have to admit I liked the look of her all over again – rain having made long, dark tendrils of hair stick to her pale face. I wanted to help her, hold her, and film her – but thought better of it.

"The young idiot she had with her, he was straight in there, arm round her waist. 'She's all right,' he kept saying, 'she's just had one too many.' I told him to take her home before she falls flat on her face again.

"She was off her head, didn't know what she was doing, staggering all over the place as the kid with the shaved head tried to hold on to her. She was having none of it, told him to 'get off', broke away, up the steps, treading on the red chips as she ran off in the rain – all very sad."

Sixteen

The redness hit me as I entered the room. On a vast white background, a concentrated mass of rich crimson pigment had dripped down the canvas like a Nitsch 'Action' painting. I had read about Hermann Nitsch, and how he orchestrates naked pagan-like ceremonies involving the ritualistic slaughter of animals. It looked like a heart had been ripped out and used like a child's potato print.

Through a door came a succession of naked women covered in red liquid – blood or paint? Perhaps they would roll on a canvas like an Yves Klein happening or was it something else? Confused, I turned around and there was Flood, naked apart from a towel round his waist, laughing.

I sat bolt upright. *It's not real. He's not here. I'm all right.*

I had expected shades of asylum: pale pea green on the lower part of the walls with dishwater grey above, but then I figured police stations should be drab, somewhere you wouldn't rush back to. To think I had been walking past that ugly pile for a good two years and had never taken much notice.

Kelly must have sensed my apprehension as she linked arms and pulled me through the doorway to a wooden counter.

"We've something to report," she said.

The duty officer had the face of a pit bull. I couldn't tell him anything.

"Is there a female officer we can see?"

Pit-bull leant towards the window. "We have the Sanctuary," he stated, passing a leaflet through the hatch. "Is that what you need?"

Kelly nodded.

"Take a seat; someone will be with you shortly."

The leaflet described a rape suite for sexual assaults. "'Rape Suite' – it sounds like they're renting out luxury space to rapists," I said. "This isn't going to work. I'll be wasting police time – they charge people for that."

"Sit." Kelly pointed at some grey chairs, and I sat, staring up at the array of posters fixed to the wall behind protective plastic: 'Drugs are no way to live!' – with a photo of a dead body on a mortuary slab; 'All of her friends said she was the life of the party. But she can't remember.' And then there were posters about terrorism and how we must be vigilant, and knife crime – saying you're more likely to be a victim if you carry a knife.

"Is that all they can do – commission posters?" I said. "I can't do this."

Kelly stopped texting and looked at me. "You're here now," she said, "so you may as well talk to someone. You might prevent it happening to someone else."

Between us we knew of four other friends who'd been victims of sexual assaults. One of Kelly's friends from home was fifteen when it happened to her. It was her brother's mate. Another friend got attacked on a date and he made out she led him on, and then I had a friend whose boyfriend had hammered her against a wall in the death-throes of their relationship and another who'd had a date go seriously wrong. So, if every woman knows at least two friends who have been raped that would suggest possibly epidemic proportions – judging by the fact none of our friends had reported the attacks, it could well be a silent epidemic. And, so far, I'd been part of that.

"Just get it logged," Kelly said. "Even if there isn't enough evidence at least they'll have it on record in case someone else one day reports him. It could even help your mate Jenny in some way, you never know."

Oh my God, she's made the same possible link I made. I felt sick and I wanted to go, get out, and run all the way up the hill home to my room and lock the door.

"Mia Jackson?" A chunky blonde woman with a nasal voice looked at us. "Would you like to come through?"

We were led down several corridors to a door labelled 'The Sanctuary'. The room, painted in a warm shade of sand with primrose yellow cushioned chairs and a vase of plastic lilies, was as comfortable as a police station gets.

"I'm DC Jan Wilson. Call me Jan. I'll be your point of contact – anything you need to ask or any problems you have, just give me a call. She punctuated her words with a kindly smile. "OK, first things first, when did the offence take place?"

The date was indelibly etched on my mind – a future unhappy anniversary. "It was Friday 27th May. I always work on Fridays."

She consulted her desk calendar. "That's three weeks ago – to be honest, the quicker these things are reported the better. The evidence will be limited."

I knew that. There was little Jan could tell me. I'd looked it all up on rape crisis websites. I knew I should have gone straight to the police after fleeing the hotel. I shouldn't have washed and I should have given blood and urine, saliva and pubic hair samples. Swabs should have been taken from my mouth, vagina and rectum. I should have been examined and probably photographed within forty-eight hours. And even then the likelihood of gaining a conviction would have been below ten per cent, and more like five.

"You understand it's too late to examine you physically. We need to think about other possible evidence. Do you still have the clothes you were wearing that night?"

That morning I'd retrieved the carefully wound plastic package I'd hidden at the back of my wardrobe. I held it up for

Jan to see. "They're cut up, I'm afraid – I couldn't help it."

Jan took the bag without looking inside. "The lab will do their best," she said. "How do you feel about making a statement?"

The night before came crashing back on me: Flood in the mirrors at Ruby's, Flood by the subway, my scattered scarlet chips and how I ran home in a panic as if Flood were chasing me, when in reality it was Tamzin and Spencer who were shouting at me to 'wait up'.

Jan-the-policewoman looked at me expectantly, and again a wave of nausea came over me. "Where's the nearest toilet? I think I'm going to be sick."

Seventeen

Interior, Flood's studio: the artist sits in his calico-covered chair, smoking. "I've had a little visit," he announces to camera. "Police hammered on my door in the early hours. I thought it was my dealer until someone shouted, 'Police, open up.' You can't wake the awake. 'Do you know **beep** **beep**?' they asked, and they wanted to know where I was on the night of Friday 27th May 2005. 'Do you like to drug women, Mr Flood? Do you like to have sex when they are semi-conscious or even half-comatose? Does rape inspire your art?'

"They were female – fat and middle-aged, Cagney and Lacey gone to seed. They did a lot of staring, but who the hell is **beep** **beep**? Finally it came to me – the waitress." He drags on his cigarette. "I have total recall – does she?

"It was her idea to go for a drink. I wasn't bothered. It was late and the bar was about to close – she suggested we take a bottle to the room. 'Why don't you freshen up a little,' she said – does she remember that? Because I know the barman will. He was delivering the champagne as she said it. It is always worth making friends with the barman – those guys remember everything." Flood shifts in his seat. "Everything consensual, although it was nothing special and so, no, I didn't call. Perhaps she felt bad about that – she let herself down. And now she's made a complaint, all these weeks later. Silly girl – she won't feel any better about herself."

Eighteen

The last day of term should have been a mere formality: turn up, sign in, have coffee, then disappear until September. Only I'd been called in for an extra crit, as had Kelly, Spencer, Charlotte and Judy.

We hung our work on the walls or laid it on the floor.

Spencer had a large stormy canvas, while Charlotte was using dolls (something to do with an alleged abortion). Judy had garish close-ups of rotting exotic fruit and I had the series of self-portraits I'd continued after the last project. There was an obvious progression; they were becoming more abstract, hazy almost, or at least I thought so. Spencer said it looked like I was disappearing, which made me think of Jenny, and brought a lump to my throat. "Don't say that," I said, as I stared vacantly at the vast seascape he'd leant against the wall.

"How long are they going to keep us waiting?" Kelly sat on one of the desks. Quarter of an hour late, the office door swung open and a pair of cowboy boots clicked onto the steps as first Mike Manners, then Mike Cherry appeared.

"Right, let's get started," Mike Cherry's bright blue eyes over-blinked as if something were irritating him. "Whose is this?" He looked around, his lips pursed.

"It's mine," I said, only daring to raise my hand a little.

"Mia, long time no see," Mike Manners said, as he stroked his greying stubble.

Mike Cherry glared. "You've been avoiding us?"

"No, not at all." I was taken aback.

"We've barely seen you. Missing in action?" Mike Manners said. "Is there anything we should know?"

How could I tell them that my life had divided into Before Flood and After Flood, and that while his show was still on at my college I was finding it hard to walk through the door?

"Cat got your tongue?" Mike Cherry asked.

"I find it easier to work at home, that's all."

"Well, that's no good to us," Mike Cherry said.

"I've been working. It's just I like to be alone."

"We need you here in person, otherwise we can't help and by the looks of it, you need all the help you can get," Mike Cherry said.

They fell silent as they contemplated my latest self-portraits.

"This is carrying on from the last project, I take it?" Mike Manners said.

"Yes, I wanted to take it further."

"Do you think you managed that?"

I shuffled from foot to foot. "I dunno, maybe."

"We're not saying they're not interesting," Mike Manners said.

Mike Cherry interrupted, "But it's not enough. They're shoddy. I'd be ashamed to show them."

Kelly gave me a sympathetic look, while I bit the inside of my cheek. *Keep it together.*

"There's nothing wrong with carrying on a project if you think you can really take it somewhere," Mike Manners said, "but I'd like you to think long and hard about where you're going with this. Your third and final year starts in September – that's only a few months away; you need to knuckle down. There's no second chance. You have to make it happen. You have to make it matter."

"And if you're not here, we can't help," Mike Cherry said. "Can we have a girl guide's promise that we'll see you in the studio on a daily basis next term?"

I bit the inside of my cheek. It was so unfair. I had been working hard only I'd done it alone in my room back at my house.

"We heard about your friend," Mike Manners said. "Has there been any news?"

I blinked hard, determined not to cry. "No, nothing."

"You can talk to us, you know," Mike Manners said, "we're always here – even if you're not."

They moved on to Kelly, and then Spencer, Charlotte and Judy. Everyone got the same treatment. Afterwards, we all gathered up our unworthy artwork and made our way out of the studio, my stomach knotted in dread as we went down the corridor towards the foyer. *Flood's bloody show* – I tried not to look but I couldn't help it. *What is going on?* There were three burly men in black T-shirts, arms folded, contemplating a particularly large piece. They were considering how best to move it. *It's being dismantled. It's over.* It was about to be packed away and shipped off somewhere, anywhere, who cares – it would be the dump if I had my way.

At last I could reclaim the space as my own. And surely now it would be less likely Flood would return to Nottingham. *Next term will be easier. I won't fail.*

"Anyone fancy a coffee?" I said; for once keen to hang around.

Nineteen

My housemates left for the summer, while I stayed on to work at Saviour's as there were few seasonal jobs in Stowe-on-Sea.

My parents came to visit. We met in the foyer of the Victoria Hotel, and Mum soon asked about "that poor girl that's gone missing".

A month had passed since Jenny had disappeared. *She's dead, I'm sure of it.* But that didn't stop me looking or dreaming. Jenny was very much alive in my head and everyone at Saviour's talked about her, attempting to remember everything she'd ever said, while I filled in the gaps, turning her into some sort of half-creation of my own, convincing myself I knew her better than I did.

I told Mum how the police call them 'mispers'. "Sounds like whisper doesn't it?"

Jenny would whisper to me in my dreams. She'd appear, always flighty and I could never quite catch up, never quite pull her back into the real world. Sometimes, the joy of seeing her would quickly diminish, as the figure of Flood would enter the frame. "Don't take a drink," I would warn her – like that would help.

I drew little girls lost in short skirts and ankle socks, sucked into dark alleys or cowering behind metal dustbins. Some were obviously young; others ambiguously older while their attire made it clear they were stranded in girlhood, forever about to go missing. *Eve Goes Missing* I, II and III.

Eve began to look more like Alice in Wonderland as I drew a champagne bottle labelled 'Drink me'. Her clothes were girlish, her hair in pigtails, but now she sat at the end of a bed without her skirt. *Eyes Wide Shut*, I called that one. Then another, similar but with legs parted, while another had blank eyes, a bottle labelled Rohypnol Fizz and a camcorder – *I Can Put You in the Movies*.

I stood in my room momentarily exhilarated by my productivity. *It's happening, really happening.* Then doubt set in, like it always did. *Are they pornographic – a paedophile's dream?* I tidied them away in my art folder to look at afresh the next day, hoping the break would provide perspective.

My parents took me out for meals all weekend and filled my fridge with luxurious food from M&S. I'd eat well for a week.

It was hard to concentrate on any artwork while they were there, and just as hard after they'd gone, as the house appeared ugly and emptier without them.

Early afternoon, my day off, and I knew I should eat something but it was too hot, stifling even. There was no movement in the air. I went to my window, forced open the rotten frame of the sash. Girls were out on the wall, itty-bitty skirts, smoking, chewing false nails. Girl-with-braids was one of them. She took out a small mirror from her tiny rucksack and checked her lovely face.

I grabbed my sketchpad and, careful I couldn't be seen, made a few fast, fluid marks on the page. She could be Cleopatra if it weren't for the backdrop of unloved terraced houses, crumbling wall with working girls and general urban decay.

I should go out, take my camera, walk around, and see what I can find. Only I felt lethargic. *It's too hot to do anything.* I withdrew from the window, switched on my portable TV, and flicked through the limited channels. News was on Three: a reporter, broadcasting by a river, and behind him, frogmen in a black dinghy. The place looked familiar but I didn't register where it was, not immediately, and then a red box appeared at the bottom of the screen: 'BREAKING NEWS: woman's body found in River Trent, Nottingham'.

Twenty

Saviour's was my first thought as I tried to take in the enormity of what I'd seen. I left immediately and arrived as the lunchtime rush drew to a close.

The bar was dark compared to the sunshine outside and it took a moment for my eyes to adjust. There were office workers sitting at tables, and men at the bar. Vivienne was serving. Her eyes locked with mine. "You're not due in today."

"You saw the news?" I asked.

She handed the man his change, and came round the side of the bar. "Nothing has been confirmed," she said. "You rushing in won't help. Jason is beside himself as it is. You'll only make it worse. It's best you go, until we hear one way or the other."

But it was too late. Donna had seen me. She smiled and then her expression faltered. "They've found a body." She welled up. "It's Jen – I know it. I've got this sickly feeling of dread."

Vivienne frowned. "We don't know anything yet. It could be anyone," she said.

"How's Jason?" I asked.

Vivienne looked heavenwards and said, "Go and see him."

Donna opened the swing door to the quietest kitchen ever.

"Table two gone yet?" Warren said.

"Just about, chef," a young lad said.

"Who's that?" I whispered.

"He's from the agency – covering for Jen," Donna said.

112

"Should have been out five minutes ago," Jason said. He noticed me then in the doorway. "Mia?"

"Can't keep away," Warren said.

"It's Jenny," Jason said. "You know something?"

"No – it's just..."

"It's her, isn't it?"

"I don't know."

After service, it was negotiated that the new temporary commis, and Clint the kitchen porter would clean up and wash down so Warren, Jason, Donna and me could take a couple of hours out to drive over to the Meadows area to see if we could locate where the body had been found and glean some information from the police.

"What about flowers?" Donna said, as we squeezed into Jason's car. We stopped en route at a petrol station and bought the best on offer – a yellow cellophane-wrapped bouquet of carnations.

Onwards past the Sixties-built shopping parade towards the rows of back-to-back terraces on Wilford Grove. "I used to live round here," I told the others. I knew the river was up ahead, beyond the playing fields. I braced myself as I watched sunbathers, kids playing and dog-walkers. "Stop here, Jase," I said, as he turned right along the embankment.

The water was calm, the River Trent lapping gently at the concrete steps. There was something municipal about this stretch of the river. It had been tamed and contained, lined in concrete on either side. Easy to spot a body, I would have thought. But then I guessed it could have been thrown in anywhere upstream and just floated down, bloated with water, to a busier stretch.

"Over there, look." Jason pointed towards a white police tent.

Donna linked arms with him.

Why didn't I think of that?

"You can hold my hand," Warren said.

"I'm all right." I gave him a look and turned away.

Jason broke into a run, and Donna struggled to keep up, as we hurried in a diagonal across the playing fields, past the men playing football, some of them bare-chested. It was hot, the hottest day of the year so far. A couple of teenage girls were sunbathing in pink bikinis and a small queue had formed at an ice-cream van. *How can people carry on as normal?*

Blue and white police incident tape marked off a small stretch of the embankment. A young policeman stood guard. In the water, some way off, there was a dinghy and men in wetsuits.

Kids on bikes had stopped to watch, along with a couple of old ladies. The oldest one, who was wearing a long knitted dress in the heat, shook her head. "Every week it's more bad news. Makes you scared to go out, doesn't it, Brenda?"

"Them frogmen – what they looking for?" a boy asked.

"Any evidence we can find," the policeman said.

And that's when Jason said, "It's Jenny Fordham, isn't it?"

Everyone turned to see who had asked such a specific question.

The policeman cleared his throat. "The body's yet to be identified."

Jason looked agitated. "You must have some idea. Is it Jenny Fordham?"

"I'm afraid I am unable to divulge any information at this early stage."

"You know though, don't you?" Jason said, "I want to speak to someone. Who's in charge?"

"Jase, they're not going to tell us anything," I said.

"My girlfriend, Jenny, she's been missing four weeks. I've a right to know." The boys on bikes looked at one another with open mouths as if to say, this is the real deal, but still the young policeman couldn't or wouldn't say a thing.

"Jase, leave it." Warren pulled him away, and Donna and I followed, leaving behind the muffled sound of whispers.

"Look, flowers already." Donna crouched down to place her

bouquet next to a bunch of white chrysanthemums. The flowers were as close to the river as the police tape would allow. Donna crossed herself in prayer, as she read out the attached note: "Sleep sweetly, dear angel."

Jason snorted. "She's not asleep. She's dead."

"What shall I write?" Donna asked.

"Jen, you're awesome, and we miss you," I said, "or, I don't know, mention what a great runner and chef she..."

"What if it's not her?" Donna said.

"For fuck's sake." Jason walked off.

"I'll go after him," Warren said.

"Just put some kisses," I said, "until we know."

We walked away, glancing back at the riverside with its white mini-marquee shielding whatever grisly finds were being made. Jason dropped Warren and Donna back at Saviour's and offered me a lift home.

"Do you want to come in for coffee?" I thought it best he wasn't left alone.

"Yeah," he said, and parked up badly with his car's back end jutting out.

Upstairs in the kitchen, he sat down at the Formica table while I filled the kettle. "Are you going back to work later?" I asked.

"Nah, fuck 'em. The bitch won't sack me at the moment, seeing as Jen went missing from her shitty restaurant." He stared down at his hands while I made the coffee. I passed him a cup and joined him at the table. "I thought by going there I'd find out if it was her." He tipped three spoonfuls of sugar into his coffee. "I can't stand not knowing." He leant his head on his right hand, a look of despair on his face. "You got anything to put in this?"

I nodded. "Give me a minute." I went up to my room to retrieve my bottle of vodka, used for preloading before club nights. And before long, our knees began to gently bump. I should pull away, I thought, but didn't.

"Where's your music?" Jason asked, and we moved up to my room. He chose Nirvana. The sound of pain and anger, I thought, as I watched him closely. He wasn't looking after himself, not shaving or spending much time on his hair. It had flattened and softened like trampled grass, and his eyes were red and sore.

"Jen really likes you, you know," he said.

"It doesn't seem real. I never thought something so awful would happen to someone I know – and someone so nice as well."

He looked towards the sash window. "I keep thinking there's a simple explanation – something we've overlooked. Like she's gone to visit her gran in Scotland and the phone's not working and she'll come back and wonder what all the fuss is about. Or that she's entered a marathon somewhere abroad and forgotten to tell anyone – nuts, I know." He ran his hand through his hair. We were side by side on my bed, backs to the wall. I turned towards him.

"People do choose to disappear. She might have wanted to get away for some reason that we don't know about."

"You don't believe that."

We looked at each other in silence as the words gave way to something else, something needier – his mouth on mine, my mouth responding. *Bad idea,* I thought as his hand cupped my breast, his mouth moving down. *We should stop.* I pulled back.

"Yeah, you're right." He looked away. And I touched his face. He turned back. It began again – with urgency this time. We pulled at each other's clothes and ended up on the floor. His fingers at my hair, angry at the world, at himself, and angry at me because I wasn't Jenny and that there was nothing he could do.

"You're hurting me."

"Sorry – I'm sorry." We moved back onto the bed and carried on until he stopped and shuddered. His body relaxed and slipped away from me. "I need a fag." He searched the pockets of his jeans and took out a folded strip of photo-booth snaps. "We had them done at the station," he said.

"Aw, like you do when you're teenagers." I felt a pang of guilt.

Jason nodded. "She'd never done the photo-booth thing before – she'd never really been out with anyone."

She looked distant already in the photos: sweet, smiling shyly, her long mousy plait hanging down the front of her sweatshirt, Jason beside her, posing like a rap star. The photos already seemed like ancient artefacts. This time had passed. She had truly gone. "She looks really pretty," I said. "She's wearing her cross."

"Fat lot of good that was," Jason said.

"You think she's gone, don't you?"

He didn't reply, though his eyes were watery as were mine.

We heard the door – a particularly loud knock.

"Who's that?" I said.

Jason pulled on his jeans. "How should I know?"

"Come with me," I said, and he followed me down where at the door stood two policemen – the same two that had come round when Jenny first went missing.

Everything has an expiry date though most things are not clearly labelled. Jenny Fordham should have said "Best before 10 June 2005" in which case there were conversations we would have had, things I should have said if only I'd realised... Only we were both young, indestructible, blissfully unaware there could possibly be a Best Before date in any way earlier than the average life expectancy. Now I know different. It's a supermarket world and we are merely stock items pre-stamped: Best Before, Display Until, Sell By, Use By – only we don't know the exact date.

I had shown the policemen into the living room, worried it was obvious we hadn't been sitting there. *Do we smell of sex?*

"Please sit down," the older officer said. He had a deeply

lined face. DCI Cameron was his name. I took it in this time.

I sat on the collapsed green sofa, Jason sat beside me and the older officer took one of the chairs with the wooden arms.

"I'll stand," said the younger one, DC Stanmore.

This is it, I thought. This is where they tell me my friend is dead – the way, when and how I'm told forever remembered.

DCI Cameron said the words. My fears confirmed. Jenny is the body fished from the River Trent, only she's not because she disappeared long ago – four weeks before in fact. The body is just a vessel; essence of Jenny vanished on the wind with the fatal moment.

"It helps to be with someone right now," DC Stanmore said.

"Close friends are you?" DCI Cameron asked.

"We work together," I said, as Jason looked at the floor.

"We've talked to you before. You're the boyfriend?"

They took DNA samples then – 'for elimination purposes'. We opened our mouths in turn; let swabs be taken from the inside of our cheeks. And I couldn't help wondering whether the recent mixing of our saliva would confuse matters. Was there a chance of cross-contamination? *Am I sure Jason had nothing to do with it?* The green flaky paint on the walls of the living room seemed to be closing in, the lack of evening light betraying the perfect sunny July day it had been.

The police told us nothing. When I asked if Jenny's murder was in any way linked to other recent local attacks, they said only that it was too early to tell. I had seen TV police dramas – they wouldn't give anything away.

"Stay," I said to Jason once the police had gone. But he was preoccupied, pacing the room, swearing under his breath.

"Fucking bastard – I can't just sit here. I have to do something."

"What can we do?"

"I can't sit and wait for the fucking police to sort it out – fucking useless, the lot of them."

"We could go back to the river?" I said, without thinking.

Jason's eyes widened and he said, "That's it; let's go back where they found her."

Twenty-one

It had gone seven by the time we arrived, the water glowing amber in the evening light. This time I took Jason's hand as we approached.

"They've gone," he said. A streamer of police tape had come loose and was flapping in the breeze. "How come they've gone?" He let go of my hand. "They've fucking fucked off already."

"I'm sure they've done all they can here." I held his arm, trying to calm him.

"No way has that been thorough. They've missed stuff. They probably needed the tent elsewhere – a stabbing or some other shit."

"The police are good at solving murders," I said. "I mean statistically it's something they're good at – shit at burglaries but all right at murders."

"What about that murder near your place, in fact, two murders – they solved them yet?"

"No, good point."

"*Cunts.*" Jason walked past the broken police tape, ignoring the mounting cellophane-wrapped bouquets. He sat down on the top concrete step, running his fingers through his wilted hair as he stared at the water.

"Pity it can't talk," I said, as the light tripped across the ripples.

"What?" Jason's voice was gruff.

"The river – pity it can't talk." It was a stupid comment. I wished I hadn't said it. And I expected Jason to tell me to shut-the-fuck-up.

"That's it." He stood up. "Who knows what happened?"

"What do you mean?" I squinted up at him.

"The only people who know who did it are the fucking cunt who did it and who else?"

"Well – Jenny, I suppose."

"Exactly."

"So?"

"We can't ask the murdering cunt because we don't know who the fuck he is and if I did know I'd kill him, but there's Jenny." He stared at me, waiting for an answer but he wasn't making any sense. My head hurt. I wanted to go home, but Jason had other ideas.

The metal lift smelt of urine.

"It's rank, I know, sorry," Jason said.

His flat on the eighth floor, however, was spotless.

"Is your brother here?" I asked, as we walked in.

He knocked on one of the beech doors off the bright white hall. "Lee, you in?" There was no answer. "Must be at Lena's," he said. "You wanna beer?"

He handed me a bottle and sat down at the small wooden kitchen table and began to write letters out on a piece of paper.

"I'm not sure about this." My voice came out whiney, so I coughed.

"You're doing it for Jenny. You ready?"

"No," I said, but still I put my hand on his.

"Just fingers," he said, pulling away so only our fingertips met on the base of the upturned glass. He took a deep breath as I held mine. "Do you think I should turn the lights off?"

"*No.*" The very thought made me panic.

"Calm down," he said. "All right, ready? How do I start? Is

121

there anyone there?"

We watched the glass.

"Is there anyone there?"

The glass remained still.

"If anyone is there could they please come through?"

There was nothing but a faint buzz from the bulb above.

"Say something else," I said.

"Like what?"

I tried to remember what I'd seen on TV. "Say we respect the spirit world, say we need their help."

"We believe in the spirit world," he said, as we held each other's gaze. "We have great respect for you spirits. We need one of you to come through. We need your help, your guidance and superior knowledge..." We waited. The only sound the dull hum from the fridge in the corner.

There was a slight tremble in the glass. Jason's hands were shaking, but it wouldn't move. It wasn't happening. Twenty minutes we sat waiting. I didn't want to be the one to stop even though my arm was aching. It had to come from Jason and he was hanging in there.

"It's no good." He knocked the glass onto its side and stared at the table, his shoulders shaking a little as he tensed his jaw. He was trying not to cry.

"Oh, Jase." I hugged him as best I could. "We'll get someone for this, you'll see." I kissed his cheek, happy to let our wet faces slide against one another, but Jason pulled away, stood up, and straightened his chair.

"It's late, I'll give you a lift back."

I didn't want to get out of the car. I didn't want to go into the house, not alone.

"Can you come in for a minute and check no one's there." I felt stupid saying it, but my imagination was working overtime. The house felt bigger and emptier than ever. I knew what sort of night lay ahead. I was under siege from my own imagination. "I hear things that aren't even there."

Jason dutifully checked through the whole house for me.

"You'll be all right," he said, as I unlocked my room.

"I'll see you at work." Jason turned to leave, then paused. "About earlier..."

"I know," I said, "we were both feeling so bad."

"Yeah."

"Forget it ever happened."

He looked at me, his face tender. "See you tomorrow."

"I'll see you out."

"There's no need."

"I want to double-lock the door." I followed him down, and he turned round at the door and I think he considered kissing my cheek but thought better of it. I watched him walk to his car; head down, as he stared at the ground. He didn't look round. And by the time I'd shut the door, applied the bolt and chain, the house had changed. It was dark, silent and foreboding. I flicked on the hall light, decided to leave it on for the night, and ran up the first flight of stairs, stopping off at the kitchen for supplies: crackers, Brie, grapes and a cup of tea, and I left another light on, and then up to my room where I locked myself in. This was all well and good but as a plan it was seriously flawed. I would at some point need the toilet. I would need to wash.

I left the tea and crackers on my desk by the lamp and looked out the window. There was a car stopped on the opposite side of the road. It was dark grey, an older model; I'm not sure what make. I sketched its dull, saloon shape and it drove away.

Twenty-two

Interior, Flood's studio: there's a large, dark canvas on an easel by the window. Flood is standing next to it, dressed in an old T-shirt and paint-splattered dungarees.

What is he painting? I want to see what it's like but the angle of the canvas makes it impossible.

Flood holds up a brush. "Sam, get us some turps?"

"You finished for the day?" It's Gecko Girl.

She stuck with him. She didn't listen to what I said.

She looks androgynous in navy overalls. "It's a bit early to stop, isn't it?"

Flood lifts a bottle of Absolut. "Fancy some?"

"Absolutely." She shakes off her overalls, revealing a white T-shirt and jeans. Flood passes her a large tumbler and she takes a gulp. "That's too much. Don't you have any mixers?"

Flood takes her glass to the kitchen area, his back to the camera. "Voila." He hands back the drink.

"That's better." She takes a deep breath, pushing her breasts up and out in her low-cut white T-shirt.

Flood reaches out and touches her with his index finger, where the bump of her right nipple is apparent. "Ouch, you're sharp." He pulls back.

Gecko Girl takes off her top and says, "Paint me."

He shakes his head, and steps back. "No," he says.

"Paint me." Her body is lean and fit.

Flood looks away, and rearranges his wet brushes.

"You paint other women, why not me?"

"It's a compulsion, something I have to feel."

Gecko Girl necks her vodka. "You want my jeans off?" She unbuttons her fly, then completes her strip and lies back on the couch.

Flood takes a rag and wipes the turps from his brushes. "I told you I'm finished for the day."

Film cuts to Gecko Girl, cigarette in hand. Flood in paint-splattered T-shirt and dungarees is sitting in his calico-covered chair. Gecko Girl, wearing only turquoise knickers, sits back down on a floor cushion at his feet.

She holds up a packet of Marlboro Lights. "You want one?"

He shakes his head. "No."

"You didn't like it?" she says.

He retrieves his Bible from an old chest of drawers.

"That's all you care about," she says. "That stuff can affect you, you know."

"Affect what?"

"Your performance."

"Drugs help."

"Not the shit you take."

He finds his glass pipe and scrabbles round for a splinter of rock. "What do you know? You're just a girl – you've barely lived."

She reaches across the floor for her shirt. "I resent that."

"What have you seen?"

"What do you mean?"

"Tell me a story, entertain me." He lifts the grubby pipe to his lips. "Tell me something that will impress me."

"Why should I?"

"You want to be an artist, right?"

"Yeah." She stubs out her cigarette and crosses her arms.

"What inspires Samantha Clark?"

She stands up and puts her jeans back on. "I don't have to tell you anything."

Flood smiles and says, "Would you like me to show you what inspires me?"

She stops and stares at him. "You mean that?"

"Sure, if that's what you want?"

Interior, a train carriage: blue seats and the number one on the window – first class.

Flood leans back to squirt Optrex in his eyes. There is triangular plastic sandwich packaging cast aside next to him.

"Do you have to do that?" Gecko Girl's voice – she must be filming.

He squirts more fluid into his eyes. "I haven't slept."

"Do you ever?"

"Some things are a lost cause." He studies a photocopied map.

"What's that?"

"The city centre."

"What have you highlighted?"

"Places of interest." He smiles, without crinkling his eyes.

Exterior: a railway station with dark Victorian brickwork, swathes of people moving, rushing footsteps and car engines. Only Flood is visible.

"That's us." He points at a white cab. And they get in.

"Sam, this is Maciek," Flood says.

The cabbie slowly turns his big, sandy head. "Where you want to go?" he says, his heavy-lidded eyes glancing at the camera.

Flood holds a finger to his lips. "Shush," he says. "I've written it down." He passes a piece of paper to Maciek, and then turns towards the camera.

"I have to blindfold you." He takes the camera. "Here Maciek, hold this."

"Why a blindfold?" Gecko Girl asks.

"You didn't think I'd give everything away, did you? Okay, Maciek, let's go."

The driver checks his mirrors and moves out, the abrupt movement making the blue bejewelled elephant hanging from his rear-view mirror swing erratically.

The car moves fast through the city streets, taking twists and turns, stopping and starting. The roads empty and darken. It must be the outskirts of town, an industrial park. They pass a packaging factory and stop in a large, deserted, gravel car park.

Flood gets out, his hand visible as he reaches out to take Gecko Girl's hand. She remains blindfolded as he leads her to a walled-off area used for waste disposal.

"Maciek, I need you to hold this." He passes the camera to Maciek so that he can remove Gecko Girl's blindfold.

She blinks and rubs at her eyes. "Where are we?" She looks annoyed and then confused as she looks around and notices there is someone else – a girl leaning against the wall smoking. *It's Girl-with-braids. What's she doing there? I don't like it. She should only be visible from my window. I can't bear it – wishing the simple act of pressing pause could stop whatever awful fate Flood has in mind.*

"You must be Sadie," Flood says.

"And you are?" She stands upright, as she flicks ash to the ground.

"We talked on the phone."

"You're not what I expected."

"Oh, why's that?" Flood asks.

"I thought you'd be alone for a start."

"Does it matter?"

"What's with the camera?"

"I'm on holiday."

"You never said nothing about filming."

"I'm prepared to pay a premium for a little holiday video?"

Girl-with-braids shrugs. "You want what we discussed?"

"Yes. But first I'd like you to tell me your name."

"It's Sadie, you know that."

"Pass me the camera, Maciek." Flood takes the camera and moves in close. "What's your surname, Sadie?"

"Sunshine – it's Sadie Fucking Sunshine. What's yours?"

Flood briefly scans the breeze-block walls and adjacent metal containers. "Tell me something about you and your life, Sadie."

"What?"

"I must know something about you."

She stamps out her cigarette. "That's not fucking normal."

"I'm sure you're used to unusual requests."

"Not like that I'm not."

"What's this all about, Jack? I don't get it," Gecko Girl says.

"You wanted to know where my work starts. It starts here."

"What is this place?" She grimaces, as the toe of her boot catches on a discarded condom.

Sadie curls her lip. "If you don't like it, you know what you can do." Girl-with-braids seems particularly affronted by another woman's presence.

"What do you see, Sam?" Flood asks Gecko Girl. "How does this look to you?"

"You do it here?" Gecko Girl asks Girl-with-braids.

"You never had it alfresco?" Girl-with-braids says.

"Sadie's spotted a gap in the market," Flood says. "A lot of the workers come out in their lunch hour or between shifts."

"Yeah, and time's money so can we get on with it?" she says.

"How old is Sadie Sunshine?" Flood zooms in on her face.

"Twenty," she says.

The camera concentrates on the eye area – not a line, not a wrinkle.

"How did Sadie Sunshine get into this line of work?"

Gecko Girl moves back to lean against the opposite wall.

"I don't need this." Sadie stomps off a few feet away. "If you want to do business, fine, let's get on with it – if not bugger off. Leave me alone."

"Give me one of your beads?"

"What?"

"I'd like one of the beads from your hair. A blue one..."

"You're fucking nuts."

"Please."

"Fuck off."

"I'll double your money."

"What you want it for?"

"A keepsake."

"What?"

"I like to collect keepsakes."

"Double you say?" She considers the offer.

"Keep you going for a day or two, won't it?" Flood says.

"Depends what shit I can get," she says.

"I want a bead."

"They're difficult to get off."

"I've got a knife," Flood says. "Here, Sam, hold the camera." He passes it over, and then takes a retractable Stanley knife from his pocket. Girl-with-braids stares ahead as he steps forward to slice a Byzantine blue bead from her plaited hair.

Twenty-three

Jenny is dead. Every day the alarm clock went off I'd open my eyes and remember that there was something I had to remember – *Jenny has gone.*

I sighed heavily. I was due in at work. I didn't want to go. But I couldn't skive, not after what happened the last time. It was another beautiful day. *How can that be?* I forced open the battered sash and wedged it open with an A4 folder. I needed light in my dark hole of a room and fresh air. Though propping the window open didn't make much difference seeing as the air was syrupy thick with heat and dust.

A girl was out already and it was only ten. She had blonde hair with black roots and wore a thin-strapped white top and short denim skirt with a frayed hem. She was slim and attractive by anyone's standards, though her eyes were hard as was the set of her jaw.

Crouched by the side of the window, on the edge of the bed, I took a black ink pen and sketched Blonde-with-black-roots as best I could. I drew her looking one way, then the other. I sketched her on the phone and pacing up and down. A car came. I drew the car. Then another – but that didn't stop.

The girl squinted up at the sun. A 4x4 arrived. I made quick decisive marks on the page. It was a Range Rover – a boxy, solid car, although my version looked jagged as if seen through a heat-haze.

The girl checked left and right and approached the car, leaning in at the open window, her back curved like a feline goddess. I got that. She walked around to the other side and got in. I struggled to keep up, my sketches frantic. She'd gone, so I sketched the empty street.

Saviour's was properly subdued. I mean the place was shady and too dark for a bright summer's day at the best of times, but the news about Jenny had made it heavy with tragedy and regret. We all wished we'd walked out with Jenny that night and seen her to the bus stop or wherever she needed to go to be out of harm's way.

I changed into my uniform and followed the usual routine: laying tables, prepping the coffee machine, sorting menus. No one expected Jason to come in. Vivienne said she'd told him to take whatever time off he needed, so it was a surprise to see him, all puffy-eyed and unshaven, his hair uncombed and flat.

"Jason, buddy, you shouldn't be here," Warren said.

"I can't sit at home and stare at the walls."

"Being here won't take your mind off anything," I said.

"Why would I want to take my mind off it? I like being with people that know Jenny. I want to talk about it – try and work out who it can be."

"You're not a cop, Jase," Donna said. "The police aren't going to tell you anything. I don't see how any of us can work it out."

Vivienne walked in then, crisp white blouse, beige trousers and high silver sandals. "Jason," she said, her concerned face firmly on. "I appreciate your dedication, but this can't be the right place for you right now."

"I have to be here." And that was the end of the subject. We all did what we had to do that day and we all worked together perfectly. There was none of the usual banter but there was the odd caring word.

I made sure I relayed all compliments to the chefs, not that they were interested. Jason merely shrugged and said, "It's only food."

Later on, as service drew to a close, Jason came over to where I was arranging some petit fours. "How was it at your place last night – everything okay?" he asked.

"Yeah, of course it was, though I can't help being jumpy. It feels like anything could happen anywhere to anyone."

Jason nodded. "I feel useless."

"Jase, you can't sort this out. I mean where do you start? We don't know enough about what happened."

He returned to his duties: wrapping up unused produce and washing down his area. He was distant, removed. I couldn't reach him. I thought about asking if he wanted a coffee somewhere afterwards but I sensed he'd refuse.

"See you same time tomorrow," he told Vivienne. "See you guys." He waved.

I felt a little put out that he hadn't asked what I was up to later. He wasn't due in that evening and neither was I. I reconsidered my plans. I couldn't stay in that house alone for another two weeks. I went to Vivienne, told her I needed to go home and see my family. She wasn't thrilled about it, but she understood.

The sea at Stowe was a milky topaz in the sunshine, and the pebbly beach was packed with locals making the most of the only thing their locality had to offer. A white-haired couple had opened up their beach hut for the day and come laden with cold meats, bread and a thermos flask. Close to the water's edge, a toddler ran in and out of the cold surf while his young dad followed behind and his mum sat guarding the towels. A couple of teenage girls lay back topless, their tanned bodies suggesting this wasn't the first time.

I sat on the wall that edged the promenade. My head felt congested, hardly able to cope with another thought. Every day started the same way – *Jenny is dead.*

I had to remind myself because in my dreams Jenny lived, filling my mind more than she ever had when she was truly alive. From time to time I would forget and think about something else. The slightest thing would then remind me. I could be chopping vegetables and think of Jenny because that was what Jenny so often did. Or it could be the straightness of somebody's hair, just like Jenny's, or anything to do with Jason. He was her boyfriend after all.

The sky had expanded; I felt smaller and everything was meaningless. Every day I walked that concrete promenade, staring at the grey-blue sea, and sat for a while. There was nothing else to do. My old friends from school were all away.

Donna called with a date for Jenny's funeral, as her body had been released for burial. *I need to get back to Nottingham.* I wanted to be with people who had known Jenny and were happy to endlessly talk about her.

It was a hard day. Jason drove Donna, Warren and me to a church not far from where Jenny was found. It was rammed with people spilling out of the door, and we were lucky enough to stand at the back. I cried throughout, and even though everyone was invited into the hall for refreshments Jason felt too uncomfortable to attend and we left and went on to a local pub.

Twenty-four

Summer gave way to September and my housemates returned ready for the final year at college.

"It feels different this beginning," I said as I sat on Tamzin's bed watching her paint her toenails a shade called 'Summer Fruits' that looked more like 'blood clot'.

"How do you mean?" She didn't look up.

"It's our final year – it's all coming to an end."

Tamzin tutted as the dark colour leaked onto her toe. Her boyfriend was coming round. She was getting ready and didn't have time to talk so I slunk back to my room and thought about calling Jason, but what would I say? I should leave well alone. He had obviously felt bad and I certainly did. Now I'd been away and let it all die down. It was a chance for a fresh start.

I'd given my room a coat of paint, like that would help. I wanted that perfect bright gallery look though I hadn't taken into account the imperfect plasterwork – every bump and blemish was highlighted by the stark brilliant blue-white paint – but it looked reasonable from a distance. You could stand back, squint and imagine you were elsewhere – not a bad idea considering... On the plus side, for the first time in ages I knew where I wanted my work to go. It would tell it like it is – what it is to be young and female. In the meantime I was concentrating on my dissertation, reading various texts I'd borrowed from the library: The Female Eunuch, The Feminine Mystique, The Blind

Side of Eden and Ways of Seeing. "All feminist bullshit" according to Slug but a lot of it made sense, such as Germaine Greer's tract about how beautiful women (or those perceived to be beautiful) are dangerous and to possess beauty is to tempt. I found a pencil on my desk and underlined a chunk of text.

I put Germaine Greer aside and retrieved my latest sketchbook from beneath the pile of papers on my desk along with a black pen and began to draw. Moving quickly, the lines spread creating a likeness of my face on the page. It looked like I was in meltdown. I ripped the page out and started again, including joke breasts topped with Cherry Bakewells. It reminded me of Sarah Lucas's *Two Fried Eggs and a Kebab*, which brought back bad memories of what Flood had said. I ripped that out too and tried again. This time it was less extreme, more obviously attractive as I let my mouth fall open, supposedly wanton. 'Hello boys' I scribbled beneath. That was it. I'd base my final year project around advertising and magazine photo-shoots – a serious comment on how women are portrayed in the media and seen in society. It would be about how just being a woman means you're considered a temptress.

I drew more, trying to convey more brazenly seductive looks, then I switched to scraping my hair back and tying it at the nape. I took a shirt from my wardrobe and put it on over my jumper, buttoning it to the neck. I was after a severe, God-fearing, no-fun look. I sketched myself and scrawled across it: 'She asked for it'.

There was a knock on my door. It was Slug. "We're all going over The Vine. You coming?" I turned him down without even considering it. "Your loss," he said, and he was right I realised, a couple of hours later when I'd sat on my own for hours achieving nothing.

Two in the morning, I crashed out after drawing several more self-portraits and flicking through every fashion magazine I could find. The photo-shoots showed innocent angels, women as predators, vain women and beautiful women that deserved to be punished. I was onto something and it was making my mind race.

Lying in bed, my thoughts shifted between Jason, Jenny and Flood. I was fantasising about revenge and how I would let the world know what Flood was really like. *What is he really like?* Fear took hold and I lay perfectly still, convinced I could hear footsteps on the stairs as I imagined Jenny's water-bloated remains rotting in the River Trent.

I had to get up and lock my door. Back in bed, I forced myself to envisage all my worries going into a brown paper bag that I then threw away and tried to sleep.

Up late, I decided to skip college and work at home, but I needed to shop and didn't want to get caught in the supermarket in college hours. *Maybe I should make an appearance after all. Let the two Mikes know there's something happening creatively back at my place.*

I could have done with a wash but I didn't have time. I had to get to the cafeteria for lunch, get myself some food and appear in the studio like I'd been there all day. I tied back my hair, applied a trace of eyeliner, packed my art folder and dashed out the door.

At the college café I ordered what I always ordered: a cheese and coleslaw roll and I imagined the woman behind the counter rolling her eyes with the boredom of it all. The studio was empty. *Am I missing something?* Work was pinned up everywhere and there were palettes thick with paint and brushes cloaked in polythene to keep them moist over lunch.

I came to my white, empty, unloved space. *Do something fast.* I took the magazine cuttings from my folder and sifted through them as I bit into my roll.

Pins – I didn't have any pins or tape or Blu-Tack. I wolfed down the remainder of my lunch and ran outside and down the road to the union building and the art shop. Drawing pins, Blu-Tack and tape, I bought the lot and papered my space in fashion photo shoots and glamorous advertising.

Later that afternoon, Beth (the one with the flicky hair who spent the summer in New York) stopped abruptly at my space, obviously surprised to find anything there, let alone full wall coverage plus artist in residence.

"Isn't it a bit intimidating being surrounded by all these beautiful women?" She said, flicking her glossy red hair over her shoulder. "It would unnerve me. Are you coming to Emily's meal tonight?" Emily was Beth's best friend.

"Yeah, I'm coming," I said, even though I wasn't bothered.

"Mia, you've banished the white walls," Graham, my studio neighbour, said.

"I know where I'm going at last."

"Half the battle." He unwrapped his brushes ready to work.

"Nice." Spencer nodded at a shot of a semi-naked Kate Moss. "What's it for?"

"I'm looking into how women are conveyed in the media."

"What you going to do?"

I shrugged. "I'm not sure yet. Watch this space."

It was nearly five o'clock and I was yet to pin up a single sketch. Somehow, that seemed a step too far. Anyhow, I needed a toilet break so I went off down the corridor to one of the cubicles. And there on the back of the door as if it were a sign placed specifically for me was a small, round, badge-like sticker bearing a number for a rape crisis helpline. I could use this – paint it up large... My phone had run out, so instead I scrabbled round in my bag, found a pen and jotted down the information.

Emily's birthday meal was at the Thai Orchid, at eight, though I didn't see the point – none of us could afford to eat out so everyone ordered less than they actually wanted and then moaned about it.

"Portion control," I said, but Emily didn't seem to know what I meant. "You have to limit the size of the portions to make a profit."

"I know that," she said. "But this is ridiculous."

"Excuse me!" Beth said to the young Asian waiter, and then

proceeded to complain while I slid down in my seat thinking the night couldn't get any worse.

"Normally people order more than one dish each," the waiter explained.

"We're so cheap," Kelly moaned.

"Should have gone down The Vine. They do Sunday roasts all week now," Spencer said. Beth made a face and said that reminded her of those footballers on the news.

"What do you mean?" I asked.

"Some footballers – I can't remember which team – have been accused of raping a girl but they reckon she consented to sleep with all four of them. They call it 'roasting'," Beth said.

"Like they're stuffing a chicken," Kelly said.

"That is terrible." I felt nauseous.

We were supposed to be going to my favourite club, Lost and Found, but Emily had the casting vote and she chose Luna. I hated the Luna Bar – there was never anyone interesting there.

"Kelly, come to Lost and Found?" I pleaded, but no, she was going to follow everyone else so I relented and did the same and we all walked in a big group past the barricaded pawnshops, bookies, crumbling pubs and kebab shops of Mansfield Road towards the city centre.

There was no queue for Luna. They let anyone in and they didn't make you wait in case you changed your mind. "Kell, I'm not going to bother," I said.

"Why not?"

"I want to do some work."

"What– now?"

"Yeah, I've got all these ideas going round my head. I don't want to forget them."

Kelly wasn't impressed but what could she do, I'd obviously decided, so I began to retrace my steps home, past shops and department stores and onto Shakespeare Street, past the YMCA where you could sometimes see pensioners enjoying a tea dance and of course my favourite bar, Ruby's.

I quickened my pace as the roads grew quieter and darker and my keys were already between my fingers as I turned right and headed uphill past the iron gates of the arboretum and the cemetery on the other side. My boots sounded loud as I pounded the pavement. Occasionally, I glanced behind pretending I needed to cross the road when really I was checking to make sure no one would jump me. There was a rustle in the undergrowth, behind the iron railings – a small animal fleeing my footsteps? I kept going on the right-hand side for as long as possible as it was well lit and then crossed over and went up Arthur Street, finally turning into Gedling Grove.

A car slowed behind me, beside me. *Too close – go away.* The driver's electric window slipped smoothly down. My heart raced.

"You doing business, love?" Within the car's dark interior I could see a light-haired, middle-aged man in a smart leather jacket. "How much, love?"

What? "Fuck off."

"I thought – you..."

"Fuck off – just fuck off!" I was right by my house and didn't want the man to see where I lived I paused and waited. *Fuck off now, you disgusting creep.*

Finally he did, and I went inside, shut the door tight, and ran up the three flights of stairs to my room where I locked the door, intending to start sketching ideas. Snatching up my sketchbook, I flicked to the inside back cover where I'd copied down the wording of the rape crisis sticker from the college toilets in tiny script. I knew how I wanted to use the sticker in my art but now on a whim I picked up my mobile and tapped in the number. It began to ring and I almost turned it off, but they answered too quickly.

"Hello, drug-rape help line, can I help you?"

It really is twenty-four hour.

"Hello, drug-rape help line, can I help? Are you okay to talk?" the voice said.

It sounds like Julie Walters.

"I know what you've been through," she said, leaving a gap for me to fill. "You're not alone."

I coughed. I couldn't help it.

"You know, it's very common. There are almost a thousand cases of drug rapes reported each year," 'Julie Walters' continued. "We suspect it could be far worse. Many women feel unable to report it."

"It happened to me," I said.

"It wasn't your fault, sweetheart." 'Julie Walters' wanted me to know that. *I didn't ask for it. I am not to blame.*

"No woman wants to be raped," 'Julie Walters' said, as tears dripped down my face. "No woman asks to be raped."

"I went back to his hotel room of my own free will," I said. "I hardly knew him. I was stupid."

"You weren't to know, my lovely. Your only crime was to be too trusting and that's no crime. You weren't to know. You've done nothing wrong."

I could picture Julie's tawny head set sympathetically to one side with her deep-set eyes emoting.

"And now my friend has been found dead..."

"Oh." Julie seemed taken aback at that and I so wanted to talk more, tell her all about it and about the mess with Jason when I heard the front door slam and then footsteps – *someone's back.* I couldn't risk being overheard.

"I've got to go, but thank you." I switched off the phone and climbed into bed fully clothed, my head under the covers, curled into a foetal position. In the kitchen below, I could hear Slug and Spencer crashing about making toast and whatever else they could find in the almost empty fridge.

Twenty-five

Saviour's was subdued, and if anyone did smile or laugh they'd quickly check themselves. I wasn't sure I could carry on working there. I still needed the money; more than ever due to the mounting costs of art materials, but it was bringing me down. Everyone was grieving and then there was the added threat that Flood could reappear at any moment, as well as my guilt over Jason.

He was understandably angry and bitter. Angry that anyone could do that to Jenny, that the police hadn't caught the culprit, and also bitter that he was a suspect. He had no alibi. He'd had a day off that fateful night and had simply stayed at home playing on his Xbox. His brother was away, so he saw no one and no one saw him. He had something to prove, so in a way it wasn't a surprise when he approached me with another desperately weird idea.

"The feds are getting nowhere," he said. "I've got to do something. You know what I said about only two people knowing who did this..."

I thought back to our last trip down by the river, to the place where Jenny was found, when we'd sat on the concrete steps and watched the amber water of the Trent flowing on regardless.

"Yes, I remember," I said.

"The murderer isn't going to help obviously, we tried the

Ouija board and that was no good, and I know it's a long shot but..."

"Where are you going with this?"

"Have you seen that spiritualist church near where Jen lived?"

"Oh, Jase – the Ouija board was bad enough."

His blue eyes pleaded with me. "I know it's freaky shit but it's got to be worth a try and say Jen or some other spirit does come through with some information the police are never going to believe me. They'll just think I'm trying to get myself off the hook. I can't do this alone. I need a witness."

I looked away, wondering what I could say to get myself out of this one.

"I'll pick you up at seven, yeah?"

"I dunno, Jase."

"Please, if not for me, do it for Jen."

The Spiritualist church was in a large four-storey Victorian villa on Park Road. It was shabby with cornflower-blue paint peeling from the doors and window frames and an overgrown front garden. By the pavement was a sealed noticeboard listing the times of meetings. Park Road was one of Nottingham's premier streets, neat with topiary gardens and executive cars. I guessed the neighbours probably weren't too thrilled to have this house of spirits in their vicinity.

"Ready?" Jason said, as we stood outside.

"No, not really."

He tugged at the old brass bell-pull, and a large woman with raven hair and a scarlet dress opened the door. "Welcome," she said with an American accent. "Come on in."

Inside, it was like a bric-a-brac shop with instruments hung from the walls: violins, a trumpet, even a cello. There was a stuffed boar's head, stag's antlers and a huge stone bust on a plinth by the staircase that looked like Sir John Gielgud or perhaps Baden-Powell.

"Marilyn Manson would love this place," I whispered.

"Old things – the spirits seem to like 'em," the woman said. I stifled a sneeze and thought of that Hollywood actor, Billy-Bob Thornton, who said he was allergic to antiques.

"The name's Andrea, by the way," she said. "Come on through... We have some newbies with us tonight," she told the people gathered in the large front room. There were heavy, dark curtains, mismatched wooden chairs placed in rows, and a scattering of seated older people and a string of fairy lights in the window.

Andrea leaned in and whispered, "Is there anyone you're hoping will come through for you tonight?"

I didn't want to say. I was sceptical and felt we'd be giving too much away. But Jason had no such qualms. "Jenny Fordham," he said. "She recently passed away."

Andrea nodded solemnly and indicated for us to take a seat, while she took up her place at the front. The lights were dimmed and she raised her hands, closed her eyes and started to sway. *Here we go – hocus pocus, mumbo jumbo.* I stole looks at the other people trying to determine how seriously they were taking it.

"Alfred," she said. "Alfred is coming through. He wants to tell Joanie everything's just fine. She mustn't worry. It will all be all right." A frail lady to my right clasped her hands together.

"Ricky is with us." Her swaying slowed. "It's time to make a fresh start. Stop living in the past."

I looked around. *Does this mean anything to anyone?* A man at the back was listening intently. *Is he Ricky's brother or perhaps his dad?*

"Ricky wants you to move on."

The man nodded.

Andrea's swaying became jittery. "This isn't too clear. There's a lot of interference. All right, sweetie, I hear you. She's new to this. It's Jenny."

How convenient.

"It's a little broken up. It's kinda faint. I gotta real concentrate here. I got it – a white man in a white van – is that right? It's a vehicle anyhow." Andrea gave a start. "She's on her way. Don't you worry, she's gonna be just fine in the summerlands..."

There were more banal messages as ambiguous as any daily horoscope and then everyone was done. Everyone had a message. One hundred per cent satisfaction guaranteed, and Andrea came round with a velvet collection net. "It takes a lot out of me, you know." She shook the collection net. "Most people give ten pounds."

"We're students," I said.

"In that case, half will do. It's a mighty expensive property to maintain."

Move somewhere smaller, I thought. "Can you tell me what it means that she's in the summerlands?" I asked, as I searched my bag for change.

"Summerlands is our name for heaven, for want of a better explanation."

"So, she's okay?" Jason asked.

"Sure." Andrea squeezed Jason's shoulder and moved on with her collection.

"Let's get out of here," I said. "Upkeep for her house, yeah right, the money probably buys all that old junk she's got stacked everywhere."

"Shut up, Mia. Why do you have to be so negative all the time? We've got a lead, at last – it's more than the police have managed."

"A white man in a white van – do you know how many bloody white van drivers there are out there? Look." I pointed across the road. "There's one over there for a start. I'm going to count them on the way back."

Jason frowned. "Maybe that's why the murdering cunt chose a white van – he won't want to get caught, so what better than use a white van? Think about it. What about that bloke who killed that little girl Sarah Payne – didn't he drive a white van?"

"Look, there's one and another. What are you going to do, Jase? Are you going to tell the police?"

"No, I'm not – you are."

"What? Hold on a minute, look, there's another one," I said. "And another – there's two more. The police will think I'm nuts."

"Remember those two girls murdered in Soham, Holly and Jessica?"

"Yeah."

"Their parents went to a medium before their bodies were found. He told them the girls were dead and it was a young guy in a red car. Ian Huntley had a red car. If the police take the piss, you tell them that." Jason drew up outside my house.

"Eight, Jason." I looked across at him.

"Eight what?"

"I counted eight white vans during a five-minute car journey."

Twenty-six

Exterior, Nottingham station. An old lady in a see-through plastic rain hat counts out her change with her purse wide open. Flood says, "You need to be careful, my dear, or you'll lose that."

People walk in front of the camera – occasionally they apologise.

"Where are you?" It's Flood's voice in the background, the camerawork shaky as he talks on his mobile. "I told you 4.30." He walks away from the station. The sky is grey and overcast. He crosses at the lights and walks through the shopping centre and back out the other side to a cobbled thoroughfare.

A short, dark-haired man smiles and raises his hand as if to stop Flood in his tracks. "Free stress test?" he says. Behind him there is a table with books and leaflets.

"Out of my face," Flood says. "Scientology bollocks."

He films the shop signs, and then directs his camera at a clinically obese woman and her matching daughter. As they shuffle past the woman narrows her eyes and says, "What you looking at?"

Flood points towards the short man. "Free stress test."

Film cuts to: Maid Marion Inn, the cheap hotel room with the tartan-covered bed. Flood is sitting on it, rocking back and forth. He hugs himself. He seems cold, possibly unwell. He takes a call. "About time," he says.

Cut to: Maciek's cab.

"Where you want to go, Jack?"

"The usual – start in Forest Fields."

"OK, we go..."

The cab moves off at speed. Flood films out the window, taking a particular interest in a group of teenage girls.

"Did you see that? Hair like cooked spaghetti."

"You need to find girl and settle down," Maciek says.

Flood films the back of Maciek's sandy head and his thick powerful bulldog neck. "Have I ever asked for your advice?" he says.

"No, you have not."

"We'll leave it at that, shall we? Turn left here, then next right." Flood makes a wincing noise.

Maciek checks Flood in his rear-view mirror. "You have problem?"

"It's nothing. Keep driving – left at the lights..."

Interior, Flood's studio: he is in his calico-covered chair, the TV on. There is rubbish strewn everywhere. The walls have been rubbed with surplus paint.

"Police say they are increasingly concerned about a young Nottingham woman who has been missing for several days. Connie Vickers was last seen on Thursday evening at about 6.40pm on Forest Road East in the Forest Fields area of the city. Connie had been known to work as a prostitute but it is out of character for her not to return home to her mother and two young children. Police say it is too early to say whether her disappearance is linked to three other recent murders in the Nottingham area."

Flood curls his lip. "Another crack-whore out on the rob." He struggles to lean over to pick up a pen and a used envelope. He writes the name 'Connie Vickers' in florid handwriting and goes to his computer in the corner of the studio. There is a pile of paper at his feet. "So much to do..."

The doorbell goes. It's a young woman with auburn spiky hair, dressed in jeans and a navy hoodie.

"Work around me, Anna."

A new cleaner – what happened to the last one?

"You want that I move things and put back?"

"Do what you like."

The young woman changes into a pair of vinyl slippers and tidies everywhere else before finally approaching Flood at his desk.

"It okay I mop under you?" He aims his camera in her direction. "Why you do that?"

"Don't you want to be in the movies?" Her face reddens as Flood focuses in for a headshot.

Flood lounges back in his calico-covered chair, his legs across the arm. He's pale, wasted and unshaven – his dark hair unkempt and in need of a cut. He looks like he hasn't eaten for days.

"'Men act, women appear' John Berger, Ways of Seeing," Flood says. "Watching you, watching me, watching you... It's hard to convey just how important a piece this is proving to be..."

He gets up and paces the room. "It's about adding layers. You start with an idea and it develops, or it doesn't and that's the difference. What I've got here is something new – I've pushed the boundaries."

Flood pauses, lights his pipe and talks straight to camera. "I've completed *Aftermath*. It's sold already, but I want feedback, and to put it on show." He takes another toke on his pipe. "More than anything, I want *her* reaction."

Twenty-seven

Martin Power, the artist who sculpts in light and soundscapes, was scheduled to give a lecture at college. We were all expected to attend, so I traipsed down to the lecture hall after lunch and found a place, halfway up the tiered seating, next to Kelly.

Mike Cherry, in a floral shirt, took centre stage. "There's been a last-minute amendment," he said. "I'm afraid Martin Power has had to postpone due to unforeseen circumstances but he has very kindly organised a more than worthy stand-in.

"I'd like to introduce a quite remarkable artist, someone who has already made big waves in the art world and continues to make exemplary and fascinating pieces. This artist has already shown here at Future Factory. I know you'll remember his recent show, *Now That You've Gone Were You Ever There?* Please join me in welcoming Jack Flood…"

Oh my God, no. Don't clap. My heart pounded. I wanted out, but I was trapped in the middle of the row, halfway up. I'd have to squeeze past everyone and go down the side steps in full view of Flood. I sank down in my seat.

"Are you okay?" Kelly whispered, as he came on stage, wearing a suit jacket over jeans and a fine-knit jersey. "What a scumbag."

"It's an honour to be invited here today to talk about my work. I never like to miss an opportunity to talk about myself." He paused for everyone to laugh. *Creep.*

"I'd like to take you through my recent exhibition and tell you a little about how I work. I'll take questions and then I'd like to give you a preview of my new work, *Aftermath*."

He wouldn't dare show anything that involved me, would he? I'd come out in a sweat as soon as I saw him but I wouldn't be taking my jumper off. Wearing only a T-shirt would feel like exposure. I wanted out, but was hemmed in. I'd have to bide my time, listen to every single thing that sad fucker had to say and then watch his latest video-art-crap.

Kelly squeezed my arm, while I imagined taking a gun from my bag and slugging him one straight between the eyes.

"This is entitled *I Owe You Nothing*. You may have seen it in my recent exhibition."

Flood's slide show commenced with a photograph of a small pot of dust, toenail clippings and pubic hairs lit from beneath by a pink light-box.

"I often use found objects or in this case human detritus and utilise constructs such as light-boxes and picture frames et cetera that we've come to recognise as signalling, 'This is art'." He babbled on for ages and after a while Graham, who was sitting two rows ahead, put his hand up and I sank lower in my seat as Flood looked upwards.

"How do you find your subject matter?" Graham asked.

Flood flicked his hair away from his face and said, "For me, it begins with the human condition. It's about how we live now and that can take in anything: the consumer society, how our identities are defined by our possessions, urban fear and alienation, the disintegration of community, the government and its need to control with more stealth taxes, et cetera."

People were taking notes while I wrote: 'Fuck off, fuck off, fuck off...' He was controlling me again. I was caught and couldn't move – couldn't leave – only this time I was awake and fully aware. The slides went on and on and then it was premiere time. The audience perked up. There's nothing like thinking you're getting a little privileged information, seeing something before anyone else, but for me it was beyond difficult. My hair stuck to the back of my neck. I felt grubby before the film had even got under way.

"*Aftermath*," he announced. The lights were dimmed, the screen flickered and there it was: that hotel room with its panelled walls, floor-to-ceiling windows and ornate cornicing. The camera felt its way round the room picking up on moved or used items as if it were recording evidence at a crime scene: the used champagne flutes, a barely touched bottle of Cristal and into the bathroom where a cream towel lay crumpled on the floor alongside a brown one. There was a designer egg-shaped bath and taps and a designer radiator. The camera swung back round into the room and slowly closed in on the bed: a satin bedspread, dishevelled sheets, possibly a stain and then moving down onto the floor, discarded underwear – *my discarded underwear*.

A strangled cough escaped my throat, and I couldn't stop. I hid my face within the neck of my jumper as a few people turned to look at me. It made it worse.

There was no mistaking them, my pale pink cotton knickers and mismatched purple bra. *God, why am I so slovenly about lingerie?* My fists clenched tight as I tried to look anywhere but at Flood. *When will it end? Get on with it. Stop.*

The camera took off again, and then a close-up – the bedside table, a twenty-pound note... *So, I'm a whore – is that it?* He had shown I was a whore, so I was a whore, and a particularly cheap one at that. It began again, focusing back on the panelled walls. The film was looped as if this exchange were never-ending.

Emily had her hand up.

"Yes, the girl with the long hair," Flood said, and Emily proceeded to completely fawn over him saying some rubbish about how intriguing it all was "and at the same time so decadent".

Flood nodded. "It's always interesting to hear interpretations of your work." Another few questions, some effusive thanks from Mike Manners and it was over.

"Hide behind me," Kelly said, as she got up and shuffled along the row before stepping out onto the steps with everyone else. I clung to the back of Kelly's jumper as we began our descent.

Flood was down at the front surrounded by young admirers looking for individual guidance on how to find success in the art world. For a moment I thought he hadn't seen me but a quick flick of his eyes let me know that he knew I was there. As I drew closer, at the most opportune moment, he turned and said, "Remember?"

I kept moving. It was all I could do. *Get out of there.*

Twenty-eight

Interior, Maciek's cab: Flood films a council estate, Sixties prefabs that lead to back-to-back Victorian terraces. There's a gang of teenage boys, a lone middle-aged woman in heels and a man walking a small dog.

Maciek glances in the rear-view mirror. "I have to tell you – it is the last time."

"What's that?" Flood isn't listening.

"I move to London."

"London?" Flood sounds irritated.

"My wife – she go to University College."

"She works in a coffee shop, right?"

"She study law in Poland. Now she start once more in London. We find house-share in Acton."

"You're kidding me? This is terrible news."

"There are plenty cab drivers – you say so yourself."

"We have an understanding, you know the ropes..."

"I save for flat deposit, now we go."

"You have no idea how heavily you have rained on my parade." Flood sighs. "Head to Forest Fields, the usual place."

Maciek glances repeatedly in his rear-view mirror.

"Is something up?" Flood asks.

"Not every day you have famous artist in back of your cab. My wife – she saw you in newspaper. You are up for big prize."

"That's right, the biggest art prize in Britain."

"There was picture in the paper also – I see the waitress."

I know what the driver is referring to – a still from Aftermath, *shot from the neck down and reprinted in the press. What a shit. But how did the cab driver know it was me?*

Flood films the university buildings, the terraced housing of Forest Fields and the crossroads with the waiting wall – *my old street.*

"Sadie, baby," Flood calls out from the car window. "Slow down, Maciek."

Sadie (Girl-with-braids), dressed in a short egg-yolk yellow skirt and low-cut T-shirt with cherries on the front, keeps walking.

"Sadie – the only sunshine in my life, jump in, sexy girl."

"Do one – fucking pervert."

"Don't be like that. You know you can't say 'no'. I pay too well for that."

"You're not filming me no more, I'm not having it. Fuck off."

"You gave me a bead from your hair – that means something."

"Just fuck off and leave me alone, I'm busy."

"Don't look busy. How much you made today – enough for your gear or are you feeling a little jittery right now?"

Sadie shoots him a look, but says nothing.

"I got candy – enough for two. Don't be silly now."

Sadie bites her thumbnail and looks around.

"OK, Maciek, she doesn't want to know, drive on."

"Wait," Sadie says. "What you offering?"

Twenty-nine

The call to the helpline did help. Drugged date rape happens – 'Julie Walters' confirmed that. I'd call again when I next had the house to myself. I'd tell her everything. And so, over and over, I rehearsed my story, determined to make it clear that I was a sensible person who had the misfortune to be momentarily duped. In the meantime, I did as 'Julie Walters' advised.

There were orange chairs at the STD clinic – the stackable, plastic type. They're everywhere: doctor's waiting rooms, the dentist and even in museums. Those chairs are institutionalised and whenever I see them I think of the time I sat, waiting to hear whether or not I was going to die prematurely of HIV/AIDS.

The waiting room posters were apocalyptic and hard to ignore. 'Been given any little gifts recently?' said one, with a picture of a purple Care Bear-type teddy with Chlamydia embroidered across its belly. 'HIV hasn't gone away,' warned another. *I know that. I'm here, aren't I?*

I tried going cross-eyed, letting the colours and words blur into each other in the hope that would make the threat go away. It was ridiculous. An AIDS test was not supposed to be part of my life.

"Mia Jackson," the receptionist called out in a girlish voice. "The counsellor will see you now – second door on the right."

Counsellor? I don't want counselling.

155

Second door on the right, and, oh no, just my luck, a great beauty's sitting there, staring at her computer.

"Take a seat," this young Elizabeth Taylor lookalike said. Glancing at her raven hair, flawless skin and lilac-blue eyes I felt grubby. *Did she forget to go to Hollywood?* She was Irish, and probably on a mission to turn bad girls good and get them on the born-again virgin train. I had seen a programme about that. Out in Texas somewhere – all these young kids taking purity pledges to remain virgins till they wed. But if they should happen to be human and fall off the sexual wagon then they could re-zip their legs and proclaim themselves secondary virgins – very convenient.

"It wasn't my fault." I didn't want Elizabeth Taylor to get the wrong idea.

"We're not here to judge you or anyone else."

"Someone spiked my drink. I don't even know what happened."

"I'm sorry to hear that," she said. And I read her name badge: Dr Ailene Shaw – not so glamorous after all.

"We're seeing more of this," she said. "You've done the right thing by coming in. When did the incident occur?"

I told her the date.

"Let me see now. Right, because it was a while ago you'll only need the one test. HIV is a virus, so if a person has contracted it, they will produce antibodies. This takes between three and six months. The HIV test looks for antibodies. We do a rapid HIV test here, which means you'll get your result back in less than half an hour." Dr Shaw went on to explain what would happen if my result were positive. I nodded politely at intervals but my mind was drifting. I was banking on a negative.

"If you'd like to follow me I'll take you through to the nurse."

Nurse – not even a doctor for this test that could change my life?

Nurse Battleaxe was more what I had expected: old, spindly and abrupt in a no-nonsense seen-it-all-before way.

"You've no veins," she said, inspecting my arm.

"I won't bother taking up heroin then."

The nurse ignored that comment. "I'll try here." She looked at my blank skin – my veins buried so deep it was like staring at the sea looking for the Channel Tunnel. Finally she found a spot and I looked away as she pushed the needle in and a dull ache ensued as a vial of my blood drained away.

Half an hour to wait – there was a cafeteria somewhere if only I could find it. I wandered through the hospital corridors – more shades of asylum, just like the police station – overcooked peas on the lower half of the wall with old string vest above. Seasons Café meanwhile had chairs and tables screwed to the floor like a young offenders' institution. There was a bloke with Down's syndrome sitting near the exit sucking loudly on a pink milkshake.

I took a tray, ordered a comforting plate of chips and a chunky flapjack and latte and sat at the other end until I spotted a CCTV camera positioned overhead in the corner. I swapped seats, turning my back on it, trying my best not to think about that shitty film *Aftermath*. *If Flood filmed that, what else has he got?* I pushed the remainder of my chips away, imagining myself on all fours; face to the wall, as Flood sat on some designer chair, beer in one hand, prick in the other, as he watched my drugged, forced performance on his forty-two-inch plasma screen. *What an arsehole.* And then it came to me – *Somehow, I'm going to make that creep pay.*

I wasn't dying as it turned out. I left the clinic feeling like I'd got away with something, caught the bus home and sat at the back, more than happy to leave the hospital with its brown-brick brutalist exterior. *Now all I have to do is get my work back on track.*

I had sketched three large self-portraits on A1-size stretched canvases. I completed them at home with my door locked – each incorporated my naked torso, onto which I daubed layers of thick acrylic paint in crimson and Prussian blue. The facial

157

features were obscured and weren't obviously me. And then onto each canvas I fixed a graphically correct replica of a section of a Rohypnol packet. On the first, the Rohypnol packet covered the eyes, on the second each ear and the third the mouth. See no evil, hear no evil, speak no evil. I needed a title. *Date Rape* seemed too obvious, as did *Sex Crime*. *Three Monkeys*?

Once again I bribed Slug to help me down the hill. Finally, I had something tangible to hang in my space. I cleared away the fashion magazine cuttings, knocked three nails into the partition and hung my triptych. I had made it in time. The two Mikes were doing the rounds. To the right, I could see Mike Manners' cowboy boots tapping away in Graham's space. We had individual crits now it was our third year. The ritual group humiliation had subsided. After ten minutes or so, Mike Cherry and Mike Manners finished with Graham and made their way over.

Mike Cherry sighed. "Mia, what have we here?" They stood in silent contemplation. "Is there a title?" Mike Cherry asked.

"*Modern Romance*," I said.

Mike Manners gave a little nod and went up close, peering into each of the canvases in turn. "Can you elaborate?"

"It's what it feels like for a girl," I said.

"Go on," Mike Manners said.

"It's like the Sixties gave us the sexual revolution and now we have the fallout. I want to address whether sexual freedom has left women too vulnerable."

"Good, keep it up," Mike Cherry said.

Did I hear that right?

"I didn't realise you were capable of such fine work," Mike Manners said.

"I agree," Mike Cherry said. "Bravo, more of this please."

'Julie Walters' wasn't there the next time I called. Someone else answered the phone. "I'll call back some other time," I told the alien voice. This other person couldn't help. Julie and me had something going. I couldn't just switch to someone else: there'd be too much to explain and I couldn't go through all that again. I thought about calling back to ask when Julie would next be in, but I could hardly call her Julie Walters. I'd have to sit tight and try to help myself.

I decided to wash early and then watch TV in my room, hoping for something to take my mind off things but everything seemed to relate to death and murder: *EastEnders*, *Holby City* and *Midsomer Murders*, just for a start. Perhaps I'd never be able to watch anything to do with murder ever again?

Jenny's brutal death had made the world a different, harsher place. I considered incorporating that loss into my work. *Disappearing Friend?* I could do some mock-up CCTV pictures and have a girl frozen in time leaving a building then in photos two, three and four she would fade to nothing.

Did it have to be Jenny or could it be any woman? Was it wrong place, wrong time or did her killer seek her out? I went through everyone at the restaurant, questioning whether they could harbour twisted fantasies or be capable of some heat of the moment mistake. Jason could certainly be hot-headed but all his reactions to her loss and murder seemed genuine. *I like Jason. It can't be him.* Warren? He was a fool whose fantasies probably didn't go beyond Page Three of *The Sun*. While Clint was more obsessed with indie bands than any girl and Duncan was loved-up with his Japanese girlfriend. *No, it's not anyone from Saviour's.*

When Jenny first went missing, the police had mentioned her interest in the Internet. Perhaps she'd met some dangerous stranger from a chat room? It didn't seem like something Jenny would do and besides why would she? She'd just started seeing Jason. Then there was the running club. Was there an oddball there? Someone who saw her every week in her shorts and T-shirt and wanted to do her harm? And what of the local attacks that had been going on for nearly a year? There was a murderer who preyed on prostitutes; could he have targeted someone else?

Outside my window, two girls paced up and down to combat the cold. One was scrawny with legs so thin there was a gap at the top of her thighs while the other was well padded – a comfort eater?

A car slowed and they both talked at the window before the heavier one got in. Scrawny continued to pace then stopped to light a fag.

She looked up. *Shit, my light's on.*

Scrawny gave me the finger.

"Sorry." I ducked away from the window.

Thirty

When I got back from college to find two police officers at my front door, I assumed Jason must have gone ahead and told them about the 'white man in a white van' and that they'd come by to get me to back his story. Then I wondered if something else had happened.

The officers were both female and I recognised one as the chunky blonde, DC Wilson, whom I'd met at the rape suite. It's about Flood I realised and it caused an instant churning in my belly.

"We hoped we'd catch you in," DC Wilson said, and I noticed her hair was now a darker mixture of blonde and brown stripes. "Can we have a quick word inside?"

I showed them through to the living room at the back, and we spaced ourselves between the collapsed sofa and wooden-framed chairs.

"This is cosy." DC Wilson's sidekick smiled.

"It's not good news," DC Wilson said. "The tests have come back negative." She was referring to the cut-up clothes: my favourite jeans and Blondie T-shirt. "I'm afraid we can't proceed."

"There was nothing – no DNA at all?" I thought DNA was wonder-evidence that's dispersed everywhere and can stand the test of time, securing convictions years later.

"Forensics could only pick up your DNA. Sometimes, items

that you assume are evidence don't come up with the goods."

I looked down at my feet in worn-out Converse trainers. They were faded blue and fraying at the edges, but at least I knew they were mine. Again I relived the horror of that moment in the hotel room when I was so out of it my own boots were unrecognisable. "I should have gone to the police sooner," I said.

"If you had come forward earlier there might have been physical evidence, some bruising perhaps. And we could have tested your blood and urine for drugs. Even so, the conviction rate for rape is depressingly low – below ten per cent."

"That's rubbish," I said. "How can it be so bad? It's the dark ages."

DC Wilson shifted in her seat. "It's notoriously hard to prove as it's often one word against another. The men always claim it was consensual and then the defence will pull the woman apart, often blaming her for being drunk. Understandably, many women can't go through with it."

"It's not good enough. Something needs to be done."

DC Wilson nodded. "Every day I feel like I personally fail women like you."

The other officer interjected, "At least you felt you could come forward and report it. More women are doing that and that's a good thing."

DC Wilson shook her head. "Day in, day out, I listen to women reporting rape and assault. I'm on antidepressants." The sidekick stared out the window at our grey backyard as DC Wilson continued, "The way I see it, men are no longer necessary."

"Jan, give it a rest."

"You're best off without them."

"Have you been through something similar?" I asked, sensing bitterness.

"My ex-husband – he was violent."

"I'm sorry."

"No man will darken my door again. It's bad enough I have to work with them. That's why I transferred to sexual crimes – to get my own back (legally, like), only it's too difficult. They keep getting away with it."

"That's enough, Jan."

Jan gave me a leaflet detailing support groups and helpline numbers, but I threw it away as soon as she left. I had 'Julie Walters' for that.

Flood's got away with it and there's nothing I can do, I thought, as I trudged back upstairs to my room to call DCI Cameron.

"A white man in a white van, that's what the psychic said," I told him, feeling foolish, but to my surprise he seemed to take it seriously. Maybe dealing with so much shit every day makes you more inclined to believe in other better worlds, or indeed a hell for all the scumbags you catch – or worse, fail to catch.

I lay back on my bed, staring up at the ceiling's textured landscape of icy peaks and troughs. *What happens to all the rapists and murderers that get away with it? Where do they go? Are they the kindly old men with twinkly eyes that I always smile at in the street? Are they the ones feeding birds in the park when they can no longer summon the strength to pull women into bushes? Do they sit on benches so they can watch the younger rapists do their stuff?*

I could see Jack Flood shuffling across a hotel room with a Zimmer frame, then struggling to set up his camera. As an ageing artist he'd probably still have access to impressionable young fans. At eighty he could still drug some poor young art student sixty years his junior, though he might have to pause to take Viagra before struggling to manoeuvre his stiff legs up onto the bed. His hairpiece would come unstuck and he'd puff and pant and worry about his dodgy ticker and she'd be so fresh and beautiful beneath him. But it wouldn't be enough any more – he couldn't get off. He'd need to do more, do worse things to get the same kick. He'd move on, try asphyxiation perhaps. That poor girl wouldn't make it and it would be my fault. I should have gone to the police the morning after. I could have stopped this, whatever it is that he does.

God, I'd love to humiliate that man – stand up in Ruby's one day, point and say, "That man drugs women. Whatever you do, don't accept a drink from that man."

Hold on, that's it, I thought, and immediately turned my room upside down, emptying boxes, my wardrobe, delving under the bed. Somewhere, I still had Flood's business card. I emptied my desk drawers onto the floor. And there, among all the old letters, postcards, photos, cinema tickets for art-house films, festival wristbands and dozens of clear lilac beads from a broken necklace, lay his simple white business card, and on it in a retro typeface his name and contact details. I slipped it into my bag and headed downhill to college.

In the library I logged on to the Internet and began my search. The Age UK site was an instant success with its pictures of incontinence pants – almost as expensive as Calvin Klein underwear. And there I found lovely 'Cosyfeet Richard' slippers and walking aids and outdoor comfort wear – everything the old git could possibly need.

I Googled 'impotency', and a few porn websites came up but I ignored those (that's not what he needs) and went for a genuine health site. I printed off an impotency quiz and the sections on ageing and impotence and the treatment options. Saga was full of possibilities. I requested their holiday brochure, health insurance and information about their credit card. And then I came across Care Homes.com – maybe he'd see sense and put himself away.

Back home, I dug out all the sexual health leaflets I'd been handed at the HIV clinic and gave Stannah Stairlifts a call: "It's my grandfather; he hasn't been upstairs for two years and the only bathroom is up there. I'd be so grateful if you could come round and show him how your wonderful product could transform his life – next Tuesday at eleven? Fantastic."

I was buzzed up at the thought of all this stuff arriving in

Spitalfields. I couldn't afford to actually order the stuff, but still I liked to imagine there really were incontinence pants and toupees turning up at Flood's door rather than just the catalogues and leaflets.

Mind you, Kelly's pragmatism brought me a little way back down to earth. "What if he knows it's you?" she said, as we sipped tea in the kitchen.

I hadn't given it a thought. "How can he know?"

"The postmark."

"I ordered it straight from the Internet. It'll be fine."

Kelly shrugged. "I guess it depends on how many girls he's upset."

I'd crossed a boundary. I knew that. I wasn't living by normal rules. Anything goes, I thought. And so what, I'm leaving soon, I can escape if things get out of hand. But I was sad about having to leave. I didn't know what to do next or where to go. I was dreading the thought of returning home to Bumblefuck.

I'll head to London, but I've got no money – can't think about this now – I've too much to do. Already I was having second thoughts about the leaflets. *What if Flood dismisses them as junk mail?* For all I knew, he might have learnt not to open certain post. *My efforts might be wasted. I need to step up a gear.*

Sod the overdraft and the student loans; I may as well put all that enforced debt to good use and actually order the stuff. And so I did, starting with a 'hernia truss and undergarment' that was basically a pair of pants with built-in hernia support that 'creates compression only where needed'. I unpacked them and photographed them and then sent the original product on to Flood.

Flood has so far received: a contraption for the infirm to steady a chair, another to help him on and off the toilet and a twelve-step guide to recovery from sex addiction. And I also arranged for someone to call about installing an upright bath with a little door so he wouldn't have to climb in any more. But I did stop short of sending round funeral directors. Kelly said it was too much and he'd probably phone the police.

Still, things were looking up. My work was really coming together though I wasn't sure how the tutors or the external examiner would take it. Anyhow, I was working hard; taking it seriously and that meant I also had to hand in my notice at Saviour's. I still needed the money of course, but I had too much to do. I was working all hours – something had to give. And besides, I thought it would be good for me to get away from the place, what with the grief hanging in the air, the guilt over Jason and the thought that Jack Flood knew where he could find me.

It would just be my luck if Flood were to turn up on my last night. *But fuck it; I'm not going to let anyone get to me, not now, no way.* Mind you, I had to bite my lip a few times especially when a demanding table of four middle-aged grouches insisted on tea. "We only offer coffee after the meal," I said, relaying company policy, but then I let them know what a big favour I was about to do them. "Seeing as it's my last night, I could make tea just this once if you don't tell anyone." I went to the kitchen to find the staff bargain basement teabags.

Jason was unimpressed. "Teabags – fucking plebs, tell them to fuck off."

"Tonight, maybe I will."

Ten minutes later Jason found me scooping a ball of vanilla ice cream to place next to his plated cheesecake. "I served that with raspberry coulis," he said.

"I know, sorry – more fussy customers."

"I need to get out of this industry. Shit hours, shit pay and no fucking respect." I could sympathise. Jason took pride in his work – each dish he sent out was a minor work of art but the punters always thought they knew better.

"That's the trouble when you're dealing with taste, it's too personal," I said.

"It's personal, all right." Jason gripped a knife like he was

Jack Nicholson in *The Shining*.

As it was my last night everyone stayed late for a drink. I had hoped they would. However, I wasn't so keen when the focus shifted to me. "We're going to miss you, Mia," Donna said, as Mags presented me with a card and gift.

"We all chipped in to get you a little something." Mags handed me a pink gift bag, and I felt myself go red, worried that I'd hate whatever they'd bought me but it was great: a set of good-quality sable hair brushes with wooden handles.

"I hope your degree show works out for you," Donna said.

"You need to find yourself a nice young man," Mags said, and I cringed, thinking of the time she tried to pair me off with her son.

Vivienne gulped at a large G&T. "If you ever need to come back, you'll be more than welcome," she said.

"I want a kiss before you go," Warren said.

I ignored that, and said I'd pop back in occasionally. "I'd like to check to see if there's any news." They all knew what I meant and we fell silent.

"I'll drop you back," Jason said, and I glanced round to see whether anyone twigged there might be more to it, but no one seemed to notice. Jenny's killer was out there and it made perfect sense to get a lift if a lift was going. Even so, I knew I'd gone red.

On the way home, I silently counted white vans. Three.

"It's just up here, isn't it?" Jason said, as he drove past the graveyard.

"Yeah, second on the left."

My street was quiet, no women or punters about. Jason stopped outside my house. "You'll still be available for seances, I take it?"

"No, but I am around if you need to talk. You've got my number." I considered inviting him in but thought better of it. "I'd better go."

"Yeah," he said too quickly.

I leant over and kissed his cheek. "See ya," I said, and got out and shut the door.

Jason held up his hand in a static wave.

Inside, I could hear my housemates in the living room. I didn't say hello; instead I ran up the three flights of stairs to my room and rushed to the window to see Jason but he'd already gone.

Girl-with-braids was there though, leaning against the wall across the road, talking into her mobile. *Shit, my light's on.* I turned it off, then peeked through the curtains once more. *What amount of bad luck do you need to end up out there walking the streets?*

A white van – oh my God.

It slowed in front of her.

It pulled away.

I tried to catch the number plate but couldn't.

It's okay. She's still there.

She put her mobile away and started to walk in the same direction as the van.

Don't say she's going to meet him somewhere? Fuck.

I checked my watch: 12.06. I wrote it down at the back of my sketchbook. It was all I could do, that and sketch the empty street.

Thirty-one

Dusk, a city street, a crowd, three or four deep – the people are mostly young, and fashionable, and are gathered outside a gallery. It's Visionary in Shoreditch. I can see the letters etched across the glass doors. There's a red rope and a few feet of red carpet ready to welcome invited guests, and to the left a skulk of photographers watching, waiting, expectant and aware that the right shot of the right person could feed their families for a month and perhaps even keep them in champagne.

The doors open. A statuesque brunette in a complicated sculpted seal-grey dress with triangular epaulettes stands by the rope. It's Amanda Darling, Marcus Hedley's assistant. She waves at a blonde couple who push forward, all big smiles for Amanda as they pass over their invites and proceed towards the door and into the gallery.

Others filter through and the photographers snap away just in case one of these guests turns out to be someone happening that they have failed to recognise.

A car arrives. The paps are alert, their lenses jostling for the most advantageous angle. Martine McCutcheon emerges, the ex-soap star, and cameras click for a moment then stop. More cars pull up. There are two recent Big Brother contestants, followed by an X-Factor finalist, some famous models: Cara, Poppy and Suki, and then Tracey Emin. "How ya doing?" she says to a young female fan, and signs her autograph.

"Tracey, Tracey, over here," a pap shouts.

Tracey turns and smiles. She's in a black shirtdress; open low at the neck to reveal a long gold chain hung with a couple of rings. The photographers click away constantly as she waves and walks into the gallery.

The Chapman Brothers saunter in looking unimpressed, and there are a few suited city types who are pleased to see that there's a crowd prepared to stand and wait simply to watch them enter an event. A young woman in a short, skin-tight dress with a couple of girlfriends grins for the cameras, followed by various other beautiful young people brandishing invites.

The focus shifts. There's a buzz in the air and people push forward. Another car draws up, the door opens, one boot with a six-inch heel emerges, then another, followed by the rest of her. Pax appears, the sphinx-like pop chanteuse and girl of the moment.

The paparazzi go into overdrive.

"Pax, Pax, over here."

"Pax, you look fabulous."

"We love you, Pax."

Pax looks above the crowd as she walks the short red carpet to the door. Her gamine, pin-thin, pop-star physique barely fills a pair of black trousers with see-through patches on her arse, and a black cowl-neck sleeveless top.

"Pax, give us a smile."

Pax pouts back at the photographer, her lips Sixties-style beige. Her long, blonde hair is backcombed and a pair of outsize, outré shades shields her eyes. The camera follows her in. No one photographs the cameraman, even though it must be Flood that is filming and this is most likely his show.

"Pax, such a pleasure to meet you, thanks so much for coming. I'm Amanda, I spoke to your assistant." Amanda Darling is gushing. "I must introduce you to Marcus Hedley. He's London's top art dealer."

Pax's face is inscrutable thanks to her sunglasses. Amanda

takes Pax to Marcus anyway, and then quickly turns back towards the camera. "Jack, for God's sake, where have you been?" she says. "I've been on tenterhooks." She smiles. "What a turnout, there are some serious buyers in tonight. You must meet them. I'm going to force you."

Marcus Hedley, his shock of white hair shorn and shaped into a micro-quiff, says, "Jack, can we lose the camera?"

Flood continues to film.

Marcus looks over his heavy framed glasses. "See that lad over there?" He points at a bearded young man with long hair, holding a camcorder. "That's Skye – just graduated from the National Film and Television School – he's filming tonight."

The camera cuts to what must be Skye's camera as Flood is now in shot. He looks better than usual. His dark hair has been cut though it's still longish, over his ears and tousled, and he's dressed in a smart dark jacket, over a shirt and jeans. He looks lean, tall and confident. He wants to be there.

"Skye, this is Jack Flood," Marcus says. "Jack's the one you need to follow this evening. Record everything. That's the way he likes it."

Flood frowns. "You're missing the point – my filming is *my filming*. It's not for anyone else to fill in the gaps."

But Marcus isn't listening. He's spotted Nicholas Drake. "Nicholas, how the devil are you?"

Drake's face is marginally plumper, his wrinkles somehow ironed out. "Is it similar to the Nottingham show?" he asks.

"There's a natural progression," Marcus says. "It's all very exciting. Check out the title piece *She Had Her Whole Life Ahead of Her* – right up your street."

"I'll let you know." Drake nods and approaches the work.

Marcus turns back to Jack. "See the woman with the long, honey-coloured hair talking to the man with the beard. That's Claire Seawood of *Art Today*: let me introduce you."

"I've nothing to say."

"She'll like that. She'll see it as a statement in itself." Marcus moves towards the art critic, but Flood doesn't follow. He's too busy watching Pax.

Tracey Emin gives Flood a nudge. "You look like you need a drink." She nods towards a tray of drinks that's circulating. "There's my friend, excuse me."

Flood remains where he is, his back against the window, watching the young pop star Pax, as Skye films from behind. Pax is talking animatedly with her friends and yet she is aware of everything around her. She turns and lowers her sunglasses for a moment. She breaks away from her group and takes a step towards Flood.

"You're the artist, yeah? That guy – is he allowed to film?"

"He's bothering you?"

"The paparazzi outside I can accept, but not in here. It's a private party and that means no press."

"I'll have a word."

She nods. "Yeah, do."

Flood approaches Skye's camera. "Game over."

The camera wobbles. "What do you mean?" Skye says.

"You're not wanted here."

The camerawork is shaky as Skye protests. "Marcus Hedley – he's employed me to film all night."

"It's my show. I'm taking back editorial control."

Interior, Flood's studio: watercolour sketches of nudes are pinned to the wall. Pax walks around in high leather boots. She takes off her sunglasses. "Who are they?" she asks.

"Nobodies."

"Really, why bother?"

"Why bother indeed?" Flood sits down in the calico-covered chair, while Pax opts for the retro leather sofa.

"I like this," she says. "It's vintage?"

"Knackered."

"Stylishly old – like you."

"I'm not that old."

"I like older men."

"I'm not old."

"Everyone over twenty-five is old."

"Your mid-life crisis will hit early."

Pax examines her nails. "I'll be okay. It's the ones who have no fun while they're young that have problems."

"Have you not heard of the quarter-life crisis?"

She shrugs and her expression hardens. "You said you had some stuff."

Flood gets up and goes towards the kitchen. There's a rap at the door. "Who the hell is that?" He checks the intercom but there's no one there. He opens the door. There's a man of about fifty in jeans and a smart navy pullover.

"James Stewart, flat four." The man is well spoken. "Someone asked me to take this in for you earlier."

"Thanks," Flood says, and shuts the door.

"A parcel, I love parcels, bring it over," Pax says.

The package is small – a jiffy bag that has been filled, folded and taped up to make it secure.

"It'll be art materials. I'll open it later."

"You can't do that. I can't like anyone who can ignore a parcel, it's not right."

Flood rips the brown padded packaging until a rattling canister falls onto the wooden floor and rolls towards Pax. She picks it up, and Flood stares open-mouthed as if he wants to say something but can't.

She looks bemused as she reads the canister's label: 'Horniman's herbal Viagra – make penile dysfunction a thing of the past – maintenance of full erection guaranteed.' Pax bites her lip, stifling a laugh. "You *really* are old."

Flood snatches it off her and throws it in a metal wastepaper basket.

The next day's tabloids were full of pictures of Pax with Flood. They made the front page of *The Daily Mail*. Pax was the main focus; her blank sunglasses-clad expression staring directly out, while Flood was pictured following behind, below the headline: 'Pax and the "Rubbish" Artist'. The copy went on to explain how conceptual artist Flood incorporates the 'rubbish' and detritus that his supposed ex-lovers have left behind into his conceptual art.

The Sun's *Bizarre* column meanwhile ran with 'Pax and Art Lover', along with an exclusive shot of Pax and Flood as they arrived at his warehouse studio.

Developments continued almost daily. Pax and Flood's accelerated relationship moved like an affair on speed (which it may well have been) from various London-based promotional events such as the launch of The Puff Pandas' new album, the opening of a new restaurant called Kyoto Kyoto and Stephen Fry's signing for his latest autobiography. They were even snapped sitting in the front row at the show for B for Beelzebub's spring/summer collection. Flood had become tabloid gold; his image combined with Pax was on fire. Add to that the newspaper-fuelled rumours of shared drug abuse; Flood and Pax as a media pairing were explosive. They sold newspapers.

I presumed it was the cataclysmic potential of their car-crash relationship that did it. The public were fascinated and so the starry couple became impossible to avoid: even though I didn't buy a daily newspaper, Slug did.

Every day, it was *The Sun*, *The Mirror* or *The Star*, but mainly *The Sun*. Always he left it on the living-room floor once he'd skimmed the features and commented on the pictures. And so I couldn't help but know that the week before Flood had been in New York with Pax while she promoted her new single and now he was happily sunning his vile, druggy white body on Sardinia's exclusive Costa Smeralda – thanks to Pax and her friendship with pop mogul Nat Withers who had offered them unlimited access to his private yacht. This was said to be a thank you after her latest song went straight into the charts at number one.

I'd like to say that all the tabloid photos of Flood at this or that banal function didn't bother me. I'd like to say my only reaction to the sight of his wasted junkie body incongruously draped across the bow of a yacht was to laugh. But such hedonistic displays of carefree freeloading were especially hard to take as the pressure of college work increased and my bank balance dipped even further into overdraft.

Time was running out. The end of degree show was looming and seeing Flood in the sun, getting away with it, made me mad. And it made me madder still that he was hanging out with someone so good-looking, famous and constantly hailed as a style icon. And that's not to mention how strange it was to suddenly know pretty much what he was doing at all times. Although there was no longer the worry of bumping into him because he was living well and truly in Pax-land – London, New York, LA, Sardinia, certainly never Nottingham – he was still unavoidably present, thanks to his new celebrity lifestyle.

Still, I assumed he'd have to check in at Flood HQ at some point so there was still the opportunity to get even.

Thirty-two

Bouquets marked the spot. It wasn't the exact spot, that was across the river on the far side where the foliage was dense, rendering it almost inaccessible.

The bouquets, their flowers turned brown and withered, marked where the policeman had stood guard on the edge of the police-tape boundary, now long gone. The flowers in cellophane had been left as close to the spot where Jenny was found – as close as friends, relatives, loved ones and onlookers were allowed. I resented the fact I hadn't been able to get closer. I wanted to claw the mud and pick through the reeds to find the clues I was convinced the police had missed.

I glanced around, as I knelt down and took a handful of damp petals and placed them between pages of my sketchbook.

I had arrived by bus, got off near the war memorial and walked. I could see the shrine as I approached. I was drawn to this place. I kept coming back day after day ever since the idea had come to me. I had spent almost the entire week sitting there on the concrete steps staring into the water.

It was another hot day. I tied my cardigan round my waist and walked in a diagonal across the playing field, well away from the shouting men playing football.

As the grass turned to tarmac at the road that ran along the river, a young man in Lycra shorts cycled past. He had the whole kit, the helmet and fluorescent socks that denoted a serious cyclist – *what a thing to be serious about.*

That Nick Cave/Kylie song was in my head: *Where The Wild Roses Grow,* about a man who takes a beautiful young woman to the river where he kisses her before hitting her over the head with a rock. Is that what happened?

I sat on the top step above where the concrete zigzagged down to meet the river's gentle lapping. The water flowed as always, glittering in the sunshine, despite what had occurred.

On the far bank a white-haired man in a black T-shirt was fishing amongst the trees. There were ducks, bobbing down for food, and a heron ready to spear unlucky fish. I opened my sketchbook.

A toddler in a pink sundress stopped and pointed at the path. "Mama, look – ladybird." She held it up triumphant, squashed between her chubby fingers.

Using charcoal I began to draw dark, dragging water that could take you down even on a glorious summer's day.

I moved on to watercolours, taking out my travel-set – a black tin filled with solid pigments. Using a small, fine brush I made watery sketches of details I could elaborate on back at college.

It was so hot my head hurt. The river had become quieter and my imagination louder as a sense of unease washed over me. *Who is that fisherman on the far bank? He's watching me – I know it. Would anyone remember seeing me here?* The cyclists sped by too fast and the mother-with-toddler only had eyes and a wishy-washy smile for her clumsy kid. *I should go.*

The bus was stifling, the walk from the bus stop to college unbearably long in the baking heat. I arrived in the calm of the studio, desperate for water and the chance to cool down. I didn't expect my tutor, Mike Manners, to find me within a matter of seconds. He was never there when I actually looked for him, so why now?

"Why don't you leave, do something else?" he said. Quite an

opener, I thought, especially so late in the day. I couldn't tell if he meant it or not, but if he did then it should have been a conversation we'd had two or three years earlier, rather than as the course drew to a close.

"Why would I do that?" I'd come into college, come straight from the river, keen to develop the sketches I'd made. I didn't expect to have to justify myself.

"You think fine art is the right course for you?"

I tried to read his expression – the laughter lines weren't laughing. *Is it just his way to fire people up to work harder at the eleventh hour or does he mean it?*

"How many people do you think manage to make a living from art?" he said.

"It depends how determined you are. I know it's competitive, anything creative is, but you shouldn't opt out just because it's difficult to get on." *You don't choose art*, I thought. It's not a choice, though I used to think it was. I'd gone to a strict academic school, and had felt that the art room was the only place I could relax and be myself. I was good at art, better than anyone else, until I went to art college, where I realised lots of people have the same talent. But that was beside the point. You are born an artist but it took me a while to realise that. All those years of feeling slightly ill at ease in the world and then it fell into place: artists are different.

After months of looking out my window and the days I'd spent by the river where Jenny was found, I finally understood that creativity is a compulsion. It's non-negotiable. *I have to highlight whatever I notice and use art to process experience as I try to make sense of the world.*

Mike Manners took a step closer to one of the canvases I'd hung temporarily to try it for size and position on the white board that delineated what would be my exhibition space. It was a painting of beautiful young people dressed in children's clothes at a party. The young men were in romper suits, the women in floral, gathered, girly dresses. One lad held a mallet and another a bottle labelled Rohypnol Fizz and, while a young woman searched the floor for a broken necklace, a guy looked on, a smirk across his face. It was entitled *While You're Down There, Love.*

Mike Manners took a step back and nodded. "What else have you got to show me?"

I sorted through the canvases I had propped against the wall and pulled out a painting of a sunlit old colonial house with a large sign in front. I turned it round slowly. "It's called *Help the Aged.*"

Mike Manners studied it closely, reading and rereading the sign in front of the house: 'Golden Sunset Gentlemen's Rest Home. Murderers, rapists and old Nazis welcome.' "Where did this come from?" he asked.

"Do I have to explain?"

He stroked his chin. "The thing is, Mia, we never see you. You rarely make an appearance. And now you are here, you have this and to my surprise I am intrigued. I would love to know your thought processes."

"Okay. It's about the little old men you see in the park. They all look so blameless but who knows? I imagined Botswana and the reported sightings of Lord Lucan and that led me to think of all the old Nazis and the Nazi-hunters still determined to track them down before they die."

He smiled – deep creases by his eyes. "We have a show."

I didn't dare say I wouldn't be using any of it.

I went home after that, keen to add my new sketches to the collection of rough work I'd already pinned to my walls.

Late that afternoon, Kelly knocked on my door. "Mia, you there?" She came in and found me sitting on the floor.

"Wow, you've been busy."

My artwork covered the floor, walls and chimney breast. There were enlarged photographs of the river, various Nottingham street signs and alleyways and then there were close-ups of impromptu shrines that had been thrown up at particular spots – death sites. There were the river paintings, sketches of the girls on the street below my window, and dozens of newspaper cuttings including various news stories about Jenny.

"Where are you going with all this?"

"I'm not sure exactly."

"We've only got a week left."

"I know. I don't know if I can pull it off in time, but I had this idea and I tried to ignore it but I can't get it out of my head."

"Then you've got to run with it, I reckon."

"Perhaps the degree isn't the most important thing."

Kelly nodded, aware that Jenny's death had shifted my perspective.

As the deadline for the end of degree loomed, the only respite from work had become the evening meal when we'd congregate in front of the TV.

Spencer sat down next to me with a plate of spaghetti bolognese: "The-family-that-TV-dinners-together-stays together."

"Shush," Slug said, as he sat forward to catch a question on *Eggheads*.

"You probably won't know it anyway," I said.

"I did know that," Slug said, "I'd have got that."

Tamzin put her plate on the floor under her chair, and picked up some mood boards that consisted of fashion drawings, a few magazine cuttings in next season's citrus colours and fabric swatches.

"Pass them over." I wanted to feel the fabrics and study the linear drawings of haughty-looking models. "I like the futuristic shoulders."

"I'm having trouble making them – bit harder than I thought."

"I'm so behind on all my work, in fact, I'd better get on with it." I returned to my room, and sat on my bed, willing myself to find the energy to continue.

It was still hot, even though it was evening. *Where's the rain when you need it?* I forced open the sash. Girl-with-braids was out, along with a stocky blonde.

I grabbed my sketchbook. I always had it to hand as it had become a project – the girls from my window and the cars that crawled by and me recording it all.

They were laughing as they smoked and checked their mobiles.

A car came. It was white with writing on the side.

I sketched it though I knew I wouldn't have time to use it.

I returned to my more advanced work. It was slow, meticulous, intricate, and I liked that juxtaposition, the unexpectedness as the subject matter was so dark. Each piece took between four and six hours, depending on the level of detail. There were to be eleven in all and I still had three left to do. I'd set myself a hard task. I'd be working through the night, as we all would, propping ourselves up with coffee and Pro Plus.

In the morning, Kelly had lines on her face that weren't normally there. I checked my own – same, though I had bigger bags under my eyes. *I'll be glad when this is over.*

In the studio, we'd been allocated two boards each in order to exhibit the culmination of three years of work. Graham's area looked complete: cast in bronze and painted, he had odd pieces of luggage. There were a couple of suitcases, a large bulging rucksack and an Adidas holdall, then there was a careful arrangement of fragments as if a case had either exploded or been the subject of a controlled explosion. Collectively, they were called *Left Luggage*. Alongside this he had sculpted a replica of a black council recycling bin, inside which he had installed a constantly ticking mechanism and called it *Everywhere*. It was all very Age of Terror post-9/11 and in my opinion, too obvious but someone liked it. Rumour had it he was being bankrolled by a mystery backer and it had to be true, as no one else could afford to work in bronze.

Emily had a series of painterly landscapes based on Somerset, where she came from. They were in earthy colours with the occasional hint of lavender – conservative, but accomplished, while Beth had turned to photography and her own face. There were twenty-five framed photos of her and her flicky hair, detailing minuscule changes of expression – nightmare, having her all over the wall.

I needed to stop looking at other people's work. It wasn't good to compare myself, not at this late stage. I returned to my designated area and began to pack away a large 3D model I'd made a few weeks before.

"Are you not using that, Mia?" Graham asked.

"No, I've moved on to something else."

"I thought it looked interesting. What's it about?"

"It's about all the dirty old men." I bubble-wrapped a giant model of a Viagra pill. I'd made an eel-shaped creature out of enlarged Viagra pills, hearing aids, and incontinence pants, porn videos and Saga holiday brochures and sprayed them all Viagra violet-blue – inspired by the items I'd sent Flood. I called it: *Whatever You Do, Don't Take Your Eyes Off It.* I'd liked it at first but changed my mind. "I'm dumping it." I kicked it aside. "Graham, can you do me a favour and hold something up for me?" I picked up an A3-size framed work that I'd finished the night before.

"Whereabouts do you want it?"

I pointed at the wall, at eye-level. "Try there."

He held up the piece, "How's that?"

"Down a little, about an inch, that's good. Hold it there while I grab a pencil." When I turned back Graham was studying it and I didn't want to interrupt. I wanted his reaction. We'd been studio neighbours for three years and I rarely felt anything impressed him.

"When did you do this, Mia?"

"It's all recent, I have a whole series."

"It's quite a departure."

"They've taken hours."

"It's feminine and yet tough. Can I see the rest of them?"

"I've only got three here. I've still got a few to do. It's going to be another all-nighter." I passed him the other two pieces I had with me.

Graham nodded. "I haven't seen you do anything like this before."

It would take all night – my own fault for getting my act together so late in the day.

Kelly came in to see me around midnight. "How's it going?"

I was at my desk in the small pool of light from the Anglepoise. It was the only way I could carry out such intricate work so late at night.

"Why didn't I think of doing this twelve months ago?"

"That's not how it is for people like us. We have to take it to the wire."

"What did we do for the last three years?"

"We had a good time." She smiled. "I'm making coffee, do you want one?" Kelly needed a break from filling the intricate display boxes she'd built. "I'm still struggling with the titles," she said. "What do you think about *Walthamstow?*"

"It's about more than where you're from though, isn't it?"

"Yeah, but I thought call one that, and then one looking at somewhere we're all supposed to aspire to, I dunno. God, I just wish it was over, I've had enough."

We sat in the kitchen with our coffee. "This time tomorrow it'll all be over."

"Yeah, roll on tomorrow. We'll be partying," Kelly said.

"Start with the free wine at the private view."

"I'll be drinking before that."

"Vodka here first, then the private view, Ruby's and a club..."

After a few hours' sleep, I woke first and gave Kelly a shout, then we packed up the last of our work and rushed down to college where the studio was abuzz with frantic activity as everyone assembled their shows.

The morning passed so fast in a Pro-Plus headachy fog. It was as though I was there but not really there. Still, my eleven works were hung in the nick of time, and my sketchbooks arranged below on a small, white box.

"Not bad, housemate." Spencer gave my arm a playful punch.

I went to see his work: three stormy canvases thick with paint. "They're certainly you."

"What are you saying?"

"Moody – unpredictable."

"I resent that." He smiled.

"It's twelve o'clock." Mike Cherry clapped his hands. "Time's up, ladies and gentlemen, everyone out, thank you very much."

The deadline had passed. There was nothing more we could do but hang out in the sunshine for the afternoon, on the grassy hill in the Arboretum alongside a hundred or so other students who were relaxing before the reality hit that they had to find something else to do with the rest of their lives.

The private view was that evening. I chose a simple, silver shift dress and pinned up my hair. Kelly went for black linen trousers and a white shirt and Tam wore a fitted black top and denim skirt.

I poured out large tumblers of vodka in my room.

"To us." Kelly made a toast.

"Thank God it's over," I said.

"I suppose we'll all end up with shitty summer jobs again," Tamzin said.

"You haven't applied for Butlins, have you?"

Tamzin shook her head. "One summer of that was enough."

Kelly looked down. "The job offers haven't exactly been

flowing in. My friend Dan, from back home – you know the one doing history – he's been offered a place on one of those graduate training schemes in the city."

"Be boring though," Tam said.

"Don't you think we'll all end up doing something boring? At least he'll get decent pay."

"Hello girls." Slug peered round the door, followed by Spencer.

"Clean out a glass and you can have some vodka," I said.

For the last month no one had washed a thing unless they needed it themselves. The sink was piled high with pans and dishes, as were the drainer and worktops.

Slug tracked down a clean saucepan. "Quarter full will do," he said, before revealing a couple of old, chipped mugs. "Who's going to be at this thing tonight then?" he said.

"I heard the two Mikes have invited a few influential people," Spencer said. "They usually sell a lot of work."

"That's because the college takes a cut," I said. "They've done a bit of marketing for once."

Kelly shrugged and said, "It's a bit of fun. I'm not expecting anything more." And neither was I. I certainly didn't expect Flood to show up.

Thirty-three

Exterior, the glass entrance to the university's Bonington Building: the camera moves into the foyer where a sign reads: 'Fine Art Degree Show', and down a corridor into a maze of board partitions that slice up the studio space.

There are paintings, installations, video art and sculptures: Spencer's seascapes, Beth's self-portraits, and Kelly's intricate boxes of found objects.

The camera slowly paces a route round the boards checking what's on show as well as filming the young crowd, some of whom turn towards the camera and nod, smile or make faces and peace signs.

"Jack, good to see you," Mike Cherry says, wine glass in hand. "Had a good look round? What do you think, a vintage year?"

"I've only just arrived. I'll get back to you on that."

The camera gently sways, taking in daubs of colour, a manic video-art piece, a bronze sculpture of a bulging rucksack and something else.

Briefly, he pauses at a set of eleven, wall-hung works. *It's my work, there on film and he's looking at it.*

He utters something under his breath and then walks back outside. He stops, his breathing heavy.

Twenty or so metres away, a large car draws up, a Bentley. A uniformed chauffeur gets out and opens the door and Nicholas

Drake climbs out.

The camera dips towards the pavement and in a wonky fashion shifts back to the glass entrance, as Flood hurries back inside.

Thirty-four

The private view for our degree show was no more than a party with free drinks, as far as I was concerned. I was up for it though. I felt good. My hair in a messy up-do had worked and my dress was flattering and despite the recent lack of sleep my skin was clear and my usual heavy liquid eyeliner had gone on in a perfect line with an upward flick at each outer corner.

"Where's the wine?" Tamzin wasn't taking any chances after the drink ran out at the post-fashion-show party the year before.

The studio-turned-art gallery was filling up fast with college staff, family, friends and the occasional interested party. Kelly joined her parents and elder brother and Spencer and Slug chatted with some guys from Photography while I looked around for Jason, Donna and Warren (whom I'd invited but were unlikely to come due to work).

"Show me round." Tam linked arms.

First up was a painted triptych with an enlarged close-up of the stamen and interior of some exotic flowers. "That's a bit Georgia O'Keeffe," Tam said.

We moved on to Graham's bronzes of left luggage.

"Impressive, aren't they?" I said. "Oh – hi, Graham." I hadn't noticed him amongst the groups of circulating people. But I should've known he wouldn't stray far from his work.

"They're good," Tam said, and she wasn't one for paying compliments.

"I really appreciate that," Graham said. "There are some serious collectors here, did you notice?" I shook my head. "See that man talking to Mike Cherry?"

We all looked over at our tutor, deep in conversation with a bald-headed man.

"That's Nicholas Drake. Mike Manners is convinced he'll buy a few pieces."

"He's a complete sleazeball," I said. "You know when I worked at Saviour's, he turned up with two prostitutes?"

"Typical short man," Tam said.

I downed my drink. "More wine?" I said, and Tam pushed ahead to the makeshift bar at the end of the studio. Two women were laughing nearby, while people on either side were pushing past me to the bar. Tam reappeared through the crowd. "Hold these, I need the loo." She handed me two glasses of wine.

I walked round to my space, curious to see if anyone was looking at my work. Emily was giving her parents a guided tour, while an older couple paused, said nothing and moved on. Spencer nodded at me through the crowd.

"I'm not enjoying this," I said.

"At least you haven't had to listen to Beth's parents telling her how fucking 'marvellous' she is."

"I'm surprised you didn't vomit."

"Your parents coming?"

"I told them not to bother as it's all going to London later on." I finished my second glass of wine and contemplated drinking Tamzin's. "Come to the bar?"

"You've still got a drink."

"It's Tam's, she's in the loo."

The bar was manned by a couple of girls from second year, one of whom Spencer had once dated. "I'm not going near that bunny boiler," he said.

"Here, hold Tam's drink a minute." I made my way over to get a drink for Spencer and yet another for myself, and as I did so, I turned and saw Flood – over to the left with the two Mikes,

189

he was there in a black suit, holding a camcorder. *What the fuck?* As far as I was concerned, Flood was now permanently ensconced in The Sun's *Bizarre* column – busy attending high-profile functions with that pop star Pax. No way was he supposed to be here, back in Nottingham, at my bloody show.

Hold on – does it matter? Don't you want him to see your work?

I took two glasses of wine, drank one and grabbed another before searching for Spencer.

I had to squeeze my way through the crowd, glancing back to check on Flood's whereabouts and sure enough, he'd broken away from the Mikes and was coming round the corner towards my space. He'd dyed his hair darker than before, and it was flopping over his right eye, casting a shadow over his pale face. He had heavy eyeliner on above and below his eyes. He looked weird, which was surprising because in the papers he had looked so well.

"Stop there a minute, Spence." I wanted to hide behind him.

"What are you doing?"

Flood was in my exhibition space. He'd spotted my photograph pinned by my work, and directed his camera lens towards it. He filmed my entire show.

"That bloke's nicking your ideas," Spencer said.

"It's not that. It's more like he's part of it."

"What?"

But I wasn't ready to answer, or perhaps not even able to, as I had to watch.

Flood let his camera drop, so as to stare close up, and then moved further back and studied the work one piece at a time.

There were eleven separate works in a series. The first showed the street from my window: the waiting-for-a-trick-wall with the bricks falling from one end and the scrawl of white graffiti and Girl-with-braids, arriving for her stint.

Number two detailed the same street, the same wall, the same girl, this time on her mobile and the arrival of another girl, the stocky blonde, in a miniskirt.

Number three: Another woman in short skirt and ankle boots joins them.

Number four: A car pulls up. Half the number plate is visible.

Number five: There are only two women.

Number six: Another car, this time blue; a girl leans in to negotiate at the driver's window.

Number seven: One girl is left, the one in skirt and boots.

Number eight: A third car arrives, this time white with lettering on the side. Again, the number plate is only partly visible.

Number nine: There is only the wall, and the gate to the Asian family's house across the road can now be seen.

Number ten is the river on a beautiful summer's evening.

Number eleven shows flowers – a spontaneous floral shrine by the river, where Jenny was found.

They were based on sketches I'd made looking from my window or down by the river, and then further developed to become more delicate and feminine with the use of silk embroidery thread on cotton. For the river piece, I'd made the water sparkle as if in the sun by sewing on sequins in gold, greens and blues.

Flood studied each piece and read the title – printed on a small white card attached to the left-hand side that said, in eleven little words: '*I Came to Find a Girl and That Girl is You* Embroidery on cotton by Mia Jackson'.

Each separate work had one of the words in sequence embroidered at the bottom. Flood stepped back, almost as if he'd faltered, and looked at the eleven pieces as a whole. He stooped down and reached for my comments book.

I could hardly breathe as he flicked through, stopped, closed the book and placed it back down where he found it. He was about to move, I could tell, so I left Spencer and walked round to the other side of the ten-foot boards.

What am I doing? Why should I hide? This is my college, my show.

As he spotted me, Flood paused, shifted a little, then started to work his way through the crowd.

"*There you are.*" Tamzin caught up with me. "Where's my wine?"

"Oh." I sounded vague because I didn't want to talk. "Sorry, I'll get you another – just give me a minute." I had to watch him.

"You bloody drank it, didn't you?"

I almost told her what I was doing, who I was watching, but Flood was approaching, and I couldn't look away.

"I hope they haven't run out. You want one?" Tamzin said.

"Yeah, whatever, if they still have any."

Tam rolled her eyes and walked off to the bar.

I was on my own and Flood only feet away. The two of us in such a small, confined space, between the ten-foot boards, trapped in a corridor of art.

I stepped back as Flood drew parallel, and he gave me a look I'd never seen on him before. Something had shifted, I was sure of it. He couldn't hold my gaze, and kept walking, his camera down. He didn't even film as he exited the studio. I stared after him. And I remained like that for a minute, watching the swing door through which he'd disappeared.

Back at my space, I checked my comments book: 'Loving your interpretation of our dodgy neighbourhood, awesome work, Kelly x', 'Weird shit, housemate – Slug', 'Could try harder – LOL, love Tam xxx'.

Apart from my friends, the pages were blank. I looked back at my work – all eleven intricate pieces. *I unnerved him?*

Kelly came over, once her family had gone. "Did you see Flood?" I nodded. "Are you all right? Did he say anything?"

"He made a pretty swift exit." I laughed.

"Did he see your work?"

"Yep."

"How did he react?"

"Minimally." I smiled. "I could be fooling myself but I think it bothered him."

We went on to Ruby's and then *Lost and Found* after that. I knew Flood could also be out somewhere in Nottingham but I didn't care. If I saw him, I could deal with it.

My time in Nottingham was nearly over, and perhaps that brought out a brave side in me, as it did in other people. Take Adrian, for example. He was someone I had rarely spoken to in three years, and he had never hit on me before. Perhaps I hadn't noticed him. He was beige from his hair to his skin to his choice of clothes and he used to share a house with Emily and Beth – enough said. Even so, now for some unknown reason, he decided he wanted to try his luck.

I was by the bar with Kelly and Tamzin when he sidled up and told me how much he liked my show. "What inspired you?" he said, running his hand through his hair.

"It's what I see from my window."

He looked as if he didn't believe me. "People say you're mixed up," he said.

"Is that what Emily and Beth said?"

"I couldn't say."

"It was them, wasn't it? Well, they would say that."

"What do you think?"

"I don't have to explain myself," I said, although if he'd been good-looking, I might have told him a few things.

He didn't give up though. "I've heard a lot about you, as in Mia the Myth – I'd love to know the reality?"

"Why don't you tell me about yourself? I don't know anything about you."

"What can I say? I like average things: beer, football, rock music, motorbikes, cycling and my mum."

I was almost asleep standing up. "I really need the loo." It was the easiest excuse. I knocked back my drink and left him alone as I went back to the chill-out room. The music was pounding as I waited to get served. Someone was next to me. I sensed them looking.

"Hello Mia, how you doing?" It was Brett, one of Slug's

friends. I didn't normally bother with Brett, though he was fit in a blonde, sporty, alpha male kind of way – that wasn't my thing, and besides he had a lousy reputation.

"You know, you frighten me," he said, with a sexy smile.

"Why's that?"

"You're smart."

"OK."

"But I'm smarter," he said.

"I doubt it."

"I hear you're pretty screwed up," he said.

No way, first Adrian and now Brett?

"Are you a lesbian?" he asked. "That's what Slug thinks."

"Every woman with an opinion gets that one thrown at them at some point. What about you? I've heard some pretty dodgy stuff about you."

"All lies."

"What about your girlfriend's sister? Slug said you got back late one night and found her drunk and half-comatose and that you took advantage."

"There are some crazy stories going round about us. I'd like to know the truth."

The city felt small. I realised I'd leave sooner than I had thought.

We did kiss, though from my point of view it was out of boredom and a lack of any better alternative. We moved away from the bar to a dark corner and kissed again. It wasn't bad.

"You're the attractive face of Millie Tant," he said.

"Milli-tant?"

"It's a cartoon character in *Viz*. She's a fat, ugly lesbian feminist who doesn't shave her armpits. I'm not saying you look like that, but I can tell you haven't got much time for men." I turned away. *Why am I even talking to him?*

"What do you want from me?" he asked.

"What? What do you want from me more like?"

"I want to fuck you. I want to fuck you long and hard."

194

"No chance." I moved away, but he followed.

He was behind me saying, "Bad boy; bad, bad boy."

"Bad?"

"Have you got a boyfriend?" he asked.

"No."

"I've got a girlfriend – bad. Bad."

Kelly and Tamzin were no longer in the chill-out bar. I'd look downstairs. Everything was blurred. I'd drunk too much.

"Have you got any money?" Brett was still following me.

"What for?"

"A packet of balloons." He smirked.

"That's presumptuous."

"Give us some money. Come on, give us some money."

I spotted Kelly and Tamzin on the dance-floor and joined them. We danced for the rest of the night, only pausing once for another drink. As the club closed, we linked arms and left, stepping out together to begin the walk home.

"Mia, wait up!" Brett shouted from the club doorway. "You coming back with me or what?"

'As if,' I said. And we laughed, and continued walking home.

Thirty-five

Interior, Flood's studio: in the large open-plan area, twenty or thirty large canvases are lined up against the wall, turned away so the paintings cannot be seen. On the floor: paper, card, paint pots, rubbish and splashes of paint – while the walls have been used to daub excess paint.

It's a mess. He's falling apart? The thought makes me smile.

Marcus Hedley and Flood are standing in the middle of the room with rubbish at their feet. "I'm excited about this," Marcus says. "Is it ready to go?"

Flood squats down by a bank of four TV screens – two black box sets placed on top of two others. "Take a seat."

It's not immediately apparent where the seating is. "Oh, there it is." Marcus lifts a pile of dust sheets from the retro leather sofa.

Across the four black screens words appear in white script: 'WHEREVER I GO, WHATEVER I DO.'

The first screen plays a speeded-up version of Flood's night-time filming around Nottingham, while the second screen is more colourful with a single pole dancer in pink-sequinned knickers twirling and gyrating round the thick metal pole as she shakes her hair extensions, feigning ecstasy. Things slow down in screen three, with a naked woman face down across a satin bedspread, the camera taking its time to linger over every dip, curve and crevice.

Is that me? I clench my fists. *Don't let it be.* Panic rises within me and I want to be sick but I also want to watch because I have to know everything.

The final screen shows a dark, damp alley. It's all in greys, black and blue, with a continuous drip from faulty guttering.

The four screens are like a giant flickering Rubik's cube.

Marcus sits forward in his seat. "I like the juxtapositions: the drab city streets, the neon of the girly bar, the naked body and then the wet alleyway. It makes you conjure stories in your head."

More words fill the screens: 'WHEREVER I GO, WHATEVER I DO, I THINK OF YOU.'

Marcus taps his chin and says, "I'd like more of a soundtrack. Music in a gallery always attracts attention. Source something moody and atmospheric."

The video begins again. Flood stares at the screens.

"The girl on the bed – it's not Pax, is it?" Marcus asks.

"No."

"Pity – could we not suggest it might be? The press would be all over it. It's just an idea, Jack." Marcus notes Flood's horrified expression. "You know since you hooked up with this Pax woman, well, you wouldn't believe the heightened interest in your work. Enquiries have increased tenfold. Your association with her has established you as an absolute brand. You're a household name. I can shift almost anything with your signature on it. It could be time to employ some help. You're not going to be able to keep up with demand otherwise."

The doorbell chimes, making Flood jump.

"It's only the door," Marcus says.

Flood kicks through the rubbish to the video-entry phone. "I'll be right down." He turns back to Marcus. "I have to sign for a package." He exits the studio and quickly returns bearing a small brown parcel. He closes the door to the studio and rips it open; causing decayed brown flowers to fall amongst the refuse already on the floor.

"*What is that?*" Marcus asks.

Flood scowls as he picks up a handful of brown petals.

He's pissed off. I got to him – all the times I thought sending him stuff was silly and puerile, I needn't have worried – it got to him.

"What is this?" Marcus asks.

Flood crushes the powdery flowers and rubs his hands together, making the flakes float to the floor. "Someone sends me stuff."

"What do you mean?"

Flood sighs and shakes his head. "I've had impotence pills, incontinence pants and colostomy bags. I even had a salesman from Stannah Stairlifts show up."

"Why would anyone go to so much trouble?" Marcus asks.

Flood wades through paper and detritus to the far window. He leans on the exposed brick wall. He looks tired.

"Have you upset someone? Do you have a stalker?"

Flood stares out the window towards lush green leaves. "I suppose that's the downside of being in the public eye; you start to attract unwanted attention. Not a jealous ex, is it?"

Flood shakes his head.

"Why rotting flowers?" Marcus asks. "What does it mean?"

A look passes over Flood's face. *He knows why it's brown flowers. He knows because he saw my show.*

"I don't know what to suggest," Marcus says. "It's unpleasant and yet juvenile. I wouldn't pay much attention. Whoever it is will soon get bored of such silliness."

No, not bored, I simply moved on.

Film cuts to Flood's studio on what I assume must be another day. It is even more crammed with art materials and litter. There are stacks of packaged canvases by the wall, thirty or so pots of paint, discarded DVD cases, screwed-up paper and other debris strewn across the floor.

Marcus rubs his hands together. "So, let's see – what have you got for us, Jack?"

Flood, his complexion grey, is tidying sketches away in a folder.

"Nicholas has taken time out to come and see your new work, Jack. He's come over especially."

Nicholas Drake is by the breakfast bar in the only patch of clear floor. "It's good of you to let me drop by," he says.

Flood doesn't look up. "Nothing's ready," he says.

"Oh, come on, Jack, you always have something to show." Marcus sifts through a pile of sketches heaped on the floor. "These are interesting – they're like storyboards." He studies a large sheet broken up into panels.

"It's not ready." Flood takes the paper from Marcus, but he moves too quickly and knocks his hip on a table laden with paints. He's in pain and unsteady on his feet. Marcus reaches out to lend his support.

"You seem a little off today, Jack."

"Nothing is ready."

Drake interjects: "I understand that it's work in progress. The thing is that you whet my appetite that time before when I came over."

Marcus looks surprised. "You've been here before?"

Flood grips the back of the calico-covered chair. He looks grey and nauseous.

"Are you all right?" Drake asks.

Flood nods but too much – it's unconvincing and he looks a mess, dressed in paint-splattered, low-slung jeans and a threadbare jumper. He rubs at his eyes. "I'm not sleeping." He grips the back of the chair.

"It doesn't normally affect you like this. Is there anything I should know? Jack never sleeps," Marcus tells Drake. "You wouldn't believe how many of my artists work strange hours."

"I guess creativity is not a nine-to-five occupation," Drake says.

"There are plenty of artists who only work by daylight," Flood says. "Painters want the natural light."

199

"You know, I would really love to see your latest work," Drake says.

Flood stands up shakily. "Bear with me."

Camera cuts to post-viewing. Drake and Marcus are sitting on the retro leather sofa.

Drake says, "I can honestly say, I didn't see that coming."

"You never cease to amaze me, Jack," Marcus says. "Jack? Where are you?"

Drake is preoccupied as he surveys a pile of prints and sketches.

Marcus seizes the moment. "What do you think, Nicholas?"

Drake looks sharply at Marcus. "It's got my name on it."

Marcus nods. "You can rest assured, that if anyone gets it, it'll be you."

"What are you saying? Is this a money issue?"

"Jack's not keen to sell at the moment. He's too attached to it. I'll talk to him – make him see sense." Marcus looks around. "Where has he got to?"

Off camera, there is rapping at a door (the bedroom or bathroom? It's unclear).

"Jack, are you okay in there?" A scuffle can be heard.

Marcus returns. "I'm not going to get any joy today," he says. "Give me a few days, Nicholas, and I'll get back to you."

"Is Jack all right?"

"He's a little fragile at the moment, a few personal issues, he'll come through."

"Well, I hope so," Drake says. "You'll let me know?"

"I'll let you know." They shake hands and Drake leaves.

Flood reappears. He traverses the studio, kicks at the rubbish, and flops down into the calico-covered chair.

"What is it, Jack, what's bothering you?" Marcus asks.

"There's something I've seen that I need to react to in a sort of semi-public conversation through art, if you like."

"Very well." Marcus pats Flood's back. "You'll find a way, and it'll be magnificent, I'm sure."

Flood forces himself out of the chair and starts to rifle through the rubbish.

"What are you looking for?"

"My Bible – have you seen it?"

"You're not still doing all that nonsense?" Marcus makes a face. "It's time I went. I won't watch that." He lets himself out, shaking his head as he goes, while Flood continues to scrabble through the chaos.

Thirty-six

The house was a tip: cigarette butts from a long-forgotten party were buried within the shag-pile on the stairs, and dirty crockery filled the kitchen. I wanted my deposit back – fat chance, unless I cleared up. I'd need some boxes. *Try the corner shop.*

Everyone had left apart from me. My folks would arrive later on as they had further to come. There was no reason to stay any longer. We had received our results a couple of days before, pinned up on the noticeboard outside Mike Manners' office.

I'd walked down with Kelly. "Good luck," I said as we approached.

"Yeah, good luck."

It took a moment before we both registered.

"A 2:2," Kelly said.

"Same," I said, "and after all that work."

"Congratulations." Mike Manners came up behind us. We turned and looked at him nonplussed. "Aren't you pleased?" he asked.

"It's crap," Kelly said.

"I'm sorry you feel like that." He smiled weakly, as he shifted from foot to foot. "The show went well, don't you think? We sold quite a few pieces and there's still London, you might get lucky down there."

"I doubt it," Kelly said. We walked away and sat on the steps by the exit. "I can't believe Beth got a first," Kelly said.

"I know, bloody typical. And after all that hard work..."

Kelly got out her phone. "I'm gonna call my mum. I want to leave tomorrow."

"Oh no, stay for the weekend – at least?"

I didn't want it to end. I had nothing to go on to, or rather back to, and wanted to remain in Nottingham as long as I could but Kelly was having none of it.

The following day, we all helped Kelly and her mum load up the family car with three years' worth of accumulated possessions and waved goodbye to Kelly Wiseman, BA Honours, who no longer wanted to be an artist.

It felt strange without her. We'd shared the top floor for two years. I entered her vacated room and sat on the floor in a pool of light, enjoying the warmth on my skin. She'd left her pine shelves. I guessed she wasn't planning on needing anything so cheap in future. There were a couple of postcards from art galleries – a Picasso line drawing of a minotaur and a sunny but smudgy painting of two figures – one playing pan pipes while the other stared mesmerised by his own reflection. I peeled it off the wall and turned it over: 'Ken Kiff, *Echo and Narcissus, Sequence 81* 1977'. *I like that.*

Kelly had also left a poster of Louise Bourgeois' giant metal spider Blu-Tacked to the chimney breast. Essence of Kelly was still in the room. It was hard to believe she'd gone; but gone she had, and soon the others left too: loading up their parents' cars while Spencer had Graham come round with a van.

No one cleared up though. The kitchen sink and worktops were piled high with unwashed crockery and the bin was overflowing with rotting debris. Did no one else care about the deposit or were they all wise to the likelihood our fat, slimy, money-grabbing landlord wouldn't pay back a penny whatever?

Ever the naïve optimist, I walked to the corner shop to get some cardboard boxes in order to clean up. I squinted in the sunlight. I didn't have my sunglasses, and neither did the albino girl with over-curled hair who sat on the wall at the crossroads. I tried not to look, but she fascinated me, sitting there in hot, shiny black clothes on a day like that.

"No cardboard boxes," the gruff shopkeeper said. "We have bin liners."

Of course he does. He can charge for those.

As I walked out, the guy in the third-floor flat next to the shop made his usual 'psst' sound. I kept walking, tucking the bin liners under my arm – I didn't want him to see what I'd bought. I didn't want him to know anything about me.

Back at the crossroads the albino was still sitting on the wall, kicking her feet out. I sneaked another glance. Her jacket and miniskirt looked like PVC, as though she'd already been wrapped in bin liners.

In the kitchen, I tipped all the crap into one of the black sacks. Plate after plate of mouldy chicken bones and the shortest cigarette butts possible. The plates went in too. They weren't worth saving, though I doubted the thin, poor-quality sack would be strong enough to hold them.

Slug's room was the only one left locked – probably a good thing. I imagined piles of porn, that nasty brown polyester sleeping bag and the lingering stench of his maggot feet.

I need a shower. I was so lethargic, hung-over, I suppose.

I stripped and climbed in behind the mildewed plastic curtain and thought about the night before. We'd gone to Zoo: Spencer, Tamzin, Graham and me.

Zoo, a huge club on two floors, wasn't as busy as usual, as so many people had already left. One of Tamzin's exes was there though. James – a handsome but dull law student was straight over, making a play for her. Tam didn't seem to mind, though she kept making faces whenever he wasn't looking.

I sat drinking and talking with the others, and more friends joined us but somehow Spencer and I splintered off. He knew I was leaving the following day, as was he (though he was only moving a matter of streets away).

"What are you planning to do next?" he asked.

I wished I could say I was staying. "I've got to go home, but I plan to move to London as soon as I can. What about you?"

"I've got a place with Graham, off Forest Road."

"What about the college show in London? Will you go?"

He shook his head. "I'm through with the whole college thing."

I nodded in agreement. "It seems weird it's all over. I'll miss it – well, not all of it, but some things." I meant him and he knew it, because after a moment's silence we kissed. It felt right. *Why did it take so long to get to this?* Few people were around, of course – no one in the way for once. We drank and talked and drank some more.

"Shall we go?" I said, and we walked back to the house we'd shared for two years, up to my room at the top where we lay down together and he touched me tenderly as if it were an act of worship rather than merely two friends saying goodbye.

The following morning we did it all again. *I like him. He likes me. It's too late.* I gathered up my clothes. "I've got to finish packing." I edged out of the bed.

I'd taken down my artwork and half-packed a couple of boxes and a suitcase of clothes but there were still piles of books, files, art equipment and other rubbish that had to be dealt with. "I can't believe how much stuff I've got."

"You'll sort it," he said.

A car horn sounded.

Spencer went to the window. "It's Graham – he's got the van for my stuff."

I stared at Spencer's tall, strong, naked frame.

"Stop looking at me like that." He grinned.

The horn went again, and Spencer forced open the sash and waved down. "Give me a minute." He pulled on his jeans, and shook out his T-shirt. "I'm going to have to go." He stroked the back of his shaved head. His soft brown eyes glanced around my shabby, part-packed room. "When are you coming back?"

"I'm not," I said. And he looked away, towards the rectangle of bright light at the window, and then back into the shady room, a soft, sad smile on his lips.

"I've got your number," he said.

We kissed again and I followed him down the three flights of stairs and helped him load up the van, ready to go.

Thirty-seven

The boredom of Bumblefuck hit me again. Stowe-on-Sea is somewhere safe you retire to if you can't afford anywhere more interesting, but even there I couldn't avoid Flood because thanks to his relationship with pop star/style icon Pax, he was news.

They had been photographed taking drugs together in the VIP lounge at top London club Fabric. In a grainy black and white shot, he could be seen smoking a glass pipe with Pax next to him, wearing oversized shades and a spaced-out smile.

The story developed and two days later, Flood was a TV news item: 'Artist Jack Flood is charged with possession of class A drugs'. And there he was, dressed in black and looking wan outside a large stone building, Thames Magistrates Court, while Marcus Hedley in a cream suit guided him down the court steps, and through a scrum of waiting photographers.

"Jack, over here," someone shouts.

"Where do you go from here, Mr Flood?" a reporter asks.

Flood puts his hand up in front of his face and, jostled by the crowd, momentarily disappears from sight.

"Is it true you're going into rehab, Jack?" a journalist asks.

"Mr Flood will not be making any comment today, thank you." Marcus Hedley tries to wave the press pack away.

"Do you believe the road to excess leads to the palace of wisdom, Mr Flood?"

"*No comment.*" Marcus Hedley guides Flood to a waiting car.

Thirty-eight

Mike Manners called. I was out at the time, walking the dog along the beach thinking about Jenny as I always do whenever I'm near water.

Mum took the call. "He wants you to contact him as soon as possible," she said.

I imagined him in his light-filled office next to the studio, cowboy boots up on the desk. Fearing the worst, I took the handset to the dining room and dialled.

"I have some good news," he said. "We've sold your work." There hadn't been a whisper of interest during the college show, but once it moved to London there'd been an approach from a third party. "Most unexpected," he said.

"Thanks," I said, affronted.

"We do sell a fair amount of work, but it's unprecedented that anyone should want to buy a student's entire output."

"They want all eleven pieces?" I pictured the eleven embroidered works hung in series at the degree show.

"They want everything: your sketchbooks and preliminary work as well as your finished pieces. It's remarkable – not even Graham's work sold so well."

"Everything?" I smiled as I said it. "Who is it?"

"No idea. An intermediary made the approach. There has been some haggling, so I assume he's a dealer working on behalf of a client. The buyer wishes to remain anonymous."

"Why?"

"Religious reasons – I'm told the works will be shipped to Dubai and must be handled in a low-key way due to the suggestive nature of the work."

Who is this creep who can't even admit to liking what he likes?

Mike said, "It's not unusual for buyers to remain anonymous, especially when collectors are bidding at auction."

"It's hardly a bidding war."

Mike laughed. "You haven't asked about price?"

It seemed beside the point, but of course I did want to know.

Finally, I'd received some validation for my work. I'd sold something, or rather everything. *I am an artist. At last I can truly call myself an artist.*

More importantly, the money meant I could escape from Stowe-on-Sea, and join Tamzin in London. She'd been staying with an aunt in Putney up to that point. But, as soon as I'd been paid we went in search of a flat together and eventually signed a short-hold tenancy agreement on a small two-bedroom basement flat down that curl of slimy steps, opposite a sauna/massage parlour in Hammersmith.

Our 'Garden Flat' was half-underground. There'd be no more watching people as I had from my top-floor window in Nottingham. From our barred front window I was limited to seeing only the legs of passers-by.

In need of a steady income I found a waitress job at Chihuahua's, a Mexican-themed restaurant off Regent Street. I hoped it wouldn't be too taxing and that the shifts would allow me enough time and energy to devote to my art.

Sunday, on my first day off from Chihuahua's, all I could hear was Tamzin and her latest boyfriend Greg going at it. *I've got to get out of here.* I dressed: jeans, T-shirt and Converse, and caught the tube into central London.

London, by the river at Embankment, is brilliant: Big Ben, the London Eye, the Savoy, St Paul's and the Gherkin, all shiny above the greenish brown water. I passed skateboarders, a man with a dreadlocked beard sitting on the ground with an upturned hat at his feet and his hand on a large brown dog, as well-fed seagulls flew above the river. Sunlight glistened on the water and as always I thought of Jenny, because to me she is forever in every river, pond and sea.

Tate Modern – power station turned art monolith was my destination. I took the escalator up to the galleries. There had been a recent, much-publicised rehang, and contemporary works jostled for attention alongside the established modern greats.

No one can like every work of art. This is where people get confused. They assume that if they don't like one contemporary artist then they can't like any, but it's not like that. Not every piece will speak to you, but if you look at a variety of work and give it all a chance, something will resonate.

The dreamy blue of a Miró attracted me first, then I moved on to a painting of a dark, foreboding wood with a childlike bird: *Forest and Dove*, 1927, Max Ernst.

The next room housed violent Bacons and Picasso's *Nude Woman with Necklace* 1968 with all her dangerous, swallowing orifices. And then there was Dora Maar – Picasso's *Weeping Woman* 1937. He made her cry, I thought.

Marlene Dumas' fresh and challenging watery paintings had their own room and in the corner next to her female nude, *Lead White* 1997, hung a long dark curtain, through which people passed. I presumed it was video art and went in and sat on one of the box stools next to a group of young Japanese women, as the night-time exterior of an English urban street with redbrick terraced houses filled the wall-sized screen.

The camerawork is fast and shaky as if the artist/filmmaker is running, while the soundscape of someone breathing becomes heavier. And the back-to-back terraces continue, until the camera takes a turn into a back alley and then another and another. They criss-cross and appear as confusing to the cameraperson as to the viewer.

The breathing is shallow and panicky, as if someone is being pursued or at least thinks they are. There is discarded rubbish: a shopping trolley, bin bags ripped open by animals, spewing nappies, beer bottles, plastic bags – and an old wheelbarrow, abandoned stepladder and branches cut from a tree.

Back out into the open streets, and the breather gets some relief. It's another seemingly endless row of redbrick terraces. It's nightmarish – a sense of entrapment. The camera moves on and the streets become familiar as the camera lingers on a short brick wall with a spray of white graffiti and bricks falling from one end. *It's the waiting wall – the waiting-for-a-trick wall, on my old street in Nottingham.* I hold my breath as my heart pounds inside my chest.

Onwards – across the crossroads and round the corner, past the corner shop and beyond to more terraced housing, an alleyway, a dead end – the camera stops, moves around. *Who is in pursuit?*

There is nothing, until a semi-naked girl emerges and freezes, as if startled, and you know she'll go, run anywhere within a moment, but for that second or two she's there on the pavement wearing only a purple bra, mismatched pink knickers and a furry, full-headed fox mask. *My knickers? My bra? Why a fox mask?*

My throat was tight, and sweat broke out across my forehead, while all around me noise was muffled. *This isn't right.*

Fox-girl is perhaps in her early twenties, her hair long, brown and deliberately unkempt over her shoulders, her feet bare, her face obscured by the mask.

And now at her feet: fresh, bright flowers in fantastical, lurid colours piled on top of others that have rotted down to brown paper mulch within their wrappings of faded cellophane. *It's Flood. It has to be Flood's work. He's got me again? How has he made it into Tate Modern?*

Somewhere, there will be a small discreet card – I have to read it.

The film had finished and was about to start again. The four

211

Japanese women began to chatter as they made their way out. I rose unsteadily to my feet and followed.

The Japanese girls gathered to take a photo outside the cubicle next to a wooden cabinet containing the fox-head mask.

I searched for the name of the video piece. A card stuck to the wall just outside the cubicle read: *The Last Haunting*, videotape on continuous loop. Jack Flood.

Why the 'last' haunting? I spun round, my head reeling. I needed to sit down. The whole room was full of Flood's work. There were old-fashioned wooden cabinets positioned on two sides of the room in an L-shape, with large information boards that detailed Flood's working processes.

I considered heading to another adjacent gallery, one with a bench. I needed to sit down.

The gallery assistant in the corner, a woman with a heavy fringe and a large mole on her upper lip was watching me, perhaps aware of my unsteadiness. I peered into another glass cabinet. There were small sketches: a naked woman, face down on the bed. *Oh my God – the underwear?* It was a dismal purple and pink combo from M&S. And next to it were test tubes holding nail cuttings, some hair and other detritus. *Is it mine? The hair's the same colour.* It was like a Victorian cabinet of curiosities with small sketches and collections of objects in pots and jars: hair, nail clippings and buttons.

Buttons? Are any of them metal? Yes, there's one and it says 'Diesel'. It's the missing button from my favourite jeans.

On the wall, to the right, was a photograph of an artist's studio: a large, light-filled room with white walls on one side and exposed brickwork on the other. It's messy, with canvases leaning against the wall and open pots of paint on the floor. While in the corner, half hidden, are brown paper packages, one of them torn open – peeking through is one of my embroidered pieces from my graduation show.

Flood's the mystery buyer. He bought my entire show.

My head was spinning; I felt faint and needed to sit down.

A guide entered and stood in the centre of the gallery. She was about forty with a gentle wave in her dark bobbed hair. She began to address a group of about ten people. "Jack Flood is one of the leading British artists working today. This particular piece follows his much lauded work: *She Had Her Whole Life Ahead of Her.*"

I can't listen to this. "Excuse me." I squeezed past. People looked askance. I was sweating – *everyone in my way, like they're walking right at me. Get out of my way. Let me pass. I've got to get out.*

The lady, the nice lady who had a black plait, dark lipstick and a Portuguese accent, told me I had fainted. I'd been taken to a small medical room and given water and a comfortable seat. "How are you feeling?" she asked.

I shrugged and tried to smile as if I were fine.

"Have some more water."

"I need to get going."

The lady pursed her lips, like she was reluctant to let me go, but I wanted to get out and escape – get as far away as I could from Flood's godforsaken trophy art.

Thirty-nine

Seventeen films of seventeen different women were found on Flood's computer, laptop and phone following a police raid. And each file was clearly labelled: Jenny Fordham, Mia Jackson, Loretta Peters, Connie Vickers, alongside another thirteen names.

The police managed to trace most of the women. Two, however, are as yet unaccounted for – missing, presumed dead.

I was so grateful to DC Jan Wilson. She was so patient when I called from outside Tate Modern. I had exited the gallery in a panic and stopped at the railings by the river, looking out towards St Paul's, while the Thames below had turned grey and choppy, and there, as always at the back of my mind at the sight of any river, was Jenny. The sky had clouded over to form a solid sheet of dark metallic grey. A storm's coming, I thought, and made the call.

Within hours the gallery had been raided, the 'artwork' seized, and the following days' headlines filled: 'Police Seize Flood's Murder Trophy Art' – *The Sun*. 'Murder and Rape Claims Close Tate Modern' – *The Guardian*.

Flood denied everything, and I was told there was a strong likelihood I'd have to go to court. I barely slept and when I did, I'd wake with images of myself in the witness box wearing a fox-head mask, unable to speak. Or, there were dreams where I was being endlessly pursued. I was aware it was Flood behind me but I could never see him and I could never get away.

I made a lousy witness. I can only remember what I can remember and it's limited. I did point that out. But then there was the film, the one with my name on it. And DC Wilson persuaded me I had a lot to offer the prosecution.

Don't look at him; don't make eye contact, I told myself over and over whilst I waited outside the courtroom. I twisted my fingers together, took my rings off and on, and bit my nails, which I don't normally do. But then I went in, took the oath and looked straight at him.

There are probably only a handful of instances in anyone's life where you can distinctly recall how it felt to meet someone's eye. With Flood, there had been a number of times: the evening I first saw him at his show, the time I ran from Ruby's after seeing him reflected repeatedly in the surrounding mirrors, at my own private view when he made a swift exit and then in court when months of dread culminated in his attempt to intimidate me – his eyes boring into me across the room. That was when all my fear about facing him dissipated as I saw him for the loser he was, flanked by prison officers and stuck behind bulletproof glass.

The formality of the court was intimidating: official, old-fashioned, wooden panels, men and women in wigs, long impenetrable arguments between lawyers and efforts to wrong-foot everyone, not least me and my hole-filled memory.

Why did I go back to Flood's hotel room? It's a question I've asked myself time and time again and it was the first question the defence lawyer asked.

He was a short, dark-haired man with blue eyes, in his early thirties and not unattractive. "Miss Jackson, what time was it when you agreed to go with Mr Flood to his hotel room?"

Whatever I say, it won't sound good. I had rehearsed this moment in my head during all the nights I couldn't sleep and yet still I sensed the wrong words were about to slip from my lips. "I didn't exactly agree to go to his room."

"You went of your own accord?"

"Yes."

"Then you agreed."

"We were going to go for a drink somewhere, that's what I agreed to do, but Mr Flood needed to change his clothes. He said someone had spilt a drink on him."

"Could you not have waited in the lobby?"

Why didn't I do that? That's what I had wanted to do. I felt myself flush, frustrated at my own stupidity and angry at Flood, the lawyer and myself.

"Mr Flood persuaded me to share a drink with him in his suite. He said we wouldn't stay long." That was it, the truth, one moment in my life when I was duped. I was stupid and it could well have been the end of me.

At that point in the courtroom, my attention slipped and again I looked at Flood. He was so still, in control as always, his dark eyes on me, watching my lips move with every word I spoke. I bit my lip and clenched my fists, determined to hold it together.

"Miss Jackson, can you hear me?" The lawyer was staring at me. Had I missed something? "Miss Jackson, I understand you left it quite some time before coming forward to make a complaint, is that correct?"

"Yes."

"Why was that?"

"I felt stupid. I couldn't remember exactly what happened." *Argh, that's not what I meant to say at all.* I knew it sounded bad.

A small, thin-lipped smirk passed across Flood's face.

"And yet here you are now to tell us you *can* remember, is that right?"

"I couldn't remember exactly because Jack Flood spiked my drink and what I do remember is waking up four hours later, naked and running out and vomiting."

There was no evidence that Flood had spiked my drink because I took so long to report the 'incident' to the police. The

216

judge (who was female) instructed the jury to disregard my comment as 'speculation'.

"That will be all, Miss Jackson," said the defence lawyer.

My evidence was all but useless. I wouldn't look at Flood again.

Stupid Girl: that song was back in my head taunting me, as I held on to the witness stand to steady myself, willing my legs to move in a reasonable fashion in order to get the hell out of there. I glanced back at the jury, tears in my eyes. I am such a failure, I thought. Is that what they're thinking? They were all watching me of course and I hoped it was empathy I could sense but I had no idea.

Forty

Interior, unspecified: Flood's face fills the screen but it's slightly fuzzy, the film quality poor and he is so close his face appears distorted; his cheeks look bigger than normal. He has a large stitched laceration to his left cheek and a swollen mouth. *Has he been attacked?*

"Who lives in a place like this?" Flood moves the camera away from his face and does a 360-degree scan of the room. There is a basic bed with a thin mattress, a small two-drawer cabinet and a heavy, locked door. The walls are bare, though there is a reasonable amount of light filtering in through the barred window.

"I've not been able to film until now." His voice is quiet, conspiratorial. "They've taken everything." He shakes his head. "Creativity is a basic human right and yet I have no creative outlet. They say it's negotiable and dependent on my behaviour." He shakes his head again. "I just got hold of this mobile that I'm filming on. I'm the prison scribe. I write letters for the illiterate inmates."

Film cuts and recommences. "This phone isn't good enough. It has an inbuilt camera but it only records short clips, not that anyone will listen. They're not used to artists. They don't understand. They tell me there will be opportunities to draw and paint but not to film. It's prohibited. But filming is my thing. I told them that I am Britain's foremost video artist.

They're philistines, especially the governor. He's the worst kind – a philistine who thinks he's cultured – his art appreciation stops with Constable and Lowry."

The camerawork is shaky. He's agitated. "The fundamental issue here is that I'm innocent. The films that they used as evidence against me are art. No one was hurt in the making of those films. They're art." Flood touches the scar across his cheek. "I have a room of my own. I'm on 'seggy'. It's a social dustbin – nonces and low-life. I am not like them."

He looks down. There are heavy bags under his eyes. His hair is greying (no more hair dye). He has aged ten years in a matter of months. There is shouting and a door bangs shut. Locks are turned.

"I'm told a lot of prisoners claim to be innocent at first, so no one listens. I write letters to the press and my MP. It's a gross miscarriage of justice. Someone has to see that. Believe me, the truth will out."

Camera cuts momentarily.

Flood remains in his cell. His tired, grey head looks up at the camera he's holding at arm's length. His baggy eyes plead. "They must let me work. It's the only way I'll get through this. Without my work I am nothing."

Forty-one

It was good to know where Flood was. I no longer needed to rely on the tabloids for information as, despite my poor courtroom performance, he was banged up for life, brought down by his own 'artwork'.

The seventeen films of seventeen different women and his magpie need to keep trophy mementoes of his victims made the evidence compelling.

Jenny, Loretta Peters and Connie Vickers all featured and that fact, along with some locks of their hair sealed in plastic, is what really did for Flood. His compulsion to record everything meant he was found guilty of three premeditated murders.

The seventeen charges of rape were not as straightforward. The jury was split, as some of them believed Flood's claims that the filmed sex (which was everything but penetrative) was consensual. As with most rape cases there was an element of ambiguity involved.

The judge said she would accept a majority verdict and after three hours of deliberation he was finally found guilty. The severity of his crimes, the sexual nature and the fact he abducted women and committed multiple murders led the judge to issue a whole life order. He wasn't getting out. Ever.

And I could let it go – or at least try to, for my own sanity.

Forget Flood. Move on. You're in London now – anything is possible.

A fortnight before the anniversary of the day Jenny went missing, an invitation arrived. There was to be a memorial service and that meant Nottingham.

I didn't want to go back but felt I couldn't say no. I tried to persuade Tamzin to accompany me but she said she couldn't get the time off work and Kelly had only just started a new job at a call centre so there was no way she could go. I would have to face it alone.

I called Kelly on her mobile. She couldn't take personal calls any other way as the company she worked for taped all calls for 'training and monitoring purposes'.

"I've been thinking of you all morning," Kelly said. "Where are you now?"

"I'm on the train – feels weird to be going back."

"You'll be all right."

"How's life in the Collections Department?" It was Kelly's job to chase people who were behind with their credit card payments.

"You have no idea. I don't know if I can last the week."

"Don't ring me looking for money."

"Have you got one of our cards?"

"It's probably the only one I haven't got. Did you hear about Tam? She's seeing someone new."

"Who is it now?"

"He's called Steve. He's a builder."

"What happened to Greg?"

"He's oblivious. I don't know how she gets away with it."

"I'd better get back to work," Kelly said. "Let me know how it goes. I'll be thinking of you."

I gazed out the window at the passing fields: cows, fencing, trees, outbuildings, flashes of train stations, car parks, busy gardens, shiny office blocks – all silver like the platinum credit cards they promote. And then I thought of Jenny and how unfair it all was. *And Jason – he'll be there. How will that go?*

The train pulled in. Lethargically, I disembarked and made

my way up the metal steps and out of the station, turning right for the city centre, and then left onto Maid Marian Way towards the Catholic cathedral.

The place was packed, but then that's untimely death for you; it stirs something even in the remotest acquaintance. I felt a lump in my throat as soon as I entered. *Get through this,* I thought, as I felt myself well up. I accepted the printed order of service from an usher, shuffled into a seat halfway back and tried to do the right thing: standing when everyone stood, kneeling and singing.

Mags from Saviour's got up and read out a poem that went something like: 'Sleep dear angel, please don't weep/ Your beautiful face is a memory we keep.'

If she were alive, Jenny would run marathons to escape all this.

Jenny's mum gave a reading. She was poised and dignified, although her voice was brittle. Then her dad said a few words, which were almost unbearably moving, and finally it was Jason's turn.

I hadn't spotted him till then. He looked good in a dark suit. I'd never seen him smart and everything he said was heartfelt. I felt guilty even being there.

Back at Jenny's parents' smart Victorian villa, with its matching cream sofas, there was tea or white wine, egg sandwiches and cake and a chance to talk to the old Saviour's crowd.

Donna's hair was puffed up in a higher cockatoo fashion than ever, but she still looked short. "You did so well, Jase. I'm so proud of you," she said.

A heavy line creased his brow. "I wanted to talk about the Jenny I knew. She wasn't the goody-goody everyone makes out. She had a wicked sense of humour." I touched his arm and felt an instant frisson. But it wasn't going anywhere. I knew that. It was good to see him again and good to see him looking so well but I just wanted the best for him and that wouldn't be me.

"How's it going at Saviour's?" I asked.

He looked around, making sure Vivienne wasn't in the vicinity. "I'm jacking it in. I don't want to be a chef any more."

"But you're so good, and we need you," Mags said.

"Shit hours, shit pay, little thanks. All this TV chef bollocks making it sound glamorous. I've got to get out while I'm still young enough to find something else."

"What are you going to do?" I asked.

"I'm going travelling round Europe with Warren – on motorbikes."

"Warren too, oh my God, Vivienne's going to freak," Donna said. "And what am I going to do? It won't be the same without you guys."

"You'll be having babies soon," Warren said.

I stayed a while longer, let the wine go to my head, before I made out I needed to catch a certain train home. I wanted to walk and take in a little of Nottingham before I left the place for good.

It was hard saying goodbye. I tried to make it easier, saying I'd be up visiting Saviour's regularly and everyone went along with it, though I'm sure they knew it wasn't true.

Jason gave me a hug. "Stay lucky."

"You too. Happy travelling. You go for it." We kissed cheeks and I left without looking back.

Outside, I walked fast – determined to once again see the good side of Nottingham. The city had become a tatty place in my mind: crumbling student digs, pawn shops, takeaways and red light areas. It was good to go back and reclaim its better side. It's all right here, I thought, as I walked through Market Square with its grand classical buildings and fountains, but I'm ready to go now.

I had about half an hour to get to the station. I crossed the street to take a pedestrian walkway, and saw the newspaper stand with its billing written out in thick black marker pen: 'KILLER ARTIST FLOOD IS DEAD'.

Forty-two

Flood is dead? I read the piece in *The Nottingham Post*, trying to contain a smile that intermittently broke out across my face. I shook my head, and almost laughed. *I have to tell someone.* I considered rushing back to Jenny's parents' place to tell them and Jason and everyone else, but how would they react? *They might think death too easy for him. Perhaps they wanted him to rot away in jail for a good thirty years or so.* I checked my watch. I was going to miss my train unless I hurried. I tucked the paper under my arm and ran.

I couldn't concentrate on anything apart from that short newspaper story announcing Flood's death. I wanted to know more. There wasn't enough detail and I wished they had a picture. I'd like to see him as a cold, grey cadaver on a metal bed. I wanted proof.

From the train window I watched the city give way to the suburbs, and smiled. *He's dead. Call Kelly. Call Tamzin. Tell everyone the good news.*

Back at my flat I flicked between news channels, watching them repeat the same information, reiterating what I already knew. *Tell me more. I want to know everything there is to know.*

The following morning I bought several newspapers. *Will there be obituaries?* I tried to remember whether other notorious criminals made the obituaries column. Well, whatever, Flood certainly did. There he was towards the back of *The Guardian*.

His life filled half a page, along with a photo of the day he left Thames Magistrates Court, convicted of possession of Class A drugs, together with a still from *Aftermath*: me naked, face down on the bed.

Jack Flood: Convicted Murderer, Sex Offender and Controversial Artist

Jack Flood, convicted serial killer, rapist, ex-partner of pop star Pax, and one of the most talked-about artists of his generation, has died in prison aged 33 from heart failure after a prolonged hunger strike.

"Jack Flood has died for his art," his art dealer and friend Marcus Hedley said in a statement read outside HM Prison Wormwood Scrubs, west London, following the announcement of Flood's death. "After a protracted hunger strike 'in the name of art' Jack Flood has died. Jack felt his treatment in prison, which ultimately curtailed his work, was inhumane and left him no choice but to protest through the rejection of all sustenance.

"Jack wanted it to be known that he was innocent of all charges. He was a great artist and friend, and I hope to soon be able to show his final work, *The More I Search the Less I Find* – a piece raising serious discussion about celebrity and the role of artists today."

Jack Flood was born in Colchester, Essex, to a Forces family. His father William rose to the level of sergeant while his Portuguese mother Adriana stayed at home to care for their only child. Flood's young life was rocked by his mother's numerous affairs. When Flood was four she temporarily left the marital home, moving in with a neighbour, only to later return after the relationship faltered. Two years later his parents divorced but this time Adriana took Jack with her and they moved to London.

A self-absorbed child, Flood later said he found an escape from childhood loneliness through art and went on to study at Goldsmith's College, London, before going on to complete a Masters at the Royal College of Art. His postgraduate show looking at the key issue of abandonment was hailed a triumph, leading to its inclusion in the infamous *Young Guns* exhibition at Visionary in 1999.

It was there that he met dealer Marcus Hedley who championed Flood's use of mixed media and edgy subject matter. With his backing, Flood set up a studio with fellow artists, Matt Piper and Dean Randall and exhibited regularly at East Sound Gallery where he gained a loyal following.

In 2004 Flood was shortlisted for the Prospect Prize and was given the opportunity to exhibit in his first one-man show *Now That You've Gone Were You Ever There?* at the Future Factory in Nottingham. Again it looked at abandonment, loss and rejection, and resulted in Flood being nominated for that year's Turner Prize, which was eventually won by Simon Starling.

Despite this disappointment, Flood was chosen to represent Britain at the Venice Biennale where his new work, *She Had Her Whole Life Ahead of Her*, was first shown. Flood had moved towards video art and his exploration of urban degradation, alienation and loss proved controversial with some critics saying he'd crossed the line and the work was unsuitable for public display. This didn't deter his greatest admirer, the collector and gallerist Nicholas Drake, who later exhibited the work in its entirety at the opening of Drake Gallery, London.

Flood exhibited globally, and as his chosen subject matter grew darker, questions of decency were raised. Were his videos too close to the mark? And even though he insisted all his models or 'muses' gave consent – should there be parameters of taste and decency placed on how the female body is used and represented in art?

His private life also came under scrutiny after the suicide of his ex-girlfriend Angela Fields, a model and actress, who died from a drug overdose on the eve of his first solo show. Their relationship had ended two months beforehand and Flood later admitted that they had briefly met earlier that day and that Angela had hoped it could be rekindled.

"Models and muses tend to have a limited life-span," he said, in an interview with Art Today that was later used in court as evidence against him.

In early 2006 Flood was accused of rape. A woman claimed personal items used in the video piece *The Last Haunting* belonged to her and were taken without her prior knowledge or consent after she was drugged and assaulted. Police immediately followed up the complaint and Flood's studio was searched and his computer seized. Seventeen suspect films were found encrypted on the hard disc. Flood was charged and later convicted of three counts of murder and seventeen counts of rape and indecent assault.

Flood, maintaining his innocence to the end, claimed it was pure coincidence that three women who had been found murdered had worked for him as models, and that they were all part of the long tradition of the artist and his muse and the sometimes questionable line between work and play.

Flood felt so strongly that he had been wrongly accused that he went on hunger strike, demanding his case be reassessed and that full artistic human rights be given to all prisoners. He went without food for thirty days and water for five before dying from heart failure. His father William died in 1990. His mother Adriana survives him.

I shoved the newspaper across the carpet towards Tamzin. "Heart failure?" I said. "He had heart failure from the word go."

Tamzin took a bite of toast, as she read the paper. "Pretty young for a heart attack – suppose the hunger strike caused it," she said.

"I don't believe in the death penalty but if some murdering bastard wants to do away with himself, let him," I said. "It's probably the best thing he's ever done."

It took me all of forty-eight hours to realise Flood's death was not a good thing, as he rose from the dead like some evil Jesus as the acres of newsprint about him began to multiply out of control. After the obituaries, there were endless features disseminating Flood's every moment as writers attempted to place his life, work and death in context. He was important, he had to be, they said so, and more famous than ever, famous for all the wrong reasons, but famous all the same. I had to face it, the man whose name I could hardly bear to say was not going to go away, but at least as a victim I remained anonymous, my identity protected. Or was it?

There were legs outside our barred window.

"Don't answer it," I told Tam, when the doorbell went. I'd already told two journalists where to go.

Tam went to the door and shouted, "*Fuck off!*" through the letterbox.

"Miss Jackson," a man's face was at the barred window. "Can you tell me your thoughts on Flood's death? Just a few words, then I'll disappear."

"Close the curtains." I backed myself up against the far wall by the kitchenette.

Tam pulled at the curtain cord, drawing together the four sections of limp beige fabric. "There – that made him disappear."

I could emigrate. It was my only option, or so I joked. Move elsewhere, somewhere, anywhere where Flood wasn't known – but where exactly? And what would I do? There's not much demand for unsuccessful artists.

Block it out, it's the only way – avoid newspapers, magazines and certain TV programmes. Keep your head down, work hard, do the waitress thing as much as necessary and hope for the break you so obviously need and deserve.

Twelve months on I thought, or rather I allowed myself to think, that my luck was about to change, when I arrived back from a particularly bad night at Chihuahua's to find a letter on my mat, inside my front door, the name DRAKE stamped

228

across the envelope.

I knew they represented Flood's estate and it could mean only one thing but still I let myself fantasise it was otherwise.

They want to see me – they must like my work.

Forty-three

I filmed as much as I could the day I went to Drake Gallery. Starting as I left my flat, I saw two skinny women holding Starbucks coffee cups enter the sauna/massage parlour with blacked-out windows across the road. I shot the back of them; heads bowed below the neon sign flashing 'Sauna'.

At Old Street, I passed three cars turning left, their indicators flashing in a pattern crying out to be set to music. I stopped to film a short sequence, before turning onto Brick Lane where I photographed a discarded leopard-print umbrella sheath lying among leaves.

There was so much of interest en route; it was almost a shame to arrive. I paused to take in the building, an old brown-brick warehouse, cleaned up and repointed with shiny steel letters spelling out DRAKE across the side, and a doorstep inscribed 'Seeing is Believing'.

"Mind your back, sweetheart." Two men carrying an oversized wrapped canvas waited for me to vacate the doorway. Then two more arrived with a crate on wheels.

I was in the way and felt like I should go and forget all about it. *But I'm here now*, I reasoned. *I may as well go in and see what it's all about.*

"Drake, London, is a leading commercial gallery representing both international names and younger innovative artists." I read the blurb and then the entire leaflet from the

Perspex box on the countertop as I waited for Little Miss Ponytail to put her copy of *Heat* aside and get off the phone.

"Anyway, it's all good; gotta go, Gracie – text me – bye." Ponytail looked my way, past the display of blood-orange flowers. "Can I help you?"

I told her my name and who I was there to see.

"You have an appointment?" she asked.

"I wouldn't just turn up."

"You'd be surprised." She checked her book. "Mia Jackson?" I nodded. "Can you sign in, and take a seat upstairs on the mezzanine level." She pointed to a flight of concrete steps.

The mezzanine was a brutalist concrete overhang furnished with one immaculate, white leather, Florence Knoll button-backed sofa – a design classic, I thought, but I didn't want to sit down. I'd made an effort, worn a black jacket with a nipped-in waist, smart trousers, a pin-tuck blouse and my red wedge shoes, but I didn't feel comfortable.

Going to the edge of the balcony, I looked down on a large white room, where a brunette in a sleeveless black dress was staring at four wall-mounted plasma TV screens. "What's going on?" she shouted. "It's supposed to be continuous."

The screens were blank. The woman folded her arms and tapped her right foot. She turned to leave, her toned upper thigh momentarily visible.

Meanwhile the top left-hand screen fired up behind her with the profile of a beautiful young blonde – perfectly still, apart from the occasional blink. A female voiceover began: "I never go out with any money." The words were out of synch with the blonde's slowly parting lips, the voice educated but regionally nondescript.

The brunette in the black dress turned back to watch, and the voiceover continued: "None of us carry money. Well, I might take a fiver but never more than that, there's no need."

The screen diagonally below came to high-definition life with an image of a naked woman; face down on a satin bedspread. The featured room is dark, the shade of the naked woman's hair unclear. *But I know it's me. It's that hotel, that night I was drugged.*

Screen two at the top lit up with the same blonde – again in profile – but this time facing the other way as if she were talking to herself.

"My mate Natalie never buys a drink," head two said.

Head one laughed. "She's a right slag."

The heads froze as the final screen filled with an image of discarded underwear.

"I never go out with any money," the voiceover repeated itself.

The film had started again – the continuous loop successfully reinstated.

"We're back in business," the brunette said.

Marcus Hedley in his signature horn-rimmed glasses and a purple shirt entered the gallery. He strode across the polished concrete floor and whispered in the brunette's ear. They both turned and looked up at me, standing at the railing above on the mezzanine floor.

"Cut the video," the brunette shouted.

"I thought you wanted it on all day," a back-room voice replied.

"Just cut the video, Oscar." She looked back at me. "You must be Mia Jackson? I'll be right with you." She joined me on the mezzanine floor. "Sorry to keep you waiting." She smiled, without crinkling her eyes. "Amanda Darling." She offered her manicured hand – her handshake weak, like an empty glove. "Let's go somewhere more private." She led the way through a side door to a larger space with massive windows and several huge sofas in citrus colours. I stared at the blank walls.

"Where's the art?" I said.

"We're between shows. We sell everything – in fact, Jack used to call Marcus the Alchemist."

She said the wrong thing.

"Jack James, the performance artist, that is," she said. "You know the one?"

I knew who she meant all right.

"We're so pleased you could come." Amanda changed the subject. "We all think it's so important." She was being nice, or trying to be. "Ah, here he is," she said, as Marcus Hedley joined us. We shook hands.

"Stunning shoes." He peered down through his horn-rimmed glasses at my round-toed red wedges. "Girls get to wear such wonderful footwear."

When I no longer recognised my feet, I finally realised something was wrong. My boots in that hotel room – and I am lost all over again. Not now, I can't think about that now.

"Are you OK?" Marcus Hedley looked concerned. In fact, they were both staring at me. Marcus suggested I sit down. "Amanda, get Mia something to drink."

Amanda looked affronted. I guess she didn't think serving drinks was part of her remit. "What would you like?" she said.

"Nothing, I'm fine, really."

But Marcus Hedley wouldn't accept that. He kept going on, said they had everything freshly-ground, freshly squeezed. He recommended the smoothies, said they were terrific.

"What is this – a café?" I tried to make a joke. "I'm fine, really. I like to make my own drinks these days."

There, I'd said it – or rather it slipped out before I could stop myself.

Marcus Hedley and Amanda Darling glanced at one another. I'd been with them less than five minutes and already they considered me unhinged.

"Look, I have to be somewhere at twelve," I lied. "Can we just – what did you want to see me about?"

"You can probably guess," Marcus said.

"It's such an important piece," Amanda said.

"We wouldn't have troubled you otherwise," Marcus said.

Oh God. My toes curled within my red shoes.

233

"We're organising a retrospective," he said. "We've been planning it for some time, haven't we, Amanda?"

Amanda nodded. "Yes, we have."

"And originally we thought we could leave out the more controversial works as it were, but as time has gone on and we've continued to look at what we've got, we realised it doesn't make sense." His words began to wash over me, but I forced myself to refocus, aware I ought to listen. And then there it was – that name, that man – the one no one will allow me to forget. "Jack Flood the artist is also Jack Flood the flawed man," Marcus said. "One does not exist without the other and the story of Jack Flood's life's work cannot be told without detailing the failings of his life. Jack Flood: a retrospective is incomplete without your permission to use *Aftermath* and perhaps even *The Last Haunting*."

Once again, Flood's godforsaken video art runs through my head: me naked on the bed, and my mismatched underwear on the girl with the fox-head mask.

Stop it. He's dead. That's the end of it. But I knew it wasn't as simple as that and really I was annoyed at myself. How naïve to think his death would provide the full stop I needed.

Marcus Hedley's expression softened. "I understand you're reluctant, but I do believe the public should be given the chance to judge for themselves. You're an artist yourself, yes?" I nodded. "Well then, you'll understand."

"Not really," I said.

"What does artistic freedom mean to you?"

"It's important," I said, aware that I was being backed into a corner.

"I'd say it's fundamental," Amanda said.

It was at that point I lost it, failing to blink back tears.

Amanda touched my arm. "How about we view the work together?"

There it was again running through my head: me spread-eagled naked.

"No. I was there, remember."

"Forgive me."

"Who owns it anyway?" I asked.

"Nicholas Drake."

That short, bald sleazeball. *Couldn't he see what Flood had done?*

"Mia, we don't want to upset you," Marcus said.

"It's just about money to you, isn't it?"

"Art is everything to me," Marcus said. "I live and breathe art. It's my life."

"This is too difficult. I need to go."

"Mia, please," Amanda said. "Don't make a decision yet."

Marcus retrieved something from a side table. "I have a copy of the *Flood Video Diaries*. If you can bear to watch them they may change your mind."

I looked down at the DVD in his hand – a bestseller, hurriedly released a few months after Flood's death. It was like the *Warhol Diaries* – only grittier, dirtier, nastier, according to reviews.

"Why would I watch that?"

"It'll help, trust me," Amanda said.

"Amanda's right," Marcus said. "It will help." I let Marcus place the DVD in my hand. "Thank you for that," he said. "I genuinely believe exhibiting this work is the right thing to do, so please take your time, have a think, that's all I ask."

I walked out then, without shaking hands.

"Can you sign out, please," Ponytail called after me.

"Fuck off," I said under my breath, as I stepped over the stupid step with its stupid inscription, relieved to walk away and turn onto Brick Lane with its jumble of Bangladeshi restaurants, shops and supermarkets. I slipped the DVD into my bag; secretly pleased I'd acquired a copy for free. Since its overhyped release I had felt a need to view its content but couldn't bring myself to buy it.

I don't give a toss about Flood's so-called 'seminal' work of art. Stuff him, stuff Marcus Hedley and stuff his artistic freedom. I only care about that when it relates to my work. And stuff Amanda bloody Darling too.

Forty-four

The flat was empty. Tamzin was out. I could put the disc on uninterrupted. Only, there were so many things I couldn't watch these days. I mean, *Crimewatch* had always been a problem but now I found myself switching over during cop shows, soap operas and even costume dramas. Reminders were everywhere. That is how it is when something happens to you.

Distracted, I looked out the window but nothing was going on, only a pair of pinstriped trousers with a black laptop case marching past.

I retrieved the DVD from my bag, studied the cover shot of a pale woman's naked torso with Celtic-style lettering round her navel that read 'The More I Search the Less I Find'. I used my Stanley knife to slice off the cellophane and returned to the living room where I knelt in front of the TV, inserted the disc and pressed 'play'.

The blue-blank screen turned black and then the words: 'The More I Search the Less I Find' – 'The Jack Flood Video Diaries'. And in the bottom right-hand corner, the date and place: 'Thursday 26 May 2005, the Merchant's House Hotel, Nottingham'.

And there he was, Flood: his pale face filling the screen, as he looks to the side. He is backlit, his dark-dyed hair framing his intense inscrutable face. He's dressed in a black shirt, open to the navel. He's fashionably thin and seems uncomfortably close.

"My name is Jack Flood and I am an artist," he pauses, slowly turning his head to look directly to camera.

Fast forward: Flood in his luxury hotel suite.

Fast forward: Nottingham's city streets and the Tesco cashier.

Fast forward: Flood in the white cab waiting.

Fast forward: Flood with his cleaner.

Fast forward: Flood in a cheaper hotel. Jenny – missing – is on the news.

Flood returns to his studio. Dora is dead.

Flood films the ketchup-coated chips.

Fast forward: Flood in his studio with Gecko Girl.

Fast-forward: another girl goes missing.

Flood gives the lecture and shows his new work, *Aftermath*.

Flood picks up Sadie Sunshine.

Flood receives an embarrassing package.

Flood visits the private view for my end of degree show.

Fast-forward: Flood outside Thames Magistrates Court.

Fast-forward: Flood in his prison cell.

Beyond the snippets of his short prison life, there is only a still of Flood lying, bone-thin and wasted, under a white sheet, his face shrunken with thin, papery skin stretched across his cheekbones like one of the ancient mummified corpses on display in the haunted catacombs of Palermo, Sicily.

The screen turns black. White typescript appears:

'Jack Flood died from heart failure after a protracted hunger strike. He professed his innocence to the end. He died in the name of art.'

Film cuts to Flood's studio: there is no longer any rubbish on the floor and the paint pots have gone. There are, however, many canvases wrapped in bubble-wrap and brown paper by the far wall.

The credits roll:

Drake Gallery Productions would like to thank:

Tatiana Polokov – *is that the Russian prostitute?*
Carmen Billings – *the Tesco cashier?*
Sadie Campbell – *Girl-with-braids?*
Samantha Clark – *that's Gecko Girl.*
Marcus Hedley – *tosser.*
Amanda Darling – *bitch.*
Nicholas Drake – *slimeball.*
Rita Karpati – *the cleaner that got upset about the cat?*
Anna Wacek – *the other cleaner?*

I don't get it. Were they all in on it? And if so, why was it different for me?

Forty-five

I didn't know what to make of Flood's DVD. I watched some of it again, trying to piece together his take on events with my own. And I even got Tamzin to watch, keen to hear her opinion.

"He's weird," she said, "and he gets weirder as the film goes on but, even so, it's hard to believe he's a murderer."

I bit my lip. "Yeah, but he did have a tape of Jenny and two other women who were found murdered. He kept locks of their hair. It's too much of a coincidence."

Tamzin frowned, and asked *the* question, the one I'd been asking myself. "How come you got away? And the other women in the credits – they must be fine? It doesn't make sense."

I went back to Nottingham to see Jan (DC Wilson) in 'The Sanctuary' at the police station. I hadn't seen her since early in the trial as once my evidence was effectively thrown out I'd gone home. Jan had phoned me with the verdict, and I was grateful for that.

"Are you sure about this?" she said, before clicking on the file.

I had asked to watch Flood's film, the one that had my name on it. And I'm glad I did because it soon became apparent that it was not as bad as I had imagined.

I did appear to be drugged, as he stripped me, filmed and photographed me in a number of compromising, awkward positions. Then he sketched me and laid odd pieces of fabric over me and other found garments.

"It's all a bit Mr Bean does porn," I said. "He's just pathetic – a seedy pervert."

Jan helped herself to a chocolate digestive. "Did I tell you what we found?"

"No." I sat up in the chair.

"He had all this stuff for impotency: leaflets, books and pills. Pathetic little man couldn't get it up."

I felt myself flush. I had to take off my jumper.

"You see the defence tried to make out he was impotent and that his impotency rendered him incapable of rape. They even got his doctor to testify that he had been diagnosed with impotency but had been refused medication because it did not relate to a specific medical condition. As I understand it, the NHS only provide prescriptions for impotency treatments if you have a condition like Parkinson's for instance. And that's where we got him." Jan nodded. "You see the defence made out he had drug-abuse-related impotency that remained untreated, rendering him incapable of rape, and yet we found all sorts of treatments at his studio. He had Viagra and herbal remedies and you wouldn't believe the amount of leaflets he had collected. He kept them all in a wastepaper bin – very cunning."

"Oh." My throat felt tight. I could hardly believe what I was hearing. "I sent him those Viagra pills," I said.

Jan looked bemused. "You what?"

"The pills, even the herbal ones and the leaflets – I sent all of them. I'm surprised he kept them."

Jan shook her head. "You've lost me; why would you send things like that?"

"He didn't rape anyone, did he?"

"Mia, you're really confusing me right now." Jan slurped from her mug of tea.

"The evidence – was it all circumstantial?" I asked.

Jan narrowed her eyes. "Rape cases are often one person's

word against another, but if you can prove that someone is capable of lying, well then sometimes, only sometimes, you can get the jury on side."

"What about Jenny, Connie and Loretta – Flood obviously killed them but was there any DNA evidence of rape?"

Jan tilted her head to one side and spoke softly. "Of course we can't be sure of much regarding your friend Jenny – her body had seriously deteriorated due to being submerged in water for a prolonged period of time. But both Loretta Peters and Connie Vickers were raped. There were traces of the lubricant you find in condoms and they both sustained heavy bruising and the kind of internal damage consistent with brutal rape."

"But no DNA evidence?"

"No."

"Then it could have been someone else that was responsible?"

Jan put down her cup of tea and folded her arms.

"Had any of the packets of Viagra been opened?" I asked.

"Mia, you've got to let this go. Flood was certainly guilty of indecent assault seventeen times over, if nothing else – we've got that on film."

"But what if he didn't commit the murders? There could be someone else still out there."

She nodded. "There's always someone out there. You can be sure of that."

Forty-six

Both Marcus Hedley and Amanda Darling phoned a few times before they finally got through to me, desperate to know whether or not I'd grant permission for the inclusion of *Aftermath* in the Jack Flood retrospective due to be held at Drake Gallery later in the year. I didn't phone back but they were persistent and eventually managed to catch me in one afternoon before I left for my shift at Chihuahua's.

"Hello, can I speak to Mia Jackson, please?" I knew it was Amanda Darling. I had come to recognise her clipped vowels and authoritative tone.

"It is Mia."

"Have you been away? I've called and left numerous messages."

"No."

Obviously put out, her voice lowered. "I wanted to touch base with you. Have you managed to watch the DVD?"

"I have."

"What do you think?" she asked.

"He was a sad, dirty pervert – pathetic really."

"You know even bad people can make great art."

"Sure," I said. "Some people believe Walter Sickert was Jack the Ripper and I don't know about that, but he's certainly a great artist."

"Where does that leave us regarding the exhibition?"

242

"I couldn't care less."

"I'm sorry you feel like that."

"I couldn't care less about his art."

"Right, does that mean we can or can't show *Aftermath*?"

"Show it, I don't care – who am I to censor anyone?"

"I applaud your broadmindedness. Awesome, absolutely awesome – Marcus will be so pleased. We will of course send you invites for the private view."

"I do have one caveat."

"Oh?" The pitch of Amanda's voice dropped even lower.

"I want you to look at my portfolio."

"Your portfolio?"

"You know I'm an artist, right? I did tell you that."

"Oh yeah, sure," she said, as if she had no recall.

"Well, I think it'll be in your interest to see my latest work. Things have really moved on for me recently."

"Is that because of Flood's death and his diaries?"

"Yeah, well, more my association with him. It inspired me in a way, and surely there has to be a marketing angle in that, especially with such a big retrospective on its way?"

Amanda agreed and said she'd be happy to take a look, but could I email her some photos as JPEGs of my latest work in the first instance.

Fine, but I won't be signing anything relating to *Aftermath* until she and Marcus have taken a proper look at *my* work.

I've moved into photography and film. Strange though it may seem in some ways I'm carrying on where Flood left off. *Temple*, I think, is a natural progression from the urban embroidery works I showed for my degree show.

I took a large-format camera and walked all of two steps outside my front door. I set it up to peek through the metal railings straight across the road to the sauna/massage parlour opposite. I used only ambient light and an exposure of ten minutes. People passing could have spoilt it but bizarrely no one was around and no one either entered or left the building.

The image has an otherworldly golden glow, the word 'Sauna' the brightest part, while the window's frosted glass offers a contrast. It is typically rundown and seedy and yet the light suggests a heavenly place where dreams could come true – or not, as the case may be.

Temple was my latest favourite piece, but apart from that I'd taken to walking round my new neighbourhood looking for things that seemed out of place: a lost shoe, an abandoned laptop case (probably dumped after the computer was stolen), a splurge of pink vomit from the night before, a fat businessman in a cashmere camel coat slugging vodka from a bottle, and a pin-thin anorexic with a backpack walking, walking all day long.

Into the Woods was me filming in the city, looking up at the towering corporate offices – very much on the outside, like the newspaper seller on the corner with his T-shirt-covered paunch and red bulbous nose.

The possibilities are endless.

There's been another murder. This time in London: the body of a woman called Janine Jones was found in an alley in Acton. And then there was another, as yet unnamed, three days ago in Ealing. Police said both women have been known to work as prostitutes.

Press reports claim the murders are linked and also bear striking, but unconfirmed similarities to the Nottingham murders. Police have so far failed to comment.

Meanwhile, CCTV footage has been released of Janine Jones' last known movements. In a grainy, ten-second film of a lamp-lit London street, a dark-haired woman of average build, dressed in a short, pale skirt and knee-length boots approaches a white family saloon. She talks for a moment at the window then walks round to the passenger door and climbs in. The car drives off, its registration number barely legible.

Police release a statement saying they are keen to trace the driver of this vehicle and are appealing for help from the public.

"Calls will be treated in the strictest confidence."

"What do you make of that?" Tamzin said, as we sat watching the news in our rented basement flat.

I shrugged, as my gaze rested on my red shoes that I'd slung across the green carpet. "There's always some evil bastard out there," I said, remembering what DC Jan Wilson had said, and then I thought of the night I went back to Flood's hotel, confused as to why we needed a cab. It was a white car, a family saloon – similar to the car shown in the clip on the news?

I went down the corridor to my room, found my college sketchbooks and looked back at the fast spontaneous mark-making that showed: half a car here, half a car there, a woman leaning in to negotiate and the odd number or letter that made up several partially recorded number-plates.

Online, I called up BBC News and watched the grainy CCTV footage repeatedly, straining to see if the car was in any way similar to my sketches. And could there even be a bejewelled blue elephant hanging from the rear-view mirror?

Acknowledgements

The genesis of this novel has been somewhat protracted, and various people have helped along the way. I'd like to say a big thank you to my editor and friend Monica Byles for her sterling work, and to Natalia Jefferson for being so generous with her time and brain power.

Fellow writers and South Bank friends: David Bausor, Christabel Cooper, Kyo Choi, Dominique Jackson, EJ Swift and Colin Tucker have provided ongoing advice and support. And I'd also like to thank Susanna Jones and Jo Shapcott at Royal Holloway, University of London, and my fellow MA students for their help and encouragement.

Writer friends Linda Buckley-Archer, Kate Harrison, Jacqui Lofthouse, Louise Voss and Stephanie Zia were there at the beginning, as was my partner Daryl Gregory and I'd like to thank all of them for their belief in this novel.

Book cover design: Simon Hunt at www.toffeemedia.com

London Tsunami & Other Stories

'I've found in London Tsunami exactly what I've been looking for – extremely talented contemporary short story authors, the modern, living, active writers with the very real potential of joining the great' Victor A. Davis, Mediascover

A random shooting, the death of Michael Jackson, and the tsunami that is ill health all feature alongside: urban runners, adulterers, lovers, haters, life, death and something in between in this collection of twenty-one contemporary London stories.

'A collection of very well written, dark comic tales. They start off innocent enough then completely throw you with a dark twist or something completely bizarre' Goodreads

'It's wonderful, very very funny, and utterly original. This writer has surprises for you' Colin Tucker

Follow/Like/Join:

Twitter: @jaqhazell
Facebook: www.facebook.com/jaqhazell
Website: www.jaqhazell.com with mailing list for latest news

Printed in Great Britain
by Amazon